JOHN HOWARD AND THE TUDOR LEGACY

John Howard Tudor Series Book 2

J.C. JARVIS

WRP

WHERRY ROAD PRESS

Get a FREE Book!

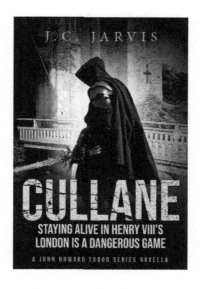

Before John Howard found sanctuary on the streets of London, Andrew Cullane formed a small band of outlawed survivors called the Underlings. Discover their fight for life for free when you join J.C. Jarvis's newsletter at jcjarvis.com/cullane

To my wife, Glenda, who is my biggest supporter and my bedrock. Without her support and encouragement none of this would have ever happened.

WHERRY ROAD PRESS

John Howard and the Tudor Legacy

John Howard Tudor Series Book 2

© 2022 by J.C Jarvis

Edited by https://safewordauthorservices.com/

Cover Design by http://www.jdsmith-design.com/

John Howard and the Tudor Legacy

by J.C. Jarvis

Quotes

"As for John Howard, I cannot find it in my heart to hold any sympathy, for I have never despised a person in my life as much as I despise that boy. My heart will not sing in peace until he is captured and killed before my very own eyes."

MARGARET COLTE, *1536.*

Foreword

Welcome to the second adventure in the John Howard Tudor Series.

Early on in my research, I made the decision to write my books in modern (British) English. If I'd kept it wholly original, nobody would have wanted to read it. So, to make it applicable to today's young adult population, I kept the Tudor period words to a minimum.

I used a few to help with the atmosphere of the novel, such as the terms "rascal" and "knave." Even though they don't illicit the same reaction today, the words reach back throughout history to a time when words such as these carried more power and demanded more attention than they do in the modern world.

To keep things authentic, I kept the street names in their original spellings, including the term "strete" instead of "street."

Marriages in Tudor times didn't always require a priest. A young couple could simply agree to take the other as their husband or wife, preferably before a witness. Once they had done this, they were legally married, and as there were no possibilities of divorce, they were married for life.

The one thing I didn't change was history itself. Any authentic events I describe are as historically accurate as possible, and when using real characters from history, I didn't have them doing anything they would have found impossible to do.

I hope you enjoy the epic adventures of John Howard and the Tudor Legacy . . .

J.C.Jarvis

Little White House

Summer 1536

THE LITTLE WHITE house on the corner of Watelying Strete and Soperlane had been busy since the death of its owner two weeks earlier.

Not many people knew that Margaret Colte had owned the house when she was alive, but thanks to Lord Asheborne's men who swarmed all over it while they searched it from top to bottom, it seemed like everyone in high society now knew her dirty little secret.

William Asheborne, the Duke of Berkshire, had posted his men in the house the day after her death at the hands of her rogue stepson, the infamous John Howard, who was now on the run with a large price on his head. His father, the Earl of Coventry, was desperately trying to find him, and even the king had men scouring the city for him.

John Howard was a member of the equally infamous Underlings, and along with their now deceased leader,

Andrew Cullane, was a murdering scum who'd sullied the names and reputations of England's elite.

But Edward Johnson knew better. He knew the truth, and he was here to find the evidence that would prove John Howard's innocence and clear his name.

It wasn't that Edward cared about John Howard; if he was being truthful, he didn't care at all. Whatever he was guilty of was between him and the Lord. All Edward cared about was carrying out his orders from his beloved master in the midlands and returning home to his pregnant wife.

At eighteen, Edward Johnson was young to be in such a prominent position of trust with his superiors. Tall and swift with straight brown hair that fell to his shoulders, Edward used his muscular physique with the precision of someone much older and more experienced. His loyalty, calmness under pressure, and his ferocious skills with the longbow and the sword had allowed him to rise rapidly to his previous role as personal guard to George Boleyn, the now executed brother of the former queen, Anne Boleyn. When George had realised his time was coming to an end, he had sent Edward to work for his cousin and best friend, James Stanton, the wealthy wool merchant from the midlands. James provided Edward with the stability he craved. He gave him a home, good pay, and a great environment in which to raise a family. They had become close during their time together, and there was nobody James Stanton trusted more than Edward, especially with the more sensitive matters such as this.

Edward Johnson loved the Stanton family, and he would gladly lay down his life for them.

His orders were simple: break into the house and find the record of events that Margaret Colte was fabled to have left behind detailing her every living moment. It was said she kept meticulous records of all her dealings with others in order to protect herself and to gain leverage should she need it.

It was Johnson's job to find the records pertaining to Lord Asheborne and his relationship with Margaret Colte. If he found them, he was to return them to Stanton with haste.

It was obvious from Edward's viewpoint high in a tree on Nederslane that Asheborne's men hadn't found anything yet. They were removing everything from the house and loading it into the back of a cart before hauling it off to goodness knows where.

That the men returned day after day told Edward they were no closer to their prize than he was.

If it was here.

If it even existed.

Edward was under no illusion that he'd find anything. He believed James had sent him on a mission that was bound to end in failure. He wasn't complaining, though. If James wanted him to waste his time breaking into an empty house in the middle of London, then he'd do it without question.

He'd watched Asheborne's men running around like headless chickens for three straight days, and now that they had emptied the house of all its belongings, there seemed to be less urgency on display. Most of them left before curfew, and the few that stayed behind didn't pay any attention to the outside world.

It should be a simple task to get in there and see if they'd missed anything, which was doubtful in the extreme.

From his observations, Edward knew he had a window of about an hour from first light until the carts returned and the house filled with men. Before that, he only had four guards to contend with, and he could easily take care of them if he had to.

Once darkness fell, Edward climbed from his perch in the tree on Nederslane and traipsed through the muddy field towards the back of the house. He kept to the shadows of the houses lining Soperlane until he reached the rear wall of the courtyard. He climbed the small tree and scrambled over the wall, dropping into the darkness between the stables and the closed gates to the outside world.

He stopped and listened for several minutes but heard nothing. Satisfied he was safe, Edward ran into the stables and sat on a pile of straw in the first available stall.

It was going to be a long night.

Dawn found the city covered in a coating of light rain as the drizzle continued. As soon as he stepped outside, Edward was soaked to the skin. But he didn't even notice. He was here to do a job.

The stretes were filled with the sounds of the city coming to life in preparation for a new day. Horses clattered their hooves on the rough cobbles, and Edward could hear traders calling to one another on their way to Cheppes Syed to market their wares.

London was waking up.

He approached the rear door, fully expecting it to be unlocked, but it wasn't. The men guarding the building were better trained than he'd given them credit for. He waited until a horse thundered by before forcing a window shutter open with a loud crack.

He crouched with his hand on his knife in case he'd been heard. The house was silent, so he climbed through the open window and took a moment for his eyes to adjust to the darkness inside.

Room after room, all he found was empty space. Everything had been taken, even down to the smallest items. There was no evidence of occupation anywhere, although Edward knew Margaret had never lived there. Her home, when she was in London, was in the aristocratic area of the Stronde. This house was used purely for her less desirable activities.

Like ordering the murder of innocent young boys.

He pressed and prodded the recesses of the panelled walls, looking for any secret doors that might be present, but found nothing.

After searching all the downstairs rooms, Edward crept slowly up the stairs. He could hear snoring coming from a room where the men slept, so that one would be off limits unless he could find a way in there after they awoke.

Being careful not to step on creaking floorboards, Edward moved silently through the narrow hallway, darting quickly in and out of the empty rooms, hoping to find a secret storage place that Asheborne's men might have missed.

Only one unoccupied room was left for him to examine, and that was right at the end of the hallway. The sleeping guards were at the other end, so he quietly cracked the door and slipped inside. The room was just like the rest—empty and dark, with the shutters closed. He felt around the panels on the wall but found nothing. Satisfied there wasn't anything of interest to be found, he turned to leave.

A creaking sound outside the door put Johnson on high alert. The hallway was barely wide enough for one person to pass at a time, so there was no way out for him there.

He ran to the window and pushed the shutters, which opened in a frenzy of noise. Edward Johnson rushed to the wall beside the door. At least two men were whispering outside.

The door opened, slowly at first, before it crashed open

with a bang. Two men rushed in with their halberds raised, screaming at the tops of their voices.

Edward knocked the halberd out of the hands of the first guard and brought his large fist crashing down into his skull. The man fell with a thud to the ground.

The second guard yelled loudly and ran at Johnson with his halberd held high. Edward ran at him to close the distance between them and rammed his knee hard into the man's groin, kicking his weapon out of the way as he fell to the floor in agony.

Edward ran into the dark, narrow hallway and headed for the stairs. Whatever he was sent to find wasn't here. Now it was time to leave.

Another guard ran at him down the hallway, which was too narrow for him to open his arms and raise his weapon. Edward lunged forward and thrust his knife into the man's right shoulder, forcing him to drop the halberd and scream in pain.

There was one more guard somewhere, and Edward was on high alert as he approached the stairs. The last remaining guard ran out of the room he was hiding in and stood in front of the stairs, blocking the path to Edward's escape.

Johnson didn't slow down. Instead, he jumped forward and kicked the man as hard as he could, sending him head-first down the stairs. He jumped over the crumpled heap at the base of the stairs and ran for the exit. His duty here was done.

He ran for the gates, intending to climb over them and lose himself in the melee of men and horses who were oblivious to the events unfolding in the little white house next to them.

As he neared the gates, they began to open.

What is this? They're early!

He diverted his run into the stables, reaching them with seconds to spare before the courtyard filled with carts and men.

There was no way out for Edward Johnson. For the first time in his life, he'd underestimated his opponents, and now he was going to pay the price.

At least my wife and child will be taken care of, he thought as he searched the stables for a good hiding place.

The stables only had eight stalls, and except for a few small piles of straw, they were empty. Except the last one.

The smell told him all he needed to know before he even got there. His eyes watered from the stink of horse-shit, and he took a deep breath and dived in with not a moment to spare.

The stall was completely full of horse manure and old straw. Whoever looked after the stables had used this stall to pile up all the filth, and now Edward found himself burrowing right into the middle of it.

His eyes burned, and his throat stung when he tried to breathe. He dug as deep as he could and held his breath.

It wasn't long before the commotion reached the stables.

"Look in here, and if you find him, drag him out. He's going to suffer for what he's done."

Johnson heard footsteps scampering around the stables until they got close to the shit mound he was hiding under. The stabbing sounds in front of him got louder as the man prodded the mound with a pitchfork. One thrust grazed his face, and he felt blood dripping down the side of his cheeks. He stifled a scream just in time.

Edward knew he wasn't the sort of man who would lie there and take a beating. The men here would have to kill him before he would give himself up. He clutched his knife in his hand and waited for the man to prod him again.

One more time and the man's throat would be sliced open from ear to ear.

Johnson buried himself even deeper into the mound until he found himself with his back to the wall, sitting on the ground. There was a small hole above him for air. Without it, he would choke to death on horse shit.

This isn't the way I want to die, he told himself as he struggled for air.

He sat in silence as the man prodded the mound several more times. More fortunate for the man than for Edward, he didn't hit any more flesh, and after a while he gave up.

"There's no one here," he shouted. "Whoever it was is long gone."

Edward heaved a sigh of relief and made a bigger hole so he could breathe without taking a mouthful of horse muck and old straw.

He rummaged around, trying to get as comfortable as he could, given that he was sitting under about a year's worth of horse turd. He used his hands to get leverage on the ground to make a bit of space for himself while he waited until dark before making his escape.

His hand touched something that felt out of place. It was cold and hard. Round.

This is metal!

Edward's hand closed around a metal ring that was set into one of the stones on the floor. He tried pulling it up, but the weight of the filth stopped him. He had to wait until he was sure it was safe.

Voices, followed by loud footsteps in the courtyard just outside the stables, alerted Edward that Asheborne's men were close by.

"Alright, men, shut up and listen." The voice sounded cultured and educated, like someone who was in charge.

"The men are adamant it was John Howard who did this, so we're not leaving until we find him. He didn't climb the gates, or we'd have seen him as we came in, so he's still here somewhere."

"Are you sure it was John Howard?" Another voice sounded sceptical.

"It was dark, so I can't be real sure, but from what the cryers say, it looked a lot like him. Who else would dare break in 'ere knowing we're all over it?"

"The man has a point," the man in charge said. "Nobody else would have the guts to try what he just did. Spread out boys, and find me John Howard. Lord Asheborne's sure to reward us well when we hand him over."

Edward had to stop himself from snorting out loud. If it hadn't been for a decaying piece of straw sticking down his throat, he probably would have done.

John Howard? I don't look nothing like John Howard. From what the cryers say, he's shorter and fatter than me. And his hair's longer. These men have been on the ale!

In any case, Edward knew where John Howard was heading, and it wasn't anywhere in London. Master Stanton had confided in him before he was given his orders that Howard and his Underlings were staying with them for a while until Duke Howard, as Edward called him, could find him somewhere more permanent. John Howard was far away from this stinking, heaving city.

"The only place we haven't looked is in here." The voice was directly in front of Edward, right in front of the large, smelly mound. "If he's here, then that's where he'll be."

Edward tightened his grip on his knife.

"Who'd want to get inside that pile of shit?" It sounded like the guard who thought Edward was John Howard.

"He'd have to be desperate to hide in there. But if he is, we're goin' to be rich."

Edward tensed as the man cackled in front of him. He pushed himself as far against the wall as he could and held his breath.

Discovery in the Dirt

The pitchfork jammed into Edward's leg, but he bit down on his arm to stop himself from making any sounds. Another stabbed into his thigh. Yet another hit his left arm. Another one hit the top of his head, making Edward feel momentarily sick and dizzy.

This was beginning to really hurt.

Yet he didn't utter a sound. He sat as still as a rock until the men stopped hacking away at the mound with their pitchforks. He heard them panting and breathing heavily.

"He ain't in here or he'd have screamed by now. No man could have suffered through that and not made any sound."

"Yea, he's not here. Let's tell the captain."

Edward's body was wracked with pain, but he forced himself to relax and sit still. He would remember that voice, and if he ever heard it again, Edward would be the last thing its owner ever saw.

"He ain't in there, Captain. We turned it over to a horse's hair."

"We found muddy footprints beside the stables, so it

looks like he got away over the rear wall," the captain said. "I want all of you to get out there and search the stretes until you find him."

"Do you think he found anything?" someone else asked.

"No," the captain replied. "We've been here for days and haven't found it, so there's no way he'd walk right in and find it straight away. Not unless he knew where it was, and that's not likely given how much they hated each other. I'm beginning to think Lord Asheborne got this one wrong and they're not here."

The voices faded, leaving Edward alone in the stables. He wanted nothing more than to get out of the stinking mound, but the metal ring intrigued him. It was probably nothing, but he wasn't leaving until he'd looked.

Satisfied he was alone, Edward tried pulling up the stone, but the weight of the mound was too much. He would have to wait until after dark so he could move the mound out of the way.

This is going to be a long day.

He made the hole at the top of the mound bigger and forced his way up so his head was clear, and he could breathe fresh air. At least as fresh as this rat-infested city would allow.

Now and again during the day someone would get close to the stables, and each time Edward sank back into the mound and covered himself until it was all clear again.

He'd planned to be in and out the previous night, so his meagre rations weren't going to last long. His throat was parched, and his nostrils were probably permanently scarred from the obnoxious onslaught being forced on them from the mound.

After what seemed like months, the daylight began to

fade, and Edward heard the cart leaving the courtyard. The captain had doubled the guards this night and ordered them to patrol the courtyard and stables in pairs until morning.

"Remember, if it is Howard, we'll all be rich. Catch him alive if you can, but if he resists, you know what to do."

"Yes, Captain," was heard loud and clear in the prison of filth, and Edward made a silent vow to himself to be extra vigilant as he made his escape.

He timed the first few patrols, counting slowly to himself until the guards returned on their next visit. It always amazed Edward how routine guards always were. In his experience, their predictability was their greatest weakness.

He counted to one thousand, and each time they returned within a few minutes. The clouds were heavy, and it felt damp and oppressive. Edward was certain they were going to get a big downpour during the night.

Because of the heavy clouds, the moonlight was obscured, and it was almost pitch dark inside the stables. After the first two circuits, the guards stopped coming inside because they couldn't see anything when they got there.

Edward climbed out of the mound and stretched himself to get his circulation going again. He pulled old straw and goodness knows what else from his ears and out of his nose. Then he pulled handfuls out from around his neck before they itched him to death.

He grabbed a pitchfork, and in total darkness, began to quietly move the mound to the side until he'd made a path big enough for him to reach down and feel the metal handle.

Making sure the guards weren't close enough to hear,

Edward pulled on the metal ring, gently at first and then with more force, as it refused to budge.

Nothing. He couldn't move it even a little bit.

He remembered seeing some rope hanging on the wall near the doorway, so he fumbled in the dark until his fingers clamped around it. He waited until the guards finished another circuit before threading it through the loop and trying again.

This time, he felt it move. Slightly at first, before an almighty pull yanked the stone from its resting place. Edward fell backwards and hit the floor. He was sure the guards had heard all the noise.

He waited for some time until he was sure he was alone before taking a deep breath and pushing his hand inside the hole in the ground.

Something was there! He felt a pouch of some kind that had something hard inside it. He pulled it out of the hole.

A cold, hard object fell from the pouch. It was a wooden box! It wasn't too big, so Edward held it in his large hands and felt around it in the darkness. He was about to open it when he heard the guards returning.

Johnson put the box back inside the pouch and threw it inside his small bag of provisions. Whatever it was, it would have to wait until he'd got away from here.

By now, the heavens had opened up and everywhere was soaked. Edward stood in the pouring rain, allowing it to cleanse the stench from his face and hair. He felt like the heavens were washing him, and he appreciated the invigorating dampness as it renewed his soul.

After one last check for the guards, who were probably sheltering inside the house, Edward made his way to the side of the stables and climbed the slippery wall before hopping onto the tree that would take him safely to the other side. From there, he would hide in the tree on Neder-slane until curfew was lifted. After that, he'd leave this smelly, nasty city and head back home to Burningtown Manor in Banbury where his beautiful bride was waiting for him.

He dropped into the muddy field and froze. The cold steel of a blade pressed against his throat, held there by someone with his arm wrapped around his neck.

"I've been waiting for you all night, John Howard," the voice of the captain whispered in Edward's ear. "I knew you were still in there somewhere, and from the smell of you, I know where it was. I knew you'd be coming out the way you came in, so I waited for you. Your father will be delighted to see you again after what you've done."

Edward sighed. It wasn't often he was taken by surprise, and he felt respect for the captain's resource-fulness.

"I'm afraid you have the wrong person. I'm not John Howard, and I've never seen him."

"If you aren't Howard, then who are you? And why are you breaking in here knowing Lord Asheborne's finest men guarded it?"

"My name is Edward Johnson," he answered truthfully. "And I came here because I thought you were gone at night and there'd be food in there. I was cold and hungry."

"I don't believe you."

The captain shifted position slightly to get a better view of his captive. "You're coming with me, and if you are John Howard, I'm going to be a very rich man."

He pushed Edward forward towards Soperlane. Edward exaggerated the push and lurched forward before stopping dead in his tracks and slamming his head back-wards as hard as he could.

His head exploded, and he struggled to remain alert

and clear his mind. He threw himself to the side and turned to face his adversary. Tall and muscular, the moustached captain looked like he was in his thirties and in great shape. He knew what he was doing.

Blood spurted from his broken nose, and although his vision must have been impaired, he flung himself at Edward with his knife raised in the air.

In a move that required extraordinary strength and precision, Edward grabbed the captain's hand and twisted, breaking his wrist with a clean snap. The captain yelled in pain as the knife fell to the ground.

Edward knelt by the injured captain. "I'm not going to kill you, Captain, so you can breathe easily. Just know that I am not the man you think I am. If Howard has any sense, he'll be miles away from London by now."

He stood up and moved away.

"What were you doing here? Who sent you?"

"I told you, I was merely trying to find shelter and food. I hope you heal well, Captain."

Edward vanished into the darkness.

Burningtown Manor

Autumn 1536

SIXTEEN-YEAR-OLD JOHN HOWARD pulled the hood of his cloak over his long, wavy dark hair and watched his breath form liquid crystals in the crisp morning air.

The leaves on the trees on either side of the lane leading up to the picturesque property in the countryside near Banbury had turned different shades of deep red and orange. John was struck by the stark contrast between this scene and those he had viewed during his recent existence in London.

Built of stone with a tiled roof, Burningtown Manor reminded John of his father's country cottages. They used to visit them together when his mother was alive.

Before the bitch ruined our lives.

John forced all thoughts of Margaret Colte from his mind. She wasn't going to ruin the serenity he felt taking in the views panning out before him.

The house wasn't Broxley. It wasn't even close, but it

gave off an aura of peacefulness and security, which were the two virtues John craved above all others after the tumultuous events that had overtaken his life in London.

After the bitch married my father.

There I go again, he thought. *I can't get her out of my mind.*

He forced himself back to the present and looked closely at Burningtown Manor, where James Stanton had graciously agreed to his uncle's request to allow him and his friends sanctuary until they could find a more permanent solution.

He saw two large windows, one on each of the two floors, and there were four chimneys in total. One of the two rear ones had smoke coming out of it. Burningtown was coming to life as daylight broke over Banbury and its surrounding villages.

The wall John was standing behind was about a hundred feet from the house. Sheep grazed in the fields all around him, and for a moment, John tried to imagine what it would be like if he were Hans Holbein, the painter, capturing the scenic beauty in an array of exquisite colours that would last for eternity.

The house sat behind a small stone wall that separated it from the large gardens that stretched all around. The morning shadows highlighted the flowers that danced around the side of the house in the gentle winds. Ivy grew along the walls on the right side, and there were a series of outbuildings to the left of the home.

Next to the outbuildings sat a smaller home that John and the others shared with Edward Johnson, Stanton's personal guard, and his heavily pregnant wife. John thought Johnson was awfully young to hold such an elevated position, but there was something about him that told John he was more than capable of taking care of himself in a fight.

"Hey, I'm talking to you." Catherine playfully shoved John with her shoulder. "I don't know where your mind was, but it wasn't here with me, where it's supposed to be." She giggled and squeezed John's arm.

John reached for the warmth of her hand, the familiar feeling of fluttering butterflies in his stomach bursting out at the merest hint of her touch.

"I'm sorry, my love. I was considering how fortunate we are to find ourselves in such a tranquil place together. After all we've been through, I never believed we could end up in a place like this."

"None of us did. We can thank your Uncle Thomas for arranging it, as well as the Stanton's for agreeing to take us in."

John reached forward and swept Catherine into his arms. Her long blonde hair flowed from beneath the cap on her head, and her warm breath made John weak at the knees. He kissed her lips, enjoying the tingling jolts her touch sent through his body.

John was head over heels in love with Catherine Devine.

"I've got to get back and help Edward with the animals," John said, reluctantly pulling himself away from the arms of his beloved.

"You mean you want to practise the longbow with him," Catherine corrected him. "Isaac's been cleaning out the stables since first light."

John smiled. "I want to practise weapons with him. Edward is the best I've ever seen with the sword and long-bow. I'm not surprised Stanton hired him as his personal guard."

"Is your shoulder up to it?" Catherine touched his right shoulder, referring to the injury he had sustained when

Margaret Colte had stabbed him in the left shoulder a few short months ago.

"Yea, it's healed now. Sybil has proven to be very good at nursing us all back to health. Both Edward and Sybil have shown themselves to be more than just good friends."

"I need to help Sybil with her duties," Catherine said. "She's so far along with child that she can't bend over anymore. I feel sad watching her struggle."

"You'd better get used to it," John flashed a cheeky smile at her.

"John Howard!" Catherine feigned disgust. "I'm an unmarried lady. There'll be none of that until you make an honest woman of me."

John's smile beamed like a thousand candles. There was nothing in the world he wanted more than to marry this beautiful girl stood before him. Of that, he was certain. Just not now. Not until he could guarantee their future together.

And he couldn't do that until he found his missing four-teen-year-old sister, Sarah Howard, and proved to his father that he was innocent of all the charges made against him. Until he did that, Catherine would never be safe with him.

They walked back to the manor in silence, arm in arm.

John sought out Edward Johnson, who was at the rear of his cottage, setting up the targets for his longbow prac-tice. Isaac was already with him, and he looked up when John approached.

"Glad you could make it, now I've cleaned out the stables already," he said with a heavy hint of sarcasm.

"Sorry," John replied. "I was enjoying an early morning stroll with Catherine."

"I know," Isaac said testily. "I saw you. You could have at least helped me first before going off with her. I know you think you're better than us, but you're not. Not anymore."

John threw his arm around his stocky friend's shoulders. "I'm sorry," he said to his shorter friend. "And I'll do better from now on. I got carried away with the peacefulness around here and I forgot myself. Why don't you let me do the stables tomorrow while you rest?"

"No need," Isaac said grumpily. "But at least help me set up these bags of straw for target practice."

Edward Johnson stood back and watched the two boys arguing playfully between themselves. They did this almost every morning, and John knew they both enjoyed it. He and Isaac were like brothers, and Isaac was the best friend John had ever had. They would die for each other if they had to.

John had become close to Edward over the last few weeks, as had Isaac. He was a man of few words, but John always knew where he stood with him. He knew Edward was a man who could be trusted.

John especially enjoyed the weapons practice alongside Edward. As proficient as he was, he knew he wasn't anywhere close to the levels of skill, strength, or precision that Edward possessed. As long as they remained there, John was determined to learn from him.

Besides his skills with weapons, Edward had proven to be a good listener. John had slowly learned to trust him, and he began to confide in him his deepest fears. Johnson rarely responded, but John knew his secrets were safe and that Edward wouldn't reveal them to anyone else.

Except, perhaps, his employer, James Stanton.

"You've been quiet today, John," Edward said in the late afternoon after they'd finished the weapon training for the day. Isaac had left to help James Stanton with some chores, so they were alone together, which was a rarity.

John, Isaac, and Edward were rarely apart during daylight hours.

"Have I?" John shrugged his shoulders.

"I know you well enough by now to know when something is bothering you. What is it?"

John shrugged again. "Every time I hold a sword, I see the faces of Ren Walden, Rolf the German, John Two, and, of course, Margaret. And yet it isn't really their faces I see. It's Sarah's. I know my uncle put himself in great danger to get us out of London, and I'm very grateful for it, just as I am to you and James for allowing us to stay here. Trust me, I know what would happen if we were to be discovered."

"And yet your sister's absence bothers you, even though you know she's safe in your uncle's care?"

"My uncle promised to tell me Sarah's whereabouts once we got out of London and things had settled down. It's been weeks and I still haven't heard anything. My uncle will only go so far, and I can never forget how he turned on his niece when the king grew tired of her. I was there the day they executed Anne Boleyn, and the look on her face as she knelt before the executioner will haunt me until the day I die. My uncle was partly responsible for that."

"You think Duke Thomas would turn on you and give you up?"

"To save himself, yes, I do. I know my father very well, and he will never stop trying to find me. If he ever gets close, my uncle won't hesitate to turn me in. That's what worries me, especially with Sarah. I need to know she's safe, and I need to know where she is so I can see her."

"And how do you think you'll do that?"

"I'm going to return to London and demand my uncle tells me where she is."

"Your bravery is your greatest asset, John Howard, but your impatience is your biggest weakness."

"What do you mean?"

"Your father must know you as well as you say you know him. He will be waiting for you to make a mistake and show yourself. He will be ready to strike, and when he does, he brings not only his own men but also those of Lord Asheborne. Even the king himself will send men after you, and that means torture and execution of all those who have gone out of their way to help you, including Master Stanton, his family, and mine. You will get us all killed if you act with your heart instead of your head. You need to think of others besides yourself sometimes, especially Catherine and Isaac, who stand beside you no matter the danger. Do not allow Margaret Colte to destroy you from her grave."

John was about to reply when Isaac ran around the corner of the house. "Master James sends word we are all to attend the manor for a gathering."

"When?" John asked.

"Now. He told me to get everyone over there."

John threw Edward a look that told him they would continue their conversation at a later time. "I'll go find Catherine and Sybil and see you over there."

He strode off with Edward's words ringing in his ears.

News from London

Edward and the heavily pregnant Sybil led the way to the great hall, followed by John and Catherine. Isaac was already there, helping himself to handfuls of lamb and vegetables. He stopped when John threw him a hard stare through the open doorway of the large room.

The door to the great hall was in the middle of the room, and as they entered, John saw the familiar tapestries adorning the walls on either side of the doorway. The large fireplace crackled and roared to their left, throwing off a warm, comforting glow that was very welcome on this chilly October afternoon.

A large window on the opposite side of the doorway filled the room with daylight, although the wooden panels and the fading sun cast shadows in all directions that danced in the glow of the flames.

The large rectangular table in the middle of the floor was filled with half empty plates that made John's stomach rumble as he realised how hungry he was.

James Stanton stood with his back to the fireplace, warming himself as his guests strolled in one by one.

Tall and lean, James looked to be somewhere in his thirties. His face bore the creased lines of a man who had experienced life to the fullest, and yet his eyes bore the hallmarks of a man filled with kindness and compassion, traits that John knew he possessed in abundance.

Joan Stanton stood next to him, and John smiled at the sight of her gently nudging her husband out of the way so she could get closer to the fire. Like her husband, Joan was a kindly woman who had made John and the rest very welcome, even though everyone knew how dangerous it was for them to be harbouring the most wanted man in England.

Joan was shorter than James, but so were most people, so that meant nothing. The most important thing was how kind and gentle she was.

Their twelve-year-old son, George, stood next to his mother. Named after his father's best friend and cousin, George Boleyn, young George looked just like his father and would no doubt one day take over the family's very successful wool business.

"Please, sit," James Stanton said. "Forgive the half empty plates, but I was entertaining a very important guest earlier and thought it a waste if we didn't finish all the food we had prepared."

Catherine pinched John playfully as they sat, causing him to jump slightly and let out a strange snort that sounded like a trapped mouse in a warm chimney.

James looked inquiringly at John. "Are you alright?" he asked, smiling at the obvious flirtation going on between them.

"Yes, thank you. I mean, I'm sorry, but this woman next to me is out of control."

Everyone laughed as they sat down to say grace. Once

it was over, James told them all to enjoy the food and that they would talk afterwards.

Eventually, the food was all gone, and everyone was satiated and stuffed to the gills. John thought he wouldn't be able to move after the amount he'd eaten.

"I've never seen as much food in all me life," Isaac said. "I've always been half-starved, and if it weren't for Andrew, and now John, I'd still be on the stretes of London starving and freezing to death. To have the greatest friends in England is a wonderful thing, and I thank you all."

Everyone raised their ale to toast Isaac's words.

"I can only repeat what Isaac has just said," John spoke. "We know how dangerous it is for you harbouring us here, and yet you accept us with open arms. We cannot thank you enough, and we will forever be indebted to you."

James Stanton waved his arms. "No need for that. You'll have us all in tears if you carry on. I invited you here not only to enjoy the feast but also to give you the news we heard today."

The room fell silent as James fixed his gaze on John.

"As you know, Thomas Howard sends word from London from time to time, normally when my good friend and trading partner, Lord Parker, travels north to talk business. Today was one of those days."

"Is he still here?" John asked.

James shook his head. "He already left so he could reach his country home before dark."

"Why can I never speak to him myself?" John asked. "I have questions he may answer."

"You are the reason I don't allow him to stay here," James replied. "The fewer people that see you, the safer it is for all of us. Lord Parker might be trustworthy, but his men might not be."

"I understand, and I appreciate your wariness, but

there are certain facts I need to know, and it would be best if I asked for them myself."

"I think Lord Parker has answered your concerns, and if you would allow me, I will tell you what he said."

The atmosphere in the room had changed. What had been jovial and relaxing had now become tense and anxious. All eyes were on John, especially those of Edward Johnson, who glared at him intently.

"What news does he bring?" John said finally, ignoring the stares that bore through him.

"King Henry is displeased with your father's failure to capture you and bring you to justice for murdering Margaret Colte."

"She deserved it," John spat the words out. The merest mention of her name sent his blood boiling.

"No doubt, but neither the king nor Robert Howard see it that way. None of the aristocracy does if you want the truth. Your father is tearing London apart trying to find you. Lord Asheborne has joined him and has pledged all his resources to Robert to assist in your capture."

"I'll bet he has Abraham looking for us," Isaac said. "He's the only one that knows what we look like."

"Who is Abraham?" James inquired.

"He is the one who betrayed us," Isaac answered. "He was one of us until he sold his soul for the reward, and now he's a traitor."

"Then he is the one Lord Parker mentioned. He said they have someone who knows what you look like since your descent into crime and poverty."

John snorted. "My descent? My father forced me into this because he believed every word the lying snake ever told him."

"Robert and Lord Asheborne still believe you are hiding in London, and we must allow them to continue believing that as long as we can. If word ever gets out that you are in this area, you must leave immediately. On that I must insist."

"We promise," John agreed. "We know how dangerous our presence here is to you. Did Lord Parker bring any news of my sister?"

James shook his head. "I told him that is your most pressing concern, but Thomas didn't give him any updates on her whereabouts. All he said was that she was safe where she was and there were no plans to move her."

John smashed his fists on the table. "Please forgive my outburst, but I must know where Sarah is being held. I shall return to London at dawn tomorrow and confront my uncle myself. I need to see Sarah and know she is safe."

"I cannot allow you to do that," Stanton said. "You will endanger all of us if you act so irrationally."

"You don't understand," John said. "It's my fault she's in this situation. If I hadn't gone back to Broxley and kidnapped her, she would be safe and sound at home."

"It didn't happen that way, John, and you know it," Isaac said. "She came with us willingly, and by your own words, she would have been in great danger from Margaret had she remained."

John sighed. "Maybe, but I'm responsible and I need to see her."

"I will keep trying, John, but for now, you must remain here. There is no other way for any of us to remain safe."

"Why are you so eager to help me?" John suddenly stood up. "Why did you agree to help me, knowing how badly everyone seems to want me in chains?"

"John!" Catherine said, grabbing his arm. "Sit down and don't be so rude."

Edward Johnson rose from his chair. He never said a word, but his gaze never left John's.

"Please, sit down," James said.

John did as he was told. Edward sat too, his gaze unwavering.

"My friendship with George Boleyn goes back all the way to our childhood. We remained close all our lives, and it was he who helped me get started in the wool business by giving me the ear of powerful men who can make or break a prospective trader.

"When the Boleyn's rose to power, my fortunes grew as theirs did. George and I remained in close contact, even when Anne became queen and George had the ear of the king. It was through George that I became friends with Thomas Howard."

John saw the sadness in James's eyes, setting off images of his own mother laying on her deathbed during her agonising last hours. He lowered his head in deference to the painful memories that were never far from the surface of his mind.

"You are not the only one who has been wrongfully accused of terrible crimes you didn't commit," James continued. "And yet you walk around as though you are the only man ever touched by the evil in this world. At least you are still alive to do something about it. Neither George nor Anne Boleyn have that privilege."

John gave a slow nod, accepting the truth of the situation. "I apologise if my actions seemed selfish. Sometimes my desire for justice clouds my judgement, and I meant no disrespect to you or your family."

John noticed Edward Johnson lower his gaze for the first time since the conversation began.

"When Thomas told me of your plight, it brought back all the memories of what happened to poor George and Anne. I couldn't stand by and watch history repeat itself, so I agreed to help you as long as I could, on the understanding that if it ever became too dangerous to keep you here, then Thomas would relocate you immediately.

"I couldn't do anything to help George or Anne, but I could do something to help you, hence the reason why you are here with us now."

"We cannot thank you enough for all you continue to do for us," John said. "We will all be forever grateful to you, and one day I hope to repay your kindness, but with all due respect, I still need to find my sister and make sure she is safe and well. She will think I have abandoned her, and that thought keeps me awake at night. Sir, I need to find Sarah."

"I understand, and I accept your reasons. I will continue to press your uncle and try to find where your sister is. But you must promise that you will do nothing to endanger us any further. You must promise that you will not attempt to return to London."

John raised his head and looked James Stanton directly in his eyes. "I promise I shall not see my uncle in London, at least not while we are staying with you. I promise I shall do nothing to put anyone here in any greater danger than you already are."

"Finally, the man sees sense," Isaac spoke up. "You do realise that I would have gone with you, don't you? That means that if they had captured you, then I'd be in chains too."

John bowed his head. "I'm sorry," was all he could think of saying.

"I have something to show you before it gets too dark," James Stanton rose from his chair. "Please, follow me."

Hiding Place

James led everyone to the outbuilding in-between the house and the cottage where Edward and Sybil made their home.

"George and Edward know about this, but I wanted to show you in case they ever attack us," Stanton gazed at John, Isaac, and Catherine, holding each of their eyes for a few seconds before moving on. "I wanted to make sure I could trust you first."

Catherine squeezed John's hand, and he squeezed back in reassurance that he meant what he had said a few moments earlier.

Stanton lit a candle and allowed George to lead the way.

"This way," George said. "Father filled the building on purpose to confuse any would be attacker."

John could see why they had done that. Furniture filled the extensive building from floor to roof. Narrow walkways branched off all over the place, but George knew where he was going, so he followed in silence, wondering what they were about to reveal.

Eventually, George stopped in front of a large bookcase at the rear of the building. He held his candle in the air and looked at John triumphantly. Then he moved out of the way as his father stepped in.

"Press the panel on the far-right side of this bookcase," he told Catherine, who was the closest to him.

James stood back and waited while Catherine pressed around on the panel. When she touched the top right corner, John heard a slight click. He watched in wide-eyed amazement as a dark hole, large enough for a grown man to squeeze through, appeared in front of them.

"What is this?" he asked.

James handed John his candle and moved out of the way. John stepped forward and peered into the black hole. Once his eyes adjusted, rough stone steps leading down into the darkness came into view.

John looked at James Stanton.

"They go to a small room where you can hide if we are ever attacked. It's small, but it's big enough for all of us."

"What about you?" John asked. "What happens if you're attacked in the house?"

"We have our own way to get out of there, so don't worry about us. I hope we never have to use it, but it's there if we need it."

"Why did you build something like that?" Isaac asked when they were standing in the fading daylight outside the building. "Is being a wool trader that dangerous?"

"No," James shook his head. "I built this when Anne fell from grace and George was arrested. Edward was George's personal guard, and he ordered him to ride here and inform me of the gravity of their situation. He ordered Edward to remain by my side in my employ from that moment on."

"I know you were friends with George Boleyn," John

said. "And I know you were his cousin, but that doesn't explain why you would build something like this. It was Anne and George who the king wanted dead, not you."

"That wasn't the only reason," James looked at his wife, who slowly nodded as though telling him it was alright to continue. "George and I were close, and everyone knew that, even the king. I am, after all, a member of the Boleyn family, even if I am only a cousin. I was, and still am, worried that there will be retributions by certain people against my family, and that is why I built this hideout."

"We know Thomas Howard is your uncle," George spoke up. "And that's why Father is not saying anything, but we don't trust him either."

John shot a look at James Stanton. "If you don't trust my uncle, then why did you agree to take us in?"

James sighed and gave his son a withering look. "When your uncle asked me if I would help, he reminded me of the guilt I felt when George and Anne were arrested and executed. As I already told you, I couldn't stand by and watch another innocent man die a painful death for something he didn't do. Thomas Howard knew this, which is why he came to me."

"But how did you know I was innocent? According to you, every aristocrat in England thinks I'm guilty."

"Not all of them," James corrected John. "Thomas Howard knows you're innocent. George never trusted Margaret Colte, so when I heard of your plight, I immediately believed in your innocence."

"So, why do you not trust my uncle?"

"As you told me, Master John," Edward Johnson spoke for the first time that evening. "Your uncle has a lot to lose if they find him helping you. He wouldn't hesitate to give you up to save himself."

John looked at James and shrugged. He was about to speak when James interrupted him.

"He betrayed Anne when it suited him. He betrayed her and condemned her to die. We all know he would do the same to us should his connection to you surface. This is my way of keeping my family safe should the need arise."

"I can't argue with you," John said softly. "The same thought has crossed my mind several times, and this is why I must find my sister. Can't you see? If my uncle betrays me like he betrayed Anne Boleyn, then Sarah will never be safe. I have to find her, or I'll never be able to rest in peace."

James placed his arms around John's shoulders. "Now that you explain it like that, I fully understand. I shall do all I can to help you find your sister and reunite you."

"Thank you. I know it is a lot to ask, especially after you have done so much already."

"Leave it with me and promise not to do anything stupid."

"I promise."

Proposal

Seven days later, John looked proudly at the masterpiece he had spent weeks creating. Today was the day he'd been waiting for.

He placed his creation back in his pocket so he wouldn't lose it and picked up the pitchfork he'd momentarily put to the side.

"It's good to see you doing some honest work for a change," Isaac said with a sly grin on his face.

"Shut up!" John threw some manure at his close friend. Even though it was a cold and misty day, sweat beaded up on John's forehead.

"Keeping up with all these animals is hard work, not that you'd know much about it," Isaac continued digging. "I suppose you'll be scurrying off somewhere to rest after this."

John shook his head. "Actually, today is a special day. I need you to come with me while I do something very important."

"What?"

"You'll find out. Just hurry and don't ask questions."

"Yes, sir."

John threw some more manure his way.

Once they'd finished their morning chores, John ordered Isaac to wait by the wall at the side of the house. A short while later, John emerged from the house with Catherine alongside him.

"What's so important that I have to leave before I finish my work?" Catherine asked. "Can't this wait until we're all done?"

"That's exactly what I said," Isaac chimed in. "What's the big secret, John? I tell you now, we're not going to London if that's what you're planning."

"I promised James I wouldn't do that, and I am a man of my word. No, this is one of the most important days of my life, and something I should have done a long time ago."

"What is it then?" Isaac asked. "I hate surprises. They normally turn out to be painfully unpleasant."

John ignored the barrage of questions and led them to the outbuildings. He had planned on doing this in the fields by the side of the house, but it had started raining again and the skies were dark and damp.

This was no time for darkness.

He led them into the entrance of the packed outbuilding and immediately turned to Catherine, dropping to his knees as he did so. Grasping her hand, he looked up into the eyes that so captivated him, and with trembling hands, he began the speech he'd rehearsed a thousand times.

Except this time his heart was pounding, and his voice cracked as he tried holding back the tears that would inevitably flow.

"Catherine Devine, you have captured my heart like no other. I know I said we had to wait until all this is over, but every time I look at you my heart melts, and I cannot hold off any longer."

Catherine looked down at John, tears streaming down her face. Her cheeks glowed bright red, and her lips parted. John thought his heart was about to burst.

Edward and Sybil joined Isaac, and even James and Joan Stanton stood with them. Isaac was quietly sobbing, holding his hands to his eyes to hide what everyone could hear. Even Edward looked touched.

"I have spent weeks making this, so I hope you like it." John reached into his pocket, fumbling because his fingers wouldn't stop tingling and shaking. "I love you with all my heart and soul, and I want to spend the rest of my life with you by my side."

Catherine gasped as John's hand slowly opened. "Will you marry me, Catherine? Will you love me as I love you? I have spent time carving this ring from a sheep's bone, so I hope you like it. It's my dedication to you."

Catherine looked shocked as she took the ring from John's outstretched hand. "John, it's beautiful. I don't know what to say." She looked at the small crowd smiling and clapping beside her.

"Just say yes," Isaac said. "Everyone knows you're made for each other. Poor John is having a heart attack waiting for your answer."

"Yes! Yes! Yes, of course I will marry you. I love you, John Howard, with all that I have. I would be proud to be your wife."

Catherine bent forward and kissed John on his lips. He stood up and embraced the love of his life, kissing her and holding himself to her. His heart was on fire, and the tears flowed as though he were standing in a storm.

"This calls for a celebration," James said. He was holding hands with Joan, and John noticed Edward and

Sybil holding hands as well. He felt sorry for Isaac, who looked as emotional as he did.

Isaac hugged his great friend before doing the same with Catherine. "It's about time," was all he could say before breaking down into tears again.

"Everyone back to the house," James said. "We all need some good cheer, so today is a good day to celebrate. Let the ale flow!"

Everyone ran through the pouring rain to Burningtown Manor for a celebration the likes of which they hadn't enjoyed for a long time. Except John and Catherine. They stood in the rain, holding each other in a passionate embrace, oblivious to everything and everyone around them.

Abraham Wylde

Twenty-year-old Abraham Wylde rode wearily into the stables in Oxford with not much daylight to spare. Tall, lean, and muscular from years of ferrying passengers across the mighty River Thames, Abraham was tired. After three days on the road with two traveling companions he despised, he was ready to change horses and get this over with.

Banbury was another day's ride north, and Abraham was hoping this was as far as they would go.

This time, anyway.

Dark grey clouds hung heavily over Banbury, most of them barely rising over the rooftops of the small market town he would call home for the evening. They mirrored Abraham's dark mood perfectly. He shivered at the thought of riding all day in freezing rain and pulled his cloak tighter around his neck as if this would prevent the coming misery.

Oh well, he thought to himself as he walked towards the welcoming sight of a nearby tavern. *It could be worse, as my two personal guards keep reminding me. I could be dangling from the end of a rope, or their favourite—my head could be hanging alongside Andrew's on London Bridge after I'd been hanged, drawn, and quartered. Anything, even putting up with these two mumpers, is better than that.*

After scouring every dark, unwelcome corner and alley of London, and spending way too many cold days and nights searching every location the Underlings were known to have used—and as their second in command, Abraham knew every secret the Underlings ever possessed—Lord Asheborne had grown impatient and widened his net.

Abraham feared his usefulness was coming to an end. After what he'd done for him, Lord Asheborne should shower him with riches, not send him out following people all over the country hoping to find the missing John Howard. *What does Asheborne want with John, anyway? I thought his problem was with the Underlings, not John Howard. He's his father's problem. But what do I know?*

These thoughts consumed Abraham as he took a seat next to the two guards Asheborne had sent with him to make sure he didn't disappear before his usefulness completely expired.

"You look like you lost a florin and found a penny," one guard said as Abraham sat down. "You should be happy you're still breathing after what you did. Nobody likes traitors, especially when it's yer best friend you betrayed."

Abraham scowled. He'd heard these words almost every day since he had turned the Underlings in to Asheborne and collected the reward.

Except he hadn't collected any reward. Not yet. Asheborne had promised him riches beyond his wildest dreams when he had betrayed his lifelong friend, Andrew Cullane, the leader of the Underlings. As yet, Asheborne had failed to deliver on that promise, even after Andrew had been hanged, drawn, and quartered at Tyburn several weeks earlier.

"I still don't know why Asheborne wants John Howard so badly." Abraham ignored the reference to his betrayal. "He had nothing to do with the duke's brother's murder, and whatever he's done, it has nothing to do with Asheborne, so why is he sending me out on useless jaunts like this?"

"It's Lord Asheborne to you," the other guard said. "And whatever his lordship's intentions are, they aren't for the likes of you to question. His lordship has generously offered to help Howard's father rid London of his murdering son. If it were up to us, we'd end you right now because even though we had no love for the Underlings, nobody should get away with betraying their best friends."

Abraham scowled. "I am tired of you always bringing this up. You do know that the Underlings didn't kill the duke's brother, right? I've told his lordship this many times. The Underlings had nothing to do with it. He was killed by Walden's strete gang, not us."

"So you keep saying," the first guard who'd spoken said. "We know it's a lie to make you feel better after betraying yer friend. Your friend is dead because of you, and nothing you say or do will change that."

"I only did it because I was tired of running. After Howard joined us, we were done for. It was only a matter of time before we were caught, and then we'd all have been executed."

"It's nothing less than any of you deserved. You're a rat who deserves to die, so think yourself lucky our orders are to protect you and not to kill you, which we'd happily do."

"I'd be much happier if I was alone. You're only here to make sure I don't run away."

The guards smiled at each other. "Concentrate on

what his lordship told you to do, and you'll be unharmed. Try anything stupid and we'll end your miserable life."

Abraham left them drinking ale and laid down on his pallet. He'd follow Lord Parker just as he'd followed many others before him. Then he'd go back to London and do it all over again.

He sighed to himself, hoping this time it would be different. The sooner he found John Howard, the better. Perhaps then Asheborne would uphold his promises and let him go.

Two days later, Abraham watched as Lord Parker and his small band of men rode their horses up the narrow tree-lined lane towards a picturesque, dreamy-looking Manor called Burningtown Manor, according to the chief guard, who could read.

Abraham hid behind a wall in a field off to the right of the house. Smoke rose from one of the four chimneys, so someone was home. Abraham clenched his teeth at the thought of Lord Parker and his men stretching out in front of a roaring fire, imagining himself feeling dry and warm. He heard the sound of a crackling fire in his mind as it warmed and soothed his cold, wet body. He sighed and allowed the thought to drift away.

Ivy grew along the right-hand side of the house, and Abraham thought it one of the most peaceful, pretty places he'd ever seen.

He shifted his eyes towards some movement from the direction of a small cottage past an outbuilding to the left of the house. A tall, strong-looking young man strode out and went behind the house, and Abraham's eyes followed him until he disappeared from view. So much of the young man reminded him of himself not too long ago. Like him, Abraham was tall and muscular, and anyone who knew him, knew he could take care of himself in a fight. The young man he'd just seen looked the same, and Abraham made a mental note to remind himself to be wary of him if they got into an altercation this day.

He stiffened. A familiar figure emerged from the cottage and went into the stables. Abraham rubbed his eyes to make sure he wasn't dreaming.

Isaac! That looked just like Isaac! It couldn't be. I'm seeing things because I want to see them.

He was about to move so he could get a better view when he stopped dead in his tracks. This time, he knew he wasn't dreaming.

A young man with long, wavy dark hair came out of the cottage with a pretty blonde-haired girl behind him. The man started walking towards the exact spot along the wall where Abraham was hiding. Abraham quietly retreated to the trees that lined the lane, where he hid again with a full view of the wall and the familiar figures that now stood behind it.

Abraham wasn't close enough to hear what they were saying, but their body language told him everything he needed to know. They obviously had feelings for each other, and this was something Abraham could use if he had to.

He watched the familiar figure pull the girl towards him in a passionate embrace, and Abraham got a good look at his face as he turned to face the girl.

John Howard! This is John Howard! The girl must be the one he rescued from Walden. *What's her name? Catherine, that's it. Her name is Catherine.*

His chin quivered slightly as he thought about the times they had shared together with Andrew.

What have I done?

47

This isn't my fault. If Andrew hadn't allowed John into the Underlings, none of this would have happened. It's Howard's fault, and he deserves what's coming.

Abraham pulled himself together and watched the couple saunter back towards the house. Catherine went inside, and John walked to the rear of the small cottage and out of sight. Abraham had seen enough, so he kept his head down and made his way back to the two guards waiting with the horses half a mile away.

"You look a lot happier," the lead guard said. "What did you see?"

"It's them," Abraham said excitedly. "I saw John Howard and Isaac, as well as the girl John rescued from Walden."

"Are you sure?"

"Positive. I've known Isaac a long time, and I'd recognise him anywhere, and I've known John long enough to recognise him whenever I see him, especially after all we went through together."

"We have to be sure it's them," the other guard said. "Let's go."

The chief guard pulled him back. "Where are you going?"

"To make sure he isn't making it up, because I don't trust him."

"And how would you know if it was John Howard or not?" Abraham asked sarcastically. "Do you know him? Have you spent time with him lately? In any case, there's someone else with them I don't recognise, and he looks like he can handle himself."

"Enough," the chief guard said. "You're not going any closer. We'll have to take his word that it's Howard. We have our orders, and we'll carry them out as his lordship commanded. He will be pleased to hear our news."

Abraham mounted his horse and prepared himself for the long journey back to Windsor. Now that he'd found them, he needed to ride swiftly back to his master.

John Howard wasn't getting away again.

A Powerful Union

Although only forty years old, a life of excess had taken its toll on the body of William Asheborne. Balding and over-weight, he still saw himself as he had been in his younger years, and no amount of encouragement from his family to take better care of himself would convince him otherwise.

William Asheborne was the Duke of Berkshire and the wealthiest man in England—except for Henry VIII, of course. Even William Asheborne wouldn't dare suggest he was worth more than the great king.

His guest today at Whitehough Court, the sprawling mansion near Windsor he called home, was a powerful lord who held the ear of the king. Robert Howard, the Earl of Coventry and head of the king's privy council, had been waiting in William's private study for over an hour.

Asheborne knew Coventry wasn't used to being made to wait, and it amused him to think of his agitation at the impertinence of his host. But William Asheborne was a duke and was a man accustomed to getting what he wanted. Robert Howard would have to wait.

"I'm sorry to keep you waiting, Robert," he said as he

finally entered his private study. "I trust my servants took good care of you."

"Indeed," Robert Howard replied, barely able to hide the anger in his voice. "I'm glad you could finally join me."

"Please accept my apologies, Robert. I had urgent business to attend to right as you arrived. I assure you I am all yours from now on. Please, sit."

Asheborne gestured to the oversized chairs adorning his spectacular study. Large oak beams ran across a ceiling that met walls lined with panels made by the finest craftsmen in England. William poured them both wine and sat back in his favourite chair, watching Robert intently.

At thirty-three, Robert was seven years younger than William, but if anyone was to have guessed their ages, they would have made the gap much larger. Robert looked young for his age, and although of only average build and height, there was nothing average about this man. His mind was as sharp as a knife, and William knew he would have to choose his words wisely if he were to be successful.

"I haven't had time to commiserate with you since the unfortunate events in London," Asheborne began.

"Yes, quite," Robert said. "I knew my son had committed terrible crimes, but even I didn't think he would sink so low as to murder his stepmother."

"A terrible affair," Asheborne agreed. "And one that shall not go unpunished. How is your search for him coming along?"

"Slowly, I'm afraid. John is proving to be elusive. He got in with those dreadful Underlings and they obviously taught him how to survive on the harsh stretes of London."

"The Underlings got what they deserved," Asheborne said. "Especially their leader. Which brings me to our meeting here today."

"I was wondering when you would get around to that," Robert said sarcastically. "I have important matters to attend to for the king."

"Once again, I apologise for my delay in getting to you." William Asheborne was enjoying himself. "I think you will like what I am about to propose."

"Go ahead."

"I don't know how to put this delicately, Robert, but as long as your son is free to wage his war on the elite of this great country, none of us are safe. It's a disgrace to the nation that he has not yet swung for his treasonous behaviour to his own kind."

"I don't appreciate your tone, but I cannot argue with your words. I disowned John some time ago, and he is an embarrassment to my family."

Robert Howard looked at William Asheborne. "I agree, he needs to be stopped by any means necessary."

"Then you won't mind if I combine my resources with yours and help you find him."

"I thought you got what you wanted when the Underling leader was caught and executed?"

"Mainly, yes, but as I just explained, John Howard needs to be caught and punished. Please remember, Margaret was on the way to my home when he killed her. What's stopping him from breaking in here and killing us all?"

"I don't see what he would benefit from doing that, but I see your point. What do you propose we do?"

Before Asheborne could answer, the door to the study burst open and William Asheborne's son, also named William, burst in. Young and athletic at twenty years of age, William junior went straight to his father and ignored the illustrious guest seated to his right.

"Father, please forgive my intrusion, but something

urgent has come up that requires your immediate attention. It shouldn't take much of your time, but it is something that cannot wait."

The duke looked visibly annoyed at this unwelcome interference, but nevertheless stood up and turned towards Robert Howard.

"Please forgive me, Robert. This should take but a moment and I will return. We still have important business to discuss."

He left the room before Robert Howard could respond.

When they got out of earshot, William turned to his son. "What was the meaning of that?" he spat the words out. "I am in the middle of very important business as you are well aware."

"I'm sorry, Father. I wouldn't have bothered you if it wasn't important."

"Well?"

"The Underling has returned from following Lord Parker to Banbury. He told me he has found John Howard and the remaining Underlings. He saw them with his own eyes."

William Asheborne's eyes bulged. "Where is the Underling now?"

"He's in the servants' entrance at the rear of the house."

"Keep him there until I am finished with Lord Howard," he said. "And tell no one about this. This is a secret only to be known to us."

"Yes, Father."

William returned to his guest. "I'm sorry about that, Robert. Please allow me to continue."

"Please do."

"As I was saying," William ignored the tension in the room. "I am willing to combine our resources to find your son and the rest of those Underthings. I have my own reasons for wanting them gone, and we need to act in haste to rid ourselves of their infestation."

"I am in agreement," Robert nodded his head slightly.

"I will send the Underling who knows your son to every building in London if necessary. He shall lead a force of my men to capture those criminals and make sure it's them. If it is, we can all celebrate."

"And if it isn't?"

"Then we continue to search until we find them. Together, we have the resources to end this once and for all."

"Agreed."

"Let us toast to a successful conclusion to our endeavours," Asheborne said, raising his glass.

"Let's find my son and end this embarrassing episode," Robert Howard raised his glass.

Once Robert Howard had been escorted to his carriage, William Asheborne scurried to another room before summoning his son and Abraham Wylde.

"Tell me everything," he demanded.

Oswyn Gare

William Asheborne slipped quietly onto Golden Lane after exiting his London home from one of the side entrances. In contrast to his normally grandiose exhibitions of power and status, this time he was alone and dressed like a strete trader. Unless you knew him, you would never know he was a duke of the realm.

He guided his horse to the inner gatehouse of the Charterhouse Priory, which the Carthusian monks had called home since 1371. But these were difficult times, and Thomas Cromwell was dissolving the monasteries and claiming them in the name of the king. After the Pope had refused to grant Henry VIII the divorce he craved from his first wife, Katherine of Aragon, the king had declared himself the Supreme Head of the newly formed Church of England, married his second wife, Anne Boleyn, and given Thomas Cromwell free rein to enact the English Reformation—including the dissolution of the monasteries.

The magnificent Charterhouse Priory was one of the

great monasteries in London, but even this holy place was not safe from Cromwell and his hated reformation.

After tethering his horse, Asheborne entered the small chapel at the head of the graveyard and knelt in silent prayer. After taking a moment to remember the three monks from the priory Henry had hanged, drawn, and quartered last year for refusing to accept him as the Supreme Head of the new church, William bowed his head and entered the priory itself.

He waited patiently in the shadow of the trees at the rear of the priory for the morning services to end and watched as the monks filed past on their way to their morning chores. He stepped out of the shadows so he could be seen and prepared himself for what was about to happen.

As the monks filed past, a pair of dull, grey eyes pierced through him as they always did. Asheborne shuddered as his soul was ripped out of his body by the cold, lifeless eyes that bore right through him.

Breathe, he told himself.

It was difficult to breathe when your heart was pumping so fast that air couldn't get into your body.

If this man brings me to this humble state, God alone knows what terror he brings to the common people. He owes me his life, and this is why I employ him. Just remember who you are and remember who he serves.

Asheborne kept telling himself this as he made his way to a small, empty building near the trees. He entered and waited for the monk.

Thirty minutes later, the monk entered the room. Asheborne wasn't used to waiting for people, especially low born people, but he made an exception for this one.

The monk was small, but even under his robes, Asheborne could see what great shape he was in. He shuddered for the umpteenth time that morning.

The monk's lifeless eyes stared at Asheborne. William was sure he was enjoying how uncomfortable he made him feel. He could have easily sent someone else, maybe even his son, but this man was Asheborne's secret weapon, and he guarded his secrets closely.

No, only he would be the one to utilise this man, the most fearsome creature he'd ever encountered. He was looking into the eyes of Oswyn Gare, the most dangerous man in England.

"Good morning, Oswyn." Asheborne composed himself by breaking eye contact. "I hope all is well with you, and the priory is serving you appropriately."

Gare nodded. "Everything is good, Master William. I like it here. It's quiet, and I am left alone. I thank you for convincing the prior to let me stay here."

"He only allowed it because I gave him a large donation," Asheborne scoffed. He took a deep breath and took control of himself. "And I promised you would find Cromwell and kill him."

The monk raised his eyebrows. "You would have me kill Cromwell?"

"Not this time. Cromwell and the reformation can wait for another day. Right now, I have a more pressing matter that needs your attention."

Gare bowed. "I am at your command, Master William."

"I'm glad you're on my side, Gare. I want you to kill John Howard."

"The aristocratic killer? You have found where he hides?"

"I have," Asheborne sneered. "He is hiding to the

north, but there is something else I need you to do as well. Something of far greater importance."

"What would you have me do?"

"Lord Parker is travelling back to London after meeting several of his wool merchants in the north. He is the one who led me to John Howard, and I believe he has further information that I need. He might know the whereabouts of the Howard girl that went missing the same time as her brother did. If you find where she is, then get her and bring her to me unharmed."

Gare bowed his head.

"There is one more thing." Asheborne shifted his weight from foot to foot. "And this is the most important part of your mission, above all else, including the killing of John Howard. What I am about to say must remain between us. Only one other person on your mission knows what I am about to tell you, and he will reveal himself to you when you leave London. Do you understand what I am saying?"

Gare bowed his head again.

"Margaret Colte left behind some very important documents when she died, and I have to find them. I'm convinced they were in a house here in London, but somebody got to them before I did. From the way he was described to me, I believe the man who found them might be hiding with the Howard boy. His name is Edward Johnson, or at least that's what he told my man during their altercation.

I want you to question Parker and find out what he knows. Kill the Howard boy and bring me the girl if you can, but most importantly, if my man confirms that Johnson is up there with Howard, I want you to question Johnson very carefully and bring me those documents. This is your true mission."

"I will do my best, Master William. If the documents are there, I will find them and deliver them to you. I will do the rest as you command."

"Good. Prepare to leave tomorrow morning at first light. My man will wait for you at the outer gatehouse on Charterhouse Lane."

Gare bowed his head one more time, turned, and left the room. William Asheborne sighed loudly. He was always glad when their meetings were over.

His plans were in place, and finally the documents Margaret Colte left behind would be in his possession. They had to be, because his life depended on it.

Gathering Evil

"Get up, yer traitor." A foot crashed through Abraham Wylde's nightmare, jolting him awake in an instant.

"Yer always talking in yer sleep. It's a big day today, maybe you can prove that yer not a coward after all."

The two men seemed to be permanently attached to Abraham's side wherever he went. "Can I not even go for a piss without you bothering me?" he groaned, glad to be rid of the recurring nightmare that had haunted him every night since Tyburn.

"Not a chance," the other guard said. "Think yourself lucky we aren't in your dreams as well."

"You are. Why do you think I have nightmares every night?"

"There's no time for small talk," the one they called Captain approached them. "Get up and get ready for action."

Abraham didn't know what the captain was talking about. He knew from the excitement amongst the men that something big was going down this day, but nobody had bothered to tell him what it was. As far as Abraham was concerned, he was only here to point out John and Isaac. The rest of it was up to them.

Abraham walked outside to relieve himself and watched as Asheborne's men huddled around the captain, who was quietly giving his orders. He stopped when he saw Abraham approaching.

"If I'm going to be involved, don't you think I should know what's going on?" he asked.

"You'll know soon enough. This doesn't involve you, so go get the horses ready and wait for us to join you."

Abraham wandered off, glad to be rid of his two shadows for a few minutes. He might not know what they were doing, but he wasn't stupid. The captain was preparing his men for battle, but against who, Abraham didn't know. It certainly wasn't to capture John because they were still two days away from him.

He had ridden to Turville, a small town between London and Oxford, with only his two companions by his side. It wasn't until the previous evening that the other men had joined them. Abraham had counted at least twenty, and he was sure there were others he hadn't yet seen.

One man caught his attention more than the rest. Small and stocky with the dullest, deadest grey eyes he had ever seen, this man looked like he was in fantastic shape and could handle himself very well. There was something else, though, something Abraham couldn't put his finger on.

The man had an aura about him, but it wasn't a good one. Whoever this man was, he had an aura of pure evil, and Abraham wanted nothing to do with him. Nor did anyone else by the look of it, because nobody went near him. Nobody that was, except the captain, who had looked uncomfortable when Abraham had watched them talking together earlier.

There was something different about this journey, and Abraham would be glad when it was over.

"Come on, traitor, we're leaving." Abraham's shadows were back.

"One of these days, I'll ram those words down your throat," Abraham said, his nostrils flaring in the weak autumn sunshine.

The two men got into position behind the main group, one in front of Abraham and the other behind, just like always.

Not long after, the captain brought his men to a halt in the middle of dense woodland at a bend in the rough road.

"This is it, boys," the captain shouted. "Our rider said Parker has left Lewknor and is on the way to Turville. You all know what to do, so may God be with you, and let's do what we're here for."

"What are we doing?" Abraham asked. "Whose Parker? What are we doing to him?"

"You aren't doing anything, so ease up" his annoyer-in-chief said. "You'll be with us, nice and quiet, out of the way. Do you hear? Nice and quiet."

"I hear loud and clear. What's he doing here? Who is he?" Abraham pointed at Oswyn Gare, who was dismounting and leading his horse away from the road.

"Him?" The two men looked at each other. "He's on his own. You just stay away from him and don't look what he's doing. It's in yer own interests to ignore him."

"I don't need to be told that," Abraham said. "There's something evil about him."

"You have no idea," the captain said, who had crept unseen right up to them. "You are to stay out of the way and have no involvement today. Just stay quiet and still. Do you understand?"

"I understand." Abraham understood perfectly well.

Some poor soul was going to get ambushed and probably killed. Why? He did not know, and frankly, he didn't care.

Tension filled the air as silence fell and the men took their positions. Not long later, Abraham heard the sounds of horses and carriages approaching from the direction of Lewknor. Abraham took a deep breath and was glad he wasn't playing a part in this deadly game.

The tension grew as the sounds grew louder. Abraham wanted to keep an eye on the frightening stranger, but he wasn't anywhere to be seen.

Probably best if I don't see him, he thought. But he kept looking for him, anyway.

Two horses came into view around the bend. The men on the horses talked and laughed, completely oblivious to what was about to happen. Abraham felt pity for them.

A carriage came into view, but Abraham couldn't see who or how many were inside it. Behind that, he could just make out two more horses.

Then all hell broke loose.

Abraham watched in morbid fascination, the scene unfolding before him taking him back to another time when he was with Andrew and the Underlings, and they were the ones being ambushed. Although one of their friends had died that day, Abraham had fond memories of himself and Andrew fighting their way out together and living to start anew.

Today was different. Andrew was dead because of his cowardice. The shadows were right to call him a traitor, because that is exactly what he was, a traitor who betrayed his best friend.

Stop it.

Abraham pulled his mind back to the events in front of him. Archers unleashed a hail of arrows, felling the four horsemen on either side of the carriage. When the carriage ground to a halt, men with swords ran to it and dragged the occupants onto the muddy road. Two more men with raised swords tried to protect their master, but they fell quickly under the onslaught.

Now only one man remained alive, and Andrew could hear him pleading for his life.

"Please," he yelled in a high-pitched voice. "I have coin, and you can have it all. Please don't kill me."

"I know who you are, Lord Parker." The intimidating spectre of Oswyn Gare emerged from the trees and approached the now-shivering man.

"I know where you've been, and who you have seen."

"I. I. I don't know what you mean," Lord Parker stammered. "I'm a wool trader, and I have been visiting my estates in the north."

"If you lie to me, it will only make it worse. I know you have seen the Howard boy, and I want you to tell me everything you know about him and his sister."

"The Howard boy? I know nothing about him."

Gare held up his hand. "I told you not to lie to me."

With lightning speed, Gare pounced on Parker and pulled him into the trees, out of sight of the rest of the men.

What happened next would live with Abraham, and probably everyone else present, for the rest of their lives.

A piercing scream, followed by sobs that could have been heard from miles away, ripped through the woodlands. Another scream. Then shouts. "Please, for the love of God!" Parker pleaded for his life, but from the screams that followed, Oswyn Gare wasn't showing any mercy.

"Please stop," the man yelled one more time. "If you stop, I'll tell you whatever you want to know."

Gare said nothing, or at least nothing Abraham could hear, but then he heard Parker talking. Fast. He couldn't make out many words, but he heard him mention John Howard, Sarah Howard, Thomas Howard, someone named Stanton, and a house in what he thought was Stratford-upon-Avon.

"What about Margaret Colte's documents?" Abraham could clearly hear Gare shouting the words at Parker.

"I don't know what you're talking about."

More screams.

"I tell you, I don't know about Margaret's documents. If they're there, Stanton never told me about them."

Another blood-curdling scream.

"I swear I'm telling the truth."

"What about the man they call Edward Johnson? Does he have them?"

"No. I don't know. He's Stanton's personal guard. That's all I know about him, I swear."

More words that Abraham couldn't make out were spoken before one last spine-tingling howl that made the hairs on Abraham's arms stand up. He looked over at his two shadows, who stared back with faces as pale and ghostly as his own must have looked. "Who, or what, is he?" one of them whispered.

Gare emerged into the road, his cloak, face, and hands covered in blood. "I've got what I want," he said to the captain, who stood staring at the aberration in front of him. "Get your men to bury him, and then we need to get to a town before dark."

The captain gestured to his men, who entered the killing fields to bury the body of the unfortunate Lord Parker. Abraham couldn't see through the trees, but he could hear seasoned soldiers vomiting and retching in the forest. Whatever this man had done, it was too much for even battle-hardened warriors to withstand. Abraham looked at his shadows and lurched forward, emptying his stomach onto the forest floor.

Oswyn Gare mounted his horse and trotted forward, seemingly oblivious to the evil he had just perpetrated.

Everyone else fell behind, silent and lost in their own thoughts. Abraham thought of John, Isaac, and the girl, and for the first time, he felt sorry for them.

Attack on Burningtown

"My coin's on John," Isaac whispered to Catherine. "I've never seen anyone as good as him with the longbow."

"I don't know," Catherine whispered back. "I think he's met his match with Edward."

"We'll see," Isaac said.

Daylight was breaking slowly over the horizon, revealing fields of pure white as the early morning frost covered the land on this cold October morning. All four huddled deep beneath their cloaks as they gathered fire-wood in preparation for what promised to be a long, cold winter.

John's heart felt light as he heard Catherine humming to herself in the early morning autumn shadows. Ever since his proposal, she had never stopped singing and dancing. It was the happiest John had ever felt in his entire life.

If only Sarah were here to see this. She would be so proud of me.

The darkness gave way to a pale blue sky, and John knew it wouldn't be long before the sun turned the white fields into a wet, soggy mess. But he didn't care. Edward and himself had been gently goading each other for days about the contest they were about to have between themselves.

Who was better with the longbow, John, or Edward? Most of the smart coin would have been on Edward, but Isaac, John's loyal and best friend, had an unswerving belief in him, and was the only one besides John himself that thought he had a chance.

"Even Catherine doesn't think I will win," John complained, watching his breath stream out of his mouth. "And she's supposed to love me!"

"I do love you," Catherine replied. "I just think Edward will win. Don't worry though, because I'll still love you even though you will be second best."

John playfully pushed Catherine as Edward and Isaac sniggered behind them.

"Let's get the targets set up so I can best you," Edward said. "I have chores to do back at the house. Sybil is so pregnant she can barely bend anymore, so I promised I would help her with her chores after we're done."

"I'll help too," Catherine said. "I told her I'd be there as soon as the contest was over."

"Let's do it then." John grabbed the apples they were going to use as targets.

He looked at Burningtown, that was emerging from the darkness off to his left. This was his favourite view of the house, with the ivy-covered wall and all four chimneys in full view from his vantage point behind the wall around a furlong away. Smoke was showing from two of the chimneys, telling John that Burningtown Manor was coming to life.

It was going to be a good day.

A slight movement from under the large tree at the rear of the house caught John's eye. Stopping in his tracks, he signalled for Edward and Isaac to join him. "Under the big tree at the back. Do you see it?"

Edward and Isaac both nodded. Catherine ducked down behind the wall as John had indicated. Staring intently, John tried making out what he had seen.

A man ducked and kept a low profile as he ran from the shelter of the tree, through the flower garden towards the ivy-covered side of the house. He wasn't too far away for John to see the glint of steel in his hand.

Edward prodded John in the ribs and pointed at the tree at the rear of the house. John counted ten men as they silently made their way to the front of the house. One stayed on the ivy sided wall while the others went to ground and crawled underneath the large windows so they wouldn't be seen from the inside.

John watched as the men split into two groups. One group gathered around the front door, with the other near the large window.

"Who are they?" Isaac whispered, but John could tell from the tone of his voice that he already knew the answer.

"They've found us," John said flatly. "They're here for us."

"What about the Stantons and Sybil?" Catherine asked.

John was about to reply when the men at the house burst into action. So too did Edward Johnson, who raised his longbow and aimed it at the man standing guard along the ivy-covered side of the house.

"Oh no," Isaac groaned, pointing at the cottage they shared with Edward and Sybil. Another group of men, at least four in number, had gathered around the cottage and were about to break in.

The sound of shattering glass exploding into a thousand pieces pierced the early morning serenity. At the same time, the first group kicked in the front door and raced inside the house. The men at the cottage vanished under a hail of shouts and screams.

An arrow whooshed from Edward's longbow, taking down the guard alongside the ivy-covered side of the house. He was over the wall and running even before the arrow hit its target.

"Stay there and don't move," John ordered Catherine, as he and Isaac jumped over the wall and ran after Edward.

Edward veered off towards the cottage while John and Isaac ran to the house. As they got near, James Stanton staggered out of the front door, clutching his side. One attacker ran after him, and Stanton turned to face him. He was giving as good as he got.

With terrifying efficiency, and without hesitation, the man ran his sword straight through James's middle, and John watched him collapse to the ground in a heap. John screamed and threw himself into battle, his sword raised high in the air.

He thudded into the man, his momentum sending the attacker flying in the air. John's sword was buried in his neck before the man could even begin to recover.

Isaac was fighting two more men who had seen them and ran to the aid of their comrade. A shadow burst past John, and in a brief second of fury, ripped the guts from the two attackers. Edward Johnson stood before John, his lips pulled back, baring his teeth in a look of blind fury the likes of which John had never seen.

Isaac fell to the ground holding his left arm, but John didn't have time to go to his aid because more men appeared from the house. Isaac saw them and struggled to his feet. Johnson let out a blood-curdling howl and threw himself at their attackers.

Moments later, eight men lay dead or dying in the courtyard of Burningtown Manor, one of them being the owner, James Stanton. Isaac moaned and fell, clutching his neck as well as his arm.

Edward ran into the house, closely followed by John, who gave a pained stare at his best friend as he ran past him. Whatever was wrong with Isaac would have to wait.

"You!" Edward spat the words out, staring at a blood-soaked man inside the manor house. "The captain. I should have killed you when I had the chance."

"Maybe you should have, but harbouring wanted murderers is a dangerous game played by fools," the man replied. "You should have known this day was coming."

Johnson didn't say another word. Instead, he lunged at the man in a frightening display of strength and skill. The man fell under Edward's furious onslaught.

"Stop!" a voice behind them snapped. "Stop, or I'll kill Catherine."

John spun around and staggered backwards, grabbing at the wall for support. "Abraham! What have you done?"

"I'll let her go if you lay down your swords and give yourselves up. It's over, John."

John's body shook, and he fought to regain control of himself. Abraham tightened his grip on Catherine, pushing his knife closer to her throat.

"Last chance, John. I swear I'll kill her if you don't lay down your sword."

"You are a dead man, Abraham," John's voice shook as he struggled to get the words out. "You betrayed us, and now they're all dead because of you."

"Catherine will be dead because of you if you don't do as I say. Lay down your swords and put your hands over your heads. Both of you."

"I swear I will kill you if it's the last thing I ever do."

John threw his sword down and put his hands over his head. "Let her go, Abraham, and I'll do as you ask."

"You too." Abraham pointed at Edward, whose face was flushed beyond recognition. He threw his sword down without a word.

Abraham gestured for them to go outside, his eyes never leaving theirs as he shuffled backwards with his knife held firmly at Catherine's throat.

A sneer, followed by a bark of laughter, followed them out of the house. A man John hadn't seen before emerged from the great hall covered in so much blood that John had to look twice to make sure he was human.

His gaze made John shudder as he felt his soul violated by the most cruel, lifeless eyes he had ever seen. It was as though his very presence sucked the humanity from John's body.

Abraham backed out into the early morning sunlight, and as he did, he let out a scream and fell to the ground. Isaac stood over him, swaying in the gentle breeze with blood dripping from the knife he held in his hand.

"Run, Catherine! Get away from here," John yelled. "You know where to go, so run."

Catherine looked at John, then spun around and ran towards the outbuilding and safety. Isaac fell back to the ground, groaning in agony, blood running down his neck.

From nowhere, a knife flashed through the air and embedded itself in John's shoulder in almost the same spot that Margaret had stabbed him just weeks earlier. He blinked rapidly and fumbled at the handle of the knife, falling to his knees beside his best friend.

The soulless eyes looked at John before turning his attention to Edward Johnson. "You have information I need, and you won't enjoy my methods of getting it from you, so it's in your best interests if you just tell me what I want to know right now and save yourself the pain."

John watched Edward, who stood his ground and said nothing.

"You took the documents Margaret Colte left behind at her house in London. What did you do with them?" The man tipped his head back with a grin that was as frightening as it was unkind. John had never seen a more terrifying man in his entire life.

Margaret? Documents? What was this man talking about? And what was Edward doing with them? Why hadn't anyone told him about them? How did Edward know the man he called captain?

Still, Edward didn't say a word. He stood there with clenched fists, as if waiting for the man to attack him. Which he did.

With frightening speed, the man threw himself at Edward, but with equally fast reflexes, Edward dodged out of the way and in an instant had produced a knife from under his cloak.

"That won't help you," the man said, and John believed him. It was as if this man wasn't human. The man lunged at Edward once again, this time catching hold of him. Edward sliced upwards with his knife, cutting the man's neck from shoulder to ear. And yet the man didn't even flinch or step backwards. Instead, he knocked the knife from Edward's hand and head-butted him violently, knocking the senses out of him. Blood spurted from Edward's nose, covering both himself and the already blood-soaked man in even more fresh blood.

"I'm going to enjoy this," the man said, dragging Edward back towards the house. John braced himself and yanked the dagger from his shoulder. Stifling a scream, he got to his feet and staggered towards the devil inside the cloak.

John threw the knife as hard as he could, burying it deep between the man's shoulder blades. This time the man slowed down, but he didn't fall or make any sounds. He turned to face John, keeping his grip tight on Edward's neck.

"I was going to enjoy taking my time when I killed you," the man snarled. "But now I'm going to enjoy it even more."

John's intervention had given Edward time to regain his senses, and he grabbed the man's wrist and twisted it as he had done to the captain weeks earlier. The man's wrist didn't crack like the captain's had, but Edward had done enough to loosen his grip. He used his other free hand to hit the man as hard as he could in the jugular.

Even this strange man couldn't stand up to this onslaught. He staggered back, gasping for breath. Edward attacked again, this time crashing a huge hand into the man's temple. The man staggered again but still refused to fall.

Edward started forward but halted abruptly. The captain appeared from inside the house, unsteady on his feet and holding his wounded arm.

"Stop." The captain pointed at the tree-lined road leading in and out of Burningtown Manor. Clouds of dust and the faint sounds of hooves crunching on the road took everyone's attention.

The fearsome man's shoulders tensed as the captain pulled the knife from his back. He turned to face John and Edward. "No matter where you hide, I will find you. I will never stop looking for you until the day I die. You will never rest in peace knowing I am out there searching for you. I give you one last chance, Edward Johnson. Tell me where Margaret's documents are, and I shall leave you alone."

Edward spat on the ground. "After what you've done to my family, it is I who will hunt you. Whoever, or whatever you are, I shall not rest until I avenge my family."

"You have been warned," the man said. "As for you, John Howard, you are a dead man walking. No matter what you do, you are a dead man. Whether it is now, or a year from now, I will find you and kill you."

"Enough," the captain said. "We have to go." He grabbed the evil one and dragged him, still staring at Edward, towards the rear of the house where they no doubt had their horses ready for their escape.

Abraham stirred from where he lay and got to his feet. "Don't leave me here, I'm coming with you." He followed the captain and the man around the side of the house.

"I'm coming after you, Abraham," John said.

"Not if he gets you first," Abraham pointed at the scary man, and John knew he was right. He sighed and fell to his knees.

"Isaac," he yelled, forcing himself back to his feet and towards his best friend lying face down on the ground.

Several horses thundered into the courtyard. John was aware of men dismounting and shouting orders that went unheard. He fell beside his friend as darkness enveloped him.

Aftermath

Hands gathered the semi-conscious John Howard and carried him into the house, struggling and screaming incoherently. For a moment, he was back on the south side of the river in the Vine brewhouse with Ren Walden and Rolf the German, and he swatted away at the helping hands that were trying to carry him.

"Take it easy, boy," someone said. "We're here to help. Your attackers are gone."

John opened his eyes and shook his head, trying to clear the heavy fog that threatened to envelop him. "Isaac," was all he could say.

"Your friend is in a bad way, but God willing he'll be alright."

"Who are you?" John asked, finally regaining his senses. "What happened? Where is Catherine?"

"I'm George Harrington, and these are my men. I'm a friend of James, and you're lucky that his cook escaped and came to me. If he hadn't, I fear you would all be dead by now."

"Catherine. Where's Catherine?" John bolted up, now

fully back in control of himself. He winced as white-hot pain seared through his shoulder.

"Steady, lad. We need to take care of that wound."

"I'm fine. Take care of Isaac and the others who need your help." John slid off the table he was lying on and took his bearings.

He was in James Stanton's private study. Clutching his shoulder, he ran to the great hall, where a small crowd was gathered around the large table. John pushed his way through and shuddered to a halt, his face ashen in disbelief at the sight in front of him.

Joan Stanton was spread out on the table, carved open like a goose at Christmas. No wonder that strange, evil man had been covered in so much blood. After his recent experiences in London, John thought he'd seen it all and that nothing could bother him again.

He was wrong. This was the vilest act of inhumanity he had ever seen. He flinched his shoulders, the sharp pain from his wound making him gasp for breath. He covered his eyes and backed away, barely reaching the fireplace before collapsing to his knees and vomiting for all he was worth.

Who was this man? No, what was this man? What kind of evil could do such a thing?

He struggled to his feet and ran to another room where their rescuers were working on Isaac. John sighed in relief when his best friend gave him the thumbs up sign. He returned the gesture and ran out of the house to the courtyard.

"Are you John?" someone yelled out as he ran past another room.

"Yes, I'm John. Who is asking?"

George Harrington pushed past the man, who yelled and gestured for John to join him inside the room. "James

Stanton is asking for you and he says it's urgent." He lowered his voice to a whisper. "He's not long left in this world, I'm afraid. His injuries are too great."

Harrington lowered his head but not before John saw the slack, heavy expression in his eyes. "What happened here? You owe me an explanation and by God, you are going to give it to me. James Stanton is a good man who doesn't deserve to die like this. And what kind of animal did that to his wife?" Harrington's voice broke up. "I mean, who in God's name commits such an act?" his eyes clouded, and he grabbed John's arm.

"I don't know who that man was," John said. "But I promise I will find him and avenge what he did here." John pulled away from George Harrington and went to James Stanton, who was laying quietly on another table. His face was as pale as moonlight, and his hands were as cold as ice.

"I'm so sorry, James. I never thought it would come to this. I would never have agreed to come here if I thought you were in this much danger."

"Promise me . . ." Blood trickled from James Stanton's mouth as he struggled to speak.

"I promise I will find the men who did this," John said.

"Promise me. Promise that you will avenge what they did to us."

John bowed his head, tears streaming down his face. "I promise you, James. This crime shall not go unpunished."

Stanton pulled John weakly towards him and whispered in his ear. "Does Edward live?"

John nodded. "Edward lives. He will help me find these men and avenge you."

Stanton shook his head. "Edward knows. He knows where the docum . . ." He lurched forward, coughing up blood and groaning in agony. Gripping John's arm as tightly as he could, Stanton pulled John even closer.

"He knows where the coin hides in the wall. You will need it if you are to survive. Hidden with the coin is a pouch with details of Margaret Colte's confessions. They are what you need to prove your innocence. Edward knows."

Stanton released his grip from John's arm, but John pulled him even tighter to him. "What do you mean, Margaret's confessions? What are you talking about?"

Stanton shook his head. "Edward knows," he repeated. His voice was failing, but he made one last effort. "Go to your sister. Find her and keep her safe. She is in Stratford. Find the Chapel of the Guild and look for the three-story house opposite. She is there."

"You knew where Sarah was all along and didn't tell me?" John pulled back, hardly able to believe what he had just heard. "Why didn't you tell me where she is?"

It was too late. James Stanton lurched forward one more time before falling backwards, his face a mask of death.

"Whatever he held back from you, he did for good reason." George Harrington placed his hands on John's arm. "I've known this man for a long time, and whatever he did was always in the best interests of those he cherished. Whatever he has done for you, he and his family have paid a heavy price for it. Never forget that."

John fought back the anger screaming at him from inside his head and shivered.

Why did Stanton hold back Sarah's whereabouts from me? Was my uncle behind it? What are these confessions that Margaret left behind, and why does Stanton have them? Why didn't he give them to me earlier? And what does Edward know that he never told me?

John's head was spinning. He had more questions than answers. *Was my uncle somehow behind all of this secrecy? If so, why? Why hold back from me the evidence I need if it proves my innocence? I never even knew of their existence. Why not tell me where Sarah was hiding?*

"James told me who you are," Harrington said softly. "I know you are John Howard, the man everyone in England is trying to find for the big rewards on offer. They say you have killed many people and are highly dangerous. And yet James took you in and loved you like a son. I don't know why he did it, but I do know what it has cost him."

Harrington gave John a withering look. "Promise me you will not let his sacrifice go in vain, and I promise I won't tell the authorities, who are on their way here as we speak, who you are. I shall plead ignorance as to your true identity."

John nodded slowly. "I am innocent of the charges made against me, and from what Stanton just told me, I can now prove it. I promise I shall find the man who did this to James, and especially to Joan, and I shall make sure he finds justice."

Harrington released his hold on John's arm and stood aside. "It is better you find your friends and leave before the sheriff gets here."

"What about George?" John asked. "What is to become of him?" He bowed his head at the thought of George losing both his parents in such a horrific way.

"I promised James I would take care of George if he's still alive. I don't know where he is, and I have men searching for him as we speak. Do you know where he could be?"

"I might, if he made it there in time. James has a safe place for times such as this. We were all taken by surprise, and most of us didn't have the time to get there. We can only hope that George made it."

"Find him and bring him to me," Harrington ordered. "Then get away from here and never come back."

"I understand." John backed away before Harrington changed his mind and held him for the sheriff and the constables.

He ran to the outbuilding and ran inside, remembering the path James had shown them in happier times. He quickly found the bookcase and pressed the lever to open the secret entrance to the stairs leading into the darkness below.

"Catherine! George! Sybil! It's me, John. Are you down here? It's safe now and I need you to come out. We have to hurry."

John waited a few moments but heard nothing, so he started down the narrow steps, wishing he had a candle to light the way.

"John?" Catherine's voice came from the darkness below. "John, is that you?"

"It is me. Are you all down there?"

Catherine's face appeared from the darkness. She threw herself at John, weeping and crying as she held him tightly. John allowed himself to tremble at her touch for a few moments before pulling himself together and pushing her away. "Where are George and Sybil? Are they down there with you?"

"I'm here." George's trembling voice sounded from the darkness.

John grabbed George and hugged him tightly. "Are you alright?" he asked, sweat pouring from his forehead.

"Where are my parents? Are they alright?"

Tears welled in John's eyes and ran down his cheeks. "Do you know who George Harrington is?"

"Yes, he's my father's friend and a good man. Why? Is he here? Where are my mother and father?"

"I'm so sorry, George," John looked at Catherine in anguish. "We were ambushed, and they didn't make it. I'm so sorry. George Harrington is waiting for you, and he will take care of you."

"What do you mean they didn't make it? Didn't you and Edward save them?" George pushed John aside and ran out of the outbuilding, shouting for his father.

John sank to his knees. "I'm so sorry." His voice cracked under the weight of the emotion.

"You're hurt," Catherine said, noticing the blood running down his arm.

"I'm fine," John said. "Where's Sybil? Is she still down there?"

Catherine shook her head. "She never made it, John. I thought she was with you."

John jumped to his feet and ran to the cottage. Four men stared up at John through lifeless eyes as he stepped over their corpses to get to Edward, who was kneeling in front of the blood-soaked body of his pregnant wife.

"Edward," he started, but Johnson ignored him. He was on his knees, cradling Sybil in his arms.

"Look what they did," he said. "Look what they did to Sybil. Who kills an innocent pregnant woman? Not even the king executes a woman who's with child."

John sank to his knees and put his hand on Edward's shoulder. He was about to speak when Edward waved him off. "I know this wasn't your fault and I'm not blaming you for it, but be warned, do not stand in my way as I go after the men who did this. The captain for one, but the other one, the evil one, is to be left to me. Do you understand?"

"I understand," John said. "And be assured that I shall be right by your side when we find the monsters who did this."

Catherine screamed and fell beside John. "Sybil!" she screamed. "Sybil. Who could do such a thing?"

"I know who they are," Edward Johnson got to his feet.

"At least I know who some of them are. As for the evil one, I do not know who he is, but I know where to look."

"Edward, we have to talk about this," John said. "The sheriff will be here any moment, and you know what that means for me. We need to hide somewhere until they've gone so we can come back and bury our loved ones."

He hesitated. "Then we need to work together to rescue my sister and find the men who did this. Once they are avenged, I will use the confessions Margaret Colte left behind to clear my name and prove my innocence."

"What?" Catherine yelled.

"You know about the documents from Margaret Colte?" Edward asked.

"James Stanton told me with his dying words. He said you know where they are."

Edward nodded. "If it was the master's dying wish, then I shall tell you, but not before I avenge my wife and unborn child."

"And I shall be with you every step of the way, my friend. You are not doing this alone."

John turned and fell into Catherine's arms. "This is all my fault," he sobbed. "Even from beyond the grave, Margaret continues to haunt me. Even being dead isn't enough for her. Everyone I come into contact with ends up dead, and it's all because of her."

John Howard sobbed and sobbed.

Wounds Run Deep

John, Edward, and Catherine half carried and half dragged the injured Isaac to the large tree at the rear of Burningtown Manor.

They barely made it before horses thundered into the front courtyard and the sheriff and his men surveyed the horrific scene that awaited them.

A narrow lane led from the rear of the house, and Edward signalled for the others to follow him along it. Isaac tried walking under his own steam, but he was barely conscious and had to be supported the whole time. Keeping to the tree line, they followed Edward along the short path until a stone tower came into view in front of them. On a different day, John would have stopped to admire the view.

But not today.

The cross on top of the tower pointed towards the heavens, and John knew this must be a church.

"This is the Church of St James-the-Less." Edward choked on the words, and John felt sorry for him. As strong as he was, his heart must be wrenching out of his body after what he'd just witnessed.

"It's been here for hundreds of years already," Edward added. "It's where we all came to pray."

"I'm so sorry." John couldn't think of anything else to say. He looked at his beloved Catherine and saw the shock and sorrow in her eyes. His heart hurting, John almost dropped Isaac as he reached out for the love of his life.

"I'm so sorry," he sobbed. "I didn't mean for any of this to happen."

"Poor Sybil didn't deserve this," Catherine said. "She was only a few weeks away from having her child, and what happened to her is unforgivable. Nobody is blaming you for what happened, but you must help Edward avenge her."

"Believe me, I will. Above all else that we do, we shall avenge Sybil."

"I'll help too." The words gurgled from Isaac's mouth, but everyone felt his passion.

"We all will," John reassured him.

Edward said nothing. He kept looking straight ahead until they reached an old wooden door with a pointed top. "This is the tower door and is always kept open in case of emergencies. Remember that if you ever need to come here again." Edward pushed through the old door and entered the church.

He made a beeline for a large, octagonal stone font that stood in front of the altar. John noticed an exquisite pattern of oak leaves carved all around it, and a dedication to the family that donated the font was etched on the base. John didn't know why he was looking at a time like this, but he was drawn to the magnificence of this mediaeval church and its wonderful ancient possessions from another time.

The font was donated to the church in 1348 by someone named Ellis Blount and his son Tobias. John wondered who they were and what kind of life they had lived. Whatever it was, he hoped it had been better than the one he was living right now.

Edward's voice pulled him back to the reality of the moment. "Help me with this. It's heavy."

Edward was behind the altar, pushing on a huge oak chest. John joined him, and together they heaved until they had moved it enough to expose an opening underneath it.

"Get in there," Edward ordered. "It's a safe place that's been there for centuries. You'll be safe."

"What about you? Where are you going?" John asked.

"I'm going back to see if any of the men who attacked us are still alive. If they are, they'll wish they weren't. I'll be back once the sheriff has gone."

John knew it was pointless trying to argue, so he simply bowed his head and complied. "Please be careful, Edward. Together, we will avenge Sybil and the Stantons."

John and Edward lowered Isaac into the dark, uninviting hole beneath them. Then they helped Catherine down, before John joined them in the darkness.

"There's candles down there, and fresh air reaches it from a small channel cut into the earth. Stay quiet, and I will be back for you after dark."

The cramped hole was barely big enough for them to sit in, and Isaac moaned quietly to himself as Edward struggled to push the heavy oak chest back into place. Once he had, the darkness was all consuming.

Isaac's whimpers cut through John like a dagger, and the pain in his shoulder was almost unbearable. Catherine sobbed quietly and held John's arm tightly.

John dug around in the darkness until his hands closed around a sack. He felt the familiar shape of candles inside the sack and pulled one of them out, along with tinder and a flint to light them. Once it was lit, he held it up so he could see where they were.

The hole was dug into the damp earth and had probably been built to provide a fast hiding place long ago in another time. John thought it sad that they still had a use for such places today in the age of the great King Henry.

The candle flickered as fresh air blew in from an unseen air hole. He hoped they wouldn't be in there long because he already felt cold, cramped, and stiff. It was going to be a long day.

"Stay strong, Isaac," John whispered. "We'll attend to your wounds just as soon as we get out of here and are sure the sheriff has gone."

Isaac moaned, which John took as an affirmative response. If his best friend was anything, he was tough, and John knew he would be alright as long as they saw to his wounds in the next few hours.

They sat in silence, each full of their own thoughts and emotions. Isaac's occasional groans broke the silence now and again, but for the most part, they all lived inside their own personal nightmares.

A faint sound above them brought John back to his senses. The dull thud of feet and muffled voices sounded like they were miles away, and yet John knew they were only a few feet above their heads.

John couldn't hear what was being spoken, but he could make out enough to know someone was shouting and probably giving orders. He braced himself for the sound of the oak chest being moved before they were discovered.

If they were, it was all over. Sybil, the Stantons, John Two, Andrew, David, Helena, Mark, Henry Colte, the list just kept growing, and all of them would have died for nothing if they were discovered now.

Eventually, the noises died down, and the church returned to silence. John sighed and settled back into his thoughts.

What documents did Margaret leave behind? Did she leave a diary confessing all of her many sins? If she did, what was James Stanton doing with them, and what did Edward know about them? James said they would prove my innocence, so why did he continue to hide me, knowing how dangerous it was for him and his family? If he'd given them to me when we first arrived here, this could all be over by now and he and his family would still be alive. As would Sybil and her unborn child.

John's head dropped at the thought of Sybil lying in Edward's arms. *Who, or more importantly, why, would someone do such a thing? And what about Joan Stanton? Who was that man? He looked and acted like the devil himself. Nothing seemed to hurt him, and no act of desecration seemed too far for him. And what about Abraham? What was he doing with such an evil man?*

And then it hit him. John slapped his forehead with the palm of his hand. "Of course," he said out loud. "Abraham was with them because they all work for Lord Asheborne. How else would Abraham know these men? Asheborne somehow found out where we were hiding and sent them to kill us."

"You think Lord Asheborne would send a man like the one you described?" Catherine asked. "Surely a man so high as him wouldn't do such a thing."

"Being a lord doesn't make you a better man," John answered. "You only have to look at my own family to realise that."

"That's true," her voice sounded sad in the darkness. "I'm sorry, John," she added quickly.

They sat in silence for hours, until John heard a faint sound above his head. The oak chest was moving!

John braced himself, hoping it was Edward, but ready in case it wasn't. Whatever happened from now on, John had decided during his hours alone with his thoughts that they would not take him alive. He knew what would happen to Catherine if they were captured, and as long as he drew breath, he wouldn't allow it.

No, if they want to capture me and parade me around London like a common criminal, they will have to kill me first.

The oak chest slid out of the way, and although it was dark outside, it wasn't as black as the hole they were about to ascend from. John could make out enough to see Edward stood over them, offering his hand to help them out.

"It is I, Edward. Take my hand, and I'll help you out."

Isaac moaned as John pushed and Edward pulled his friend out of the hole. Catherine followed, and John came out last.

"What happened?" John asked. "Has the sheriff captured the men who attacked us?"

"Sit down." Edward pointed to a row of pews in the dark church.

"What happened?" John repeated the question. "Did you at least bury Sybil and the Stantons?"

Edward sighed. "The captain remained at the house after the evil one escaped. He produced letters from the king proclaiming they were acting on his authority because James was aiding a known murderer. That made all of us guilty of harbouring you, and therefore, we were all to be arrested and captured, either dead or alive."

"What lies!" Catherine shouted.

"Furthermore, the sheriff has now proclaimed that as I

am an accomplice to murder, I am to be captured or killed on sight. I am wanted almost as much as you are now."

"What about Joan? How did he explain the pure evil of her death? I've never even heard of such barbarity before, much less witnessed it," John said. "Not to mention Sybil. I'm sorry, Edward, but not even the king would order the murder of a woman with child."

Edward's lips curled into a snarl. "The captain said that when they got here, James and Joan decided to turn you over to them, and when you learned they had betrayed you, it was you who butchered Joan and murdered James."

"And they believed such lies? What about Sybil?"

Edward sighed. "The captain said he wounded you in the shoulder when he caught you murdering Sybil. He said he was trying to stop you, and it was you who injured him when you assaulted him."

"Why would he say I killed Sybil? What benefit would I gain from that?"

"The captain said you bragged to him that you would blame her murder on him so I would help you kill them all and escape."

"And the sheriff believed all this?" John threw his hands in the air in disbelief.

"Yes, he did. When the captain produced the orders from the king, what else was he supposed to do?"

"What did you say to him? Surely you told him it was all lies?" John was almost screaming now.

"I was hiding close by. The sheriff issued an order that I am to be detained, either dead or alive, for aiding you. He said they would give me a fair trial because of what you did to Sybil, and if I assist in your capture, then I would receive a full pardon."

John looked at Edward. "And what do you propose to do about that?"

"Nothing, of course. We all know it's lies just to get me to help them capture you. The captain is working for Lord Asheborne, that much I know, and he will make sure I die if I turn myself in because I know too much."

"Yes, you do," John said. "And there is much you and I need to discuss, but now is not the time."

"I agree," Edward bowed his head.

"What about the friend of James, the one who came to our aid?" John asked. "Didn't he tell him what happened?"

Edward threw his hands in the air. "He didn't get there until the slaughter was over. Kenneth, the cook, told him the men who attacked us were there to kill us, but the captain said they were doing it in self-defence. George Harrington could only say what he saw, which wasn't much."

Edward looked up at the heavens. "And then there was George Stanton."

"What did he say?" John waved his fists in the air. "Didn't anyone tell the truth?"

"He was upset when he ran into the house, and from what I heard, he forced his way past Harrington into the great hall. When I saw him he was delirious with grief."

"Oh no," John said. "They should have stopped him from seeing that. It will live with him for the rest of his life."

"George was hysterical, and he blamed you for everything." Edward lowered his head again. "He told them that you forced him into the hiding place, and Catherine held him there while his family was murdered. He told the sheriff that he'd always hated you, and that he believed what the captain said about his parents' murder."

"The poor boy is suffering. He's just saying that because of his grief," Catherine said in the darkness. "He's lashing out at John because none of this would have happened if we weren't there."

"She's right," Edward said. "I wouldn't hold too much against him for what he said."

"I don't," John answered. "It's perfectly understandable. My own half-brother, Arthur, will no doubt grow up hating me for killing his mother, so I understand George's anger. I hope he gets the support he needs with Harrington and his family."

"Did they bury the bodies?" John asked.

"They did," Edward replied. "They buried them all behind the house under the shade of the tree. The captain took the bodies of his men with him when he left."

"So what now?" Catherine asked. "What do we do now?"

John looked at Edward. "I know you want to avenge Sybil, and I promise you I shall be by your side when that happens, but right now, we need your help. If you refuse, then Sybil, James, and Joan will have all died in vain because we will be captured and killed for yet another crime that we didn't commit."

Edward Johnson nodded his head. "I am at your service, John Howard. Together, we will either prevail and gain our vengeance, or we will fail and fall. Either way, we are in this together."

"Your loyalty and friendship will not go unrewarded once I have proven my innocence."

"So what do we do?" Catherine asked again.

"The first thing we are doing is returning to Burningtown Manor," John said. "We need to collect whatever supplies we can muster as well as their honey so we can treat our wounds."

"Yes, good idea," Catherine said. "You all need help,

but I don't think Isaac will make it if we don't heal his wounds."

"Then we retrieve the coin and Margaret's documents that James hid behind a wall somewhere in the house." John said. "Edward knows where it is?"

Edward nodded at John, their eyes locked.

"Then we head for Stratford to rescue my sister."

"There's one more thing," Edward said.

John raised his eyebrows and turned his palms facing upwards.

"The captain said that cryers all over England would announce what happened here today. He said they would tell everyone about a big reward for John Howard and the Underlings."

Cryptic Clues

The small group remained in St James's Church all night. John and Edward prepared to leave for the manor and the cottage before daylight, in case the sheriff had left someone behind to guard the house.

Catherine was to stay behind at the church with the injured Isaac. "Promise me you won't leave us here," she ordered John during their final embrace.

"I promise," John said. "I'll be back before you know it."

John and Edward left the church via the pointed tower door and kept to the protection of the trees on the brief journey back to Burningtown Manor.

Everything was in darkness when they arrived. They split up, with Edward watching the house from the side of the cottage, and John taking his post behind the wall where all this had begun just one day earlier.

Then they waited.

In daylight, it was obvious that the sheriff had posted one of his men to stay behind to guard the house. He walked around the yard at different times, making it impossible to time him and learn his schedule.

John watched Edward sneak up close to him and put him to sleep with a crashing right hand. They joined forces and tied the guard against a tree so he couldn't escape.

Once the guard was restrained, Edward led John to the rear of the house, where it joined the ivy-covered east wall. John kept watch as Edward dropped to his knees and pulled a knife from his cloak, counted three stones up from the bottom, and began scraping away at the daub between the stones. When he had cleared enough out, he started working the stone with his fingers. Eventually, it popped out and fell to the ground.

Reaching inside, Edward pulled out a sack that John could see held a box. Without missing a beat, Edward handed the box to John and replaced the stone back in the wall so as not to make it obvious why they had come back to the house.

John felt a strange tingling sensation in his fingers, and his heart was racing a little. *Am I holding the evidence I need to finally prove my innocence?*

He shivered and placed the sack inside his cloak. Whatever was in there would have to wait until it was safe for him to open it. Wherever that was, it wasn't here, because the sheriff or Harrington could show up at any moment.

"Let's get the supplies and get out of here," Edward said, getting back to his feet. John made sure their prisoner was still tied to the tree before running inside Burningtown Manor one last time.

John walked heavy-footed into the kitchen, trying hard not to look inside the blood-soaked rooms and stir up all the sights and emotions from yesterday. He focused his eyes in front of him and found what he was looking for: bread, honey, and whatever else he could carry that would help them until they reached Stratford, which was at least a day's ride, if not two.

He found Edward on his knees at the side of Sybil's freshly dug grave at the rear of the house. He left him to say his last goodbye and ran to the stables to steal two of the horses that were still there. One of them was already saddled up and obviously belonged to the sheriff's guard, but John didn't care.

He gathered their weapons together and waited for Edward.

Edward didn't speak when he joined John at the stables. Instead, he mounted the horse John had prepared for him and rode off. John followed closely behind, he himself feeling the intense weight of sorrow bearing down on them as they left.

After collecting Isaac and Catherine, they rode for several miles until John pulled off the muddy track and came to a halt by a cluster of trees by the side of a small stream.

"Let's stop here and give the horses a rest," he said. "We'll tend to our wounds and see what's inside this box."

Catherine had ridden with John, while the larger horse belonging to the sheriff's guard carried Edward and Isaac, who had not spoken a word all day. John helped Edward slide Isaac from the horse and laid him down under a tree.

For the first time, John could look at Isaac's wounds. He scrunched up his face into a ball when he saw the state his friend was in. They gently removed Isaac's cloak and laid his head back so they could see the wound on his neck, which John thought was the one causing all his problems.

After rinsing the wound with river water, Catherine and John gently smeared his neck with honey to prevent him from having an apoplexy or some other fatal ailment.

Isaac opened his eyes and squeezed Catherine's hand. "I'm alright," he croaked. "Don't worry about me."

"Always the hero," Catherine said, smiling. "We're taking care of you whether you like it or not, so you can complain all you like because I'm not listening."

Isaac gave a faint smile and coughed. "Just so long as you take care of John first."

"I'm fine, my friend," John leant over Isaac so he could hear him better. "I'm right here and we're going to make you better."

"There's nothing wrong with me." Isaac's voice was raspy, so John reached for the ale he'd brought and sat Isaac up so he could take a drink.

Catherine next looked at his left arm. The wound was deep, and Isaac had lost a lot of blood, which was probably why he was so weak. She washed it and smeared it with honey, just as she had the wound on his neck. She wrapped his arm with linen and gave him more ale to drink.

"You'll be running around again in a few days, but until then I'm ordering you to rest and regain your strength."

"Yes, boss!" Isaac was feeling better already.

John walked away with his hand inside his cloak, but Catherine pulled him back. "Not so fast, John Howard. I want to look at your wound as well."

"I'm fine."

"You sound just like Isaac. Take your cloak off and let me look."

John sighed loudly and looked at the sadness etched all over Edward's face. "I'll do as I'm told," he said.

Once Catherine had tended his wound, he sat by a tree and opened the sack that was burning a hole in his brain.

"What can you tell me about this, Edward?" he asked. "James told me you knew."

Edward pulled a face and sat next to John, who, along with Catherine and the recovering Isaac, was all ears.

"Master James didn't trust Duke Howard after the queen and my former master, George Boleyn, died. After I went to work for him, James always told me that while he liked the duke, after what he did to the queen, he wouldn't trust him again.

When Duke Thomas asked James if he would take you in for a short while, he refused at first. He and I talked about it often, and in the end, he remembered what he'd felt like when George and Anne stood accused of crimes they weren't guilty of."

"How did he know I wasn't guilty?" John asked.

"He didn't, but he took the duke's word for it. He believed him, and that's why he agreed to take you in. But he still didn't trust your uncle."

"How did he get these documents?" John asked.

"He thought your uncle might betray him and claim no knowledge if you were discovered. So when he heard the rumours of Lord Asheborne searching a house in London for some documents of confession from the woman you supposedly killed, he sent me to see if I could find them. Asheborne's men clearly couldn't because they were still searching, so I went and looked."

"And you found them when Asheborne and all his men couldn't?"

"Only by pure chance. I was forced to hide under a mound of horseshit, and I found a ring in a stone under the mound. That's where I found them. I had a run in with the captain as I was leaving, and I knew I should have killed him when I had the chance. I swear I will see him again, and when I do, I will be the last thing he ever sees."

John emptied the contents of the sack onto the ground.

A pouch full of coins fell out first, followed by a wooden box he recognised instantly.

He tossed the bag of coins to Edward, who set about counting them and whistled after he'd finished. "There's a fortune in here," he said. "There's almost ten pounds."

"James Stanton is very generous," John said. "That amount is enough to get us through this and help us escape afterwards, should we need to."

"It's more than enough," Edward said. "This is two years' wage for most of us."

"Hiring horses and constantly running is expensive," John reminded him. "Ask me how I know."

Edward shrugged and replaced the coin in the pouch before throwing it back to John. "Coin doesn't interest me, especially now. I don't need coin for what I want to do."

John pursed his lips and held up the box that he knew so well. A sound like a half grunt, half squeal, forced itself from his throat, and he hit the ground hard with his fist, causing spasms of pain to shoot through his injured shoulder.

"What is it, John?" Catherine asked.

John held out the box in front of him. About ten inches long by eight inches wide, the sides were intricately carved with dolphins spouting water from their mouths. There were two of them, one on each side of the lock, with both facing inwards.

The top was carved with a deep red shield with a white diagonal stripe running from left to right. Each side of the stripe held three white crosses, which followed the diagonal line down the shield.

"That is the most beautiful thing I have ever seen," Catherine said. "What is it, John?"

John's face was deep red, and the flame in his eyes made way to clouds of moisture. "This is my mother's jewellery box. The shield on top is my family's crest. The bitch used my mother's jewellery box."

"Maybe she used it for a good purpose," Catherine spoke softly.

"She didn't know the meaning of good," John spat out the words.

The box was locked, so John forced his knife under the lid and snapped it open. He sighed and shivered, his spine tingling.

Is this it? Is this the proof I need to finally put an end to this nightmare?

Ignoring his quivering muscles, John pulled out the pouch that lay inside the box. He closed his eyes and removed the bundle of documents from inside the pouch.

Catherine, Edward, and Isaac waited patiently while John read them to himself.

"Well?" Catherine asked finally. "What do they say? Did Margaret confess to anything?"

John looked up. "It's definitely Margaret's handwriting, because I'd recognise the devil's work anywhere."

"What does it say?" Isaac croaked.

John began reading out loud.

Confessions

The confessions I am writing are for God alone, as only He can grant me the forgiveness I crave. I pray I may enter His kingdom after my passing.

If someone else is reading my confessions, I am already dead, or I am about to be; the punishment for my many crimes will carry the ultimate penalty.

Either way, my soul will stand before God, waiting for His judgement. I am under no illusions as to my good Christian character because I have none, and He knows I have sinned many times during my life. My confessions are my admission of my guilt to the Lord Almighty in the hope that He forgives me.

My confessions detail the many indiscretions I committed during my life. In the physical world I bear no regret, for everything I did was for the betterment of my life, and to that end, I achieved what I wanted. That I hurt people along the way is a mere consequence that God alone may judge.

My confessions begin with Isobel and follow me throughout my life—from Dawn Browne to Henry Colte, and from Thomas Colte to Robert Howard and his son, the despicable John Howard.

God may demand atonement for what I did to John Howard, but for that I offer no apology, for I would never have achieved my objectives had I not condemned him to a life of poverty and destitution. That he still lives is my worst regret, and it remains the biggest failure of my life.

That other innocent boys had to die in his name is John's own fault and the blame must lie with him, because if he hadn't resisted the way he did, then none of this would have been necessary. He would have gone to France and died over there as he was supposed to have done. Instead, he ran away and caused me endless problems.

What else was I supposed to do?

William Asheborne agreed with me, and he assisted me every step of the way. My life would have been very different if William hadn't found me and shown me the way forward, even when it meant making the difficult decisions regarding the young boys brought to me by the Walden gang.

God alone knows that William has been involved in my life for more years than anyone could ever know. He has been my lover and my partner ever since I left Saddleworth.

Many of my confessions involve William, and he was rightly worried when he discovered I was writing them down. He insisted on keeping them for safekeeping, but as much as I love him, I don't trust him. So my confessions are as much for my protection as they are for my confession to God.

As for John Howard, I cannot find it in my heart to hold any sympathy, for I have never despised a person in my life as much as I despise that boy. My heart will not sing in peace until he is captured and killed before my very eyes.

So, my Lord, the following pages contain my confessions. My hope is that once You have read my life story, You will find forgiveness and allow my soul to rest in Your everlasting glory.

This letter I keep here, at my little white house in London. The rest of my confessions lie safely with T.B where they will never be found during my lifetime. After my death, they will lie in darkness, *waiting to be found one day to reveal the truth. The one thing of which I am certain is that history will remember my name.*

Margaret Colte

JOHN LOOKED up at the faces staring back at him.

"Yea, it looks like you can finally clear your name and claim back your heritage," Isaac said.

"Until we find where she hid the rest of them, we don't have anything," John said.

"This proves your innocence!" Catherine clapped her hands together. "We did it, John. She said plainly in her letter what she did to you."

"Not quite," John said. "We still have to find the rest of them before Asheborne does or we'll never be free of him. No wonder he's sending his worst people after us; he believes we have her confessions, and he's not going to stop until we're dead."

"Let them come," Edward said. "I look forward to it."

"Where are they, then?" Isaac asked, sitting up and looking like he might actually survive his injuries.

"I don't know," John said. "Edward, do you know who T.B. is?"

Edward shook his head. "I never heard Master James mention anyone with those initials. I have no clue who that could be."

"We need to think about it," John said, "but first we need to hurry and rescue Sarah. Once we are all together, we'll find somewhere to hide while we work out who this person is."

"Sounds like a good idea," Isaac said. "Let's go find Lady Sarah. I would love to see her again."

"Yea, we all saw how taken by her you were the last time," Catherine giggled.

Isaac sneered and shook his head at Catherine. He struggled to get to his feet, so John helped him up.

"You are looking better, my friend. Are you good to travel with us?"

"A wild boar wouldn't stop me," Isaac said. "Now help me up onto that horse and let's go find Lady Sarah."

They rode through the night until they reached the outskirts of Stratford, where they waited until first light before making their move to find Sarah Howard.

Stratford-upon-Avon

As dawn broke, the four weary travellers stopped by the side of the River Avon, next to the old medieval parish church. John dismounted and helped Catherine down from their horse.

"Isaac, I know you want to be with us when we rescue Sarah, but you're injured and will slow us down. I need you to stay here with Catherine and take care of the horses."

"I'm going with you." Isaac scowled. "There's nothing wrong with me."

"Please, my friend, do this one thing for me," John pleaded. "There will be plenty of times we need you with us, but now isn't one of them."

Isaac sighed. "Just this once, but if you're not back soon, I'm coming after you."

"Aye, that's fair enough." John nodded. "Are you ready, Edward?"

Edward Johnson, who had barely spoken a word since they left Burningtown, nodded his head. "I'm ready."

"We're looking for the Chapel of the Guild. Sarah's

place is a three-storey house opposite the chapel. Stratford isn't a large place, so it shouldn't be hard to find."

They strode past the old college, followed by an orchard and some more houses, before they came to a turn in the road. Heavy rains had made the road so muddy that John could hear his feet squelching in the mud as he walked.

Looking around to get his bearings in the early morning light, Edward pointed to a stone tower. "I don't know if that is the chapel you spoke of, but it looks like it could be."

John nodded and pushed his way through the mud towards the stone tower. A clock set in the stone rang out, jolting him and making him jump.

"I wasn't expecting that," he whispered to Edward. "It must chime every hour." He pointed to a three-storey house across the strete and to the right a short way.

"That must be it. Are you ready?"

Johnson nodded.

John led them to the gardens at the rear of the house and stopped behind a tree that gave him a good view of what they were facing. Edward took up position behind a bush further to John's right.

The house was in complete darkness. John couldn't see even a hint of a shadow or a flicker from a candle.

He ran to Edward and whispered in his ear. "Everyone must still be asleep, which is unusual, but I can't see any movement at all."

"Neither can I," Edward whispered back.

"Let's go." John stepped forward, with Edward right behind him.

A calmness fell over John, which wasn't unusual at times like this, but this felt different. He felt it because he knew Edward was behind him. Of all the people he had known throughout his life, Edward was the most skilled he had ever seen. To know that he was right behind him going into a dangerous situation such as this was one of the most comforting feelings John had ever experienced. He hoped Edward would stay with him for a long time.

They tried a door on the right side of the gardens, and to John's surprise, it swung open, revealing a dark, uninviting entrance..

Something isn't right.

John's spine tingled, warning him that danger lurked ahead. He turned left into one of the dark downstairs rooms and almost fell over the prone body of a man lying still on the ground.

He blinked, trying to get his eyes to adjust to the dark of the room. Once they had adjusted, he dropped to his knees to look at the man lying before him.

His hands touched the floor and were immediately covered with a thick, sticky fluid.

Blood!

John stood up and removed his sword, noticing that Edward already had his weapon at the ready. John kicked the man over and saw the gaping wound in his chest that told him all he needed to know. He looked at Edward, who was gesturing for him to move forward to the inner sanctum of the house.

John crept quietly into the next room but found nothing. Another slain man was in the study, and John's entire body was shaking.

Sarah! Where's Sarah? No, no, no! This can't be happening. Sarah has to be safe.

Abandoning all stealth, John ran from room to room. He counted at least five dead bodies strewn all over the floors, tables, and furniture. He ran to the stairs, where he found Edward already ahead of him. Two more men lay dead on the stairs, and by now John's head was exploding.

"Sarah! Sarah!" he yelled at the top of his lungs. "Sarah, where are you? It's me, John, and I'm here to rescue you."

Nothing, not a sound, came back at him.

The carnage upstairs was the same as it was downstairs. Twelve men in total lay dead in the house, and there was no sign of Sarah.

What he saw in one bedroom forced John to stop and sink to his knees. Girls' clothes lay scattered around the room, and John recognised the hairbrush on a nearby table.

This was Sarah's room!

"Sarah! Sarah!" he shouted as loud as he could. "If you are here, please come out. It is I, John."

Silence.

Once John stopped shaking, he looked closer at the aftermath of what must have been a terrifying encounter for all those who had witnessed it. Furniture was turned over, and every room had been ransacked. Items from each room were scattered all over the floors, telling John that whoever had done this had been in a violent rage.

"John. John, come down here," Edward shouted from downstairs.

John bounded down the stairs, hoping he'd found Sarah. Instead, what he saw made him bend in half and vomit on the floor.

One victim was stretched out on a long table in what must have been the dining room. Like Joan Stanton before him, he had been tortured and violated in a manner that the devil himself would find sinful. John felt himself turning green with nausea.

"Only one man could have done this," he spat the

words out, his chest heaving. "They must have come here after they left Burningtown."

"Or before," Edward said. "Remember, he was injured when he left Burningtown."

"That may be why there was so much anger when he broke in here," John said. "Look at what they did. What happened here goes way beyond any assassination I've ever seen or heard about. Whoever did this was angry, and from the looks of it, he took it out on these poor people."

"Did you see any signs of your sister?"

"No," John shook his head. "She was definitely here because I recognised her hairbrush, but she isn't here. My guess is they've taken her, so I'll be forced to hand myself in."

"What do you propose we do now?"

"I want to go to Asheborne's home and kill them all," John sneered. "But I know we can't. We'd need a small army to do that."

"It is what I must do, even if I die."

"No, we need to be smarter than that," John said. "We have to find the confessions that Margaret referred to in the letter we found. If what she wrote is true, she left detailed evidence proving that Asheborne was helping her, even when she was murdering all those boys in my name. That, by itself, is enough to get him arrested and executed. We have to find those documents."

"What about your sister?"

John sighed. "I fear greatly for her safety. I must see my uncle and tell him what has happened here."

"Know this, my friend, that what happened here will be blamed on you," Edward said. "Maybe even this very morn, cryers all over England will shout out your name, offering a big reward for your capture."

"You're right. Let's get out of here and find somewhere

to hide. We're in deep trouble, and we need to consider carefully what we do next because one wrong move could mean the death of all of us."

Edward bowed his head and started to leave. As they got near the rear door from which they had entered, John froze and prodded Edward, who indicated that he'd heard it too. Someone was trying the front door, and it wasn't locked.

"Quick," Edward whispered.

They ran out of the back door, and no sooner had they closed it than several men burst into the house from the front. John knew it had to be the sheriff and his constables.

They ran down the muddy strete and back to the old church as fast as they could. Shouts and screams from behind told them the news of the barbaric murders were spreading around the town.

"We don't have time to explain," John panted, out of breath. "We've got to get out of here."

They mounted their horses and galloped off as fast as they could.

Regrouping

They rode all day, barely stopping to rest the horses and eat some of the meagre rations they had scrounged from Burningtown. As darkness fell, the horses were at the point of exhaustion, and they knew they couldn't continue.

In any case, they didn't know where they were going.

A large house loomed in front of them in the fading light. John spotted a sign that told them they were approaching a town called Middleton Cheney, but it didn't mean anything to him. He didn't have a clue where he was. All he knew was that he was nowhere near either of the two danger areas of Burningtown Manor or Stratford-upon-Avon, and that would have to do for now.

They tethered the horses and rested behind a line of trees that hid them from view of the house. They took turns watching for signs of movement while the rest of them slept.

John handed out the last of the rations they'd brought, and he knew they were in desperate trouble. Drizzle came with the darkness, making for a miserable, chilly night for the small group of weary travellers. They huddled together under shelter of the branches, but it didn't stop them from getting wet and freezing cold.

Late into the night, John came back from his watch on the house. "There's been no sign of anyone, and I think it's safe to move closer and at least find a barn or something for the night. If there's still no signs tomorrow, we can break in and perhaps stay here a few days while we decide what to do."

Nobody argued, so they allowed the horses to roam free in the field and traipsed to the buildings at the rear of the house. John watched intently to make sure no lights appeared at any of the windows as they approached.

None did.

Isaac pushed open a large barn door, and using the faint moonlight, he found a pile of straw in the corner of the barn.

"Hey, over here," he said way too loudly for John's liking. "There's a pile of straw we can use for tonight. It's a lot better than being outside."

"Shhh." John put his finger to his lips, but Isaac wasn't listening. Instead, he threw himself onto the straw and was snoring within seconds.

"He needs to rest so he can regain his strength," John whispered. "Why don't you join him, my love, and Edward and I will keep watch."

"I don't mind taking my turn," Catherine offered, but John was having none of it.

"No, I need you to rest because you have to take care of us every time we come back injured. I love you and I want you to rest while I look after you."

John bent forward and whispered in her ear. "You look more beautiful than a morning sunrise over Broxley when the moonlight catches you sleeping."

Catherine kissed him lightly on the cheek. "You are a

good man, John Howard, and don't let anyone tell you otherwise."

John kissed her one more time and went to the door, where Edward was already on watch.

"What do you think we should do?" Edward spoke softly when they were sure Catherine and Isaac were both fast asleep. "We have no supplies, and we don't even know where we are going."

"I know, but we had to get away from Stratford because I fear you were correct. I wouldn't be surprised if the man you called the captain was there, telling the sheriff that I was responsible for killing them all and kidnapping my own sister. It won't be the first time they have accused me of taking her against her own will."

"So I heard. Perhaps we can stay here for a few days while we resupply ourselves in the town close by, and while we're here, we can decide what to do about finding Margaret's confessions."

"That's what I was thinking, too," John said. "We need fresh horses as well, because the ones we have are spent. Another hard day with them and they will collapse under us. I think you should go into the town and secure us four horses when we are ready to move. I'd go myself, but I've no doubt my description has been spread throughout the land by now . . . Again," he added.

By mid-morning, John was convinced the house was empty, so he decided to try his luck and see if there was anything they could use inside.

"I'm coming with you, and you're not stopping me." Isaac was adamant that he was feeling better, so John didn't resist.

"I'll remain here with Catherine and keep a lookout in case anyone approaches," Edward said.

The house had one front entrance and four front

windows, two on each floor. John ignored the front and went around the back, where he forced open a downstairs window. Slipping inside, he helped Isaac through the window and stood still, listening. If anyone was in the house, they would have surely heard the commotion they had just made.

Satisfied they were alone, John and Isaac went from empty room to empty room. The house was completely barren, and whoever had lived here hadn't even left a single piece of straw behind. It had been swept clean of everything and was seemingly abandoned.

It was perfect.

"It's completely empty," Isaac said when they returned to the barn. "Whoever lived here abandoned it, but not before they cleaned it out. They didn't even leave a crumb behind for the mice."

"It's just what we need," John said. "We can take some of the straw inside and use it for pallets. There's plenty of windows and doors, so we can escape if anyone comes."

"How long are we staying?" Isaac asked. "I'm sorry I've been quiet the last few days, and that I wasn't there for you when you needed me."

John laughed at his friend's humble apology. "You fought bravely against vastly superior forces, and you lost a lot of blood. Yet here you are, apologising for not being there for me? My friend, you were there when I needed you the most, and it almost cost your life. You have nothing to be sorry for. We're just glad you are regaining your strength and acting more like your old self."

"You didn't answer my question," Isaac said gruffly.

"Not long. We need to regroup, resupply ourselves, and make our plans. Once we've done that, we'll leave here. No matter where we go, we can't stay in the same place for long or we'll be discovered."

"We've lived this nightmare before," Isaac said. "It seems like running and hiding is all we ever do, afraid of staying in the same place too long in case we either get killed ourselves or, even worse, we get good people who help us killed. The only place we were ever safe were the crypts in London."

"They were horrible." Catherine shivered. "I'll stay anywhere but there again."

"The first thing we need to do is get supplies," John changed the subject. "The town must be close to here, but it's too dangerous if I go because I'm sure they have yelled my name and description all over England by now."

"I'll go." All three said it at the same time.

"Edward, why don't you take Catherine and get us what you can. You look like an ordinary couple, so nobody should give you a second glance. While you're there, see what you can find out without giving yourselves away."

Edward nodded. "Consider it done."

John gave his beloved Catherine a long, passionate kiss and whispered in her ear.

"For goodness' sake, man, put her down," Isaac complained. "You're putting me off my breakfast."

"That's a good thing because we don't have any breakfast," John laughed. He threw Edward a handful of coins and wished them well.

John watched them go until Catherine vanished from sight. He sighed and got to work carrying the straw from the barn into a room on the ground floor of the house. Isaac tried to help, but he soon grew tired. John ordered him to sit and rest and to watch out for anyone approaching the house, especially his beloved Catherine.

A few hours later, the dull sound of hooves splattering in the muddy lane leading to the house woke John from his deep slumber. Isaac was shaking him, trying to wake him up.

"John, someone is coming. Come on, we have to hurry."

John rubbed his eyes and jumped up. That was the first sleep he'd grabbed in several days, and he'd obviously needed it. He shook his head to clear out the mist and ran after Isaac.

They ran back to the barn and hid behind it, ready to bolt if they had to. John grabbed his longbow and prepared himself, but he lowered it as the sounds became louder and the riders came into view.

It was Edward and Catherine, and they had four horses between them.

"Whoa," John ran out to help with the horses when they got close. "Where did you get these from? They are fine animals."

"We traded the ones we had for these at the horse fair. Along with extra payment, of course," Edward said. "The trader was very interested in the big destrier we took from the guard at Burningtown, so I told him he could keep it if he allowed us a trade."

"It might raise suspicions," John said. "What did you tell him about us?"

"I told him that my wife and I were on a pilgrimage north and that our horses were tired. We took an extra two so we can rest them in between towns without the need to change them too often. He understood, and I think he accepted my explanation."

"We got enough food and supplies to last us a long time," Catherine beamed. "This is a delightful town, John, and I wouldn't mind living here once all this mess is over."

John smiled at the love of his life. Seeing her happy made his heart melt, and God alone knew she'd had little to smile about recently. Certainly not since she had met him.

Once darkness fell and they were safely hidden away from the world, John gathered everyone around to discuss their next move.

"As much as we like it here, we can't stay for long. In fact," he cut off and looked around at them all. "In fact, this has to be our last night here. If we stay any longer, we're sure to bring attention to ourselves and we all know what that brings. We have to leave tomorrow."

"Where will we go?" Isaac asked. "Nowhere is safe, and until we find out who this mysterious T.B is, we don't have a plan."

"Actually, I do." John looked at them all again. "But you won't like what I'm about to say."

"Well?" Isaac raised his palms in the air. "What is it?"

John squeezed Catherine's hand. "You won't like it either, but it's the only thing I can think of that can help us find both Margaret's confessions and Sarah quickly. And that's the important thing. We have to do this quickly because every day we waste, Sarah and ourselves are in greater danger."

"Do you know where Sarah is?" Edward asked.

"No, but I know someone who can find out," John said. "He might also know who T.B is."

"Who?" Isaac asked. "Your uncle?"

"Yes, my uncle, Thomas Howard. He has spies everywhere and always seems to know what's going on. I suppose he has to in order to survive in these troubled times."

"So, we're going to Norwich?" Catherine asked.

"No, and this is the part you won't like. We have to return to London. My uncle is most likely there, and we have Gamaliell who can safely arrange a meeting for us.

It's the only way I can get close to my uncle without being captured."

"Are you mad?" Isaac shouted. "London is the last place we need to go. Everyone is looking for you there and you won't last a day. We barely got out last time, so why do you think it's any better now? It's suicide."

"I understand the risks better than most," John said. "Which is why you won't like the second part of my plan."

Isaac raised his eyebrows.

"It is best if we find somewhere outside London where Edward can protect you while I find my uncle. Once I've seen him, I will return to you when it's safe."

"No. Not doing it." Isaac said.

"I'm not leaving you, John," Catherine said. "I'd rather die with you than live without you."

"It's a gracious gesture, but it isn't happening," Edward said. "I'm a soldier built for conflict, not sitting back hiding while others go into battle for me. No, John, if we go to London, then we go together or not at all. I think you're right in what you say, but we either go together or I go alone."

"How do we get in?" Isaac asked. "You know every entrance will be guarded."

"We can rent a boatman to take us down the river under cover," John said. "Andrew told us many a tale of when he and Abraham worked as wherrymen."

"Can't we use our secret entrance?" Catherine asked.

Abraham might have men watching that," John said. "Although he probably kept it to himself in case he ever has to get out quickly. I know that's what I would have done."

"You wouldn't have betrayed us in the first place," Isaac said.

Edward stood up. "London it is, then."

The Howard Girl

William Asheborne the younger entered his father's resplendent private study and found him standing by the window with his hands on his hips and his elbows splayed out like he was about to take flight.

"You look very smug today, Father. Pray tell me what pleases you so much."

"As you know, I sent the Underling along with my most personal assistant to the north to carry out my instructions," William the elder said. "Not everything went to plan, but I am pleased with what they accomplished."

"What happened, Father? You know I have been eager to find out ever since they left, although I didn't know you had sent that ghastly creature who serves you so well."

"He is a necessary evil I use sparingly when I have to."

"He is an aberration that needs to be destroyed," the younger William corrected him. "He is an affront to God and is as evil as any man can be."

"That he is, but he has a purpose, and thankfully he serves that purpose for me alone."

"Well, what happened? Did he kill the Howard boy?

What about the documents the Colte woman left behind? Did he bring them to you?"

"The answer is no on both counts," his father said.

"Then why are you so satisfied with his mission? If he failed on both counts, then what do you have to be happy about?"

"We have much to celebrate, my son. Sometimes victories come in surprising ways, and this is one of them."

"So, what happened?"

"The Underling was correct when he identified Howard at the wool trader's estate in Burningtown. I had Gare intercept Lord Parker on the way back from meeting the trader so he could extract what he knew about Stanton and his association with the Howard family."

"That's the problem I have with Gare—I don't like his methods for extracting information."

"Nobody does, but he's effective. Anyway, it turns out that Stanton is friendly with Norfolk and agreed to keep the Howard boy as a favour to him. This is great information that we can use, William.

With this, we can have the Howard family at war with each other, and when the king steps in and removes Coventry from the privy council, I will be there to step into what is rightfully mine. And then one day, yours."

"This is indeed wonderful news, Father, but what of Margaret's confessions? We will never be safe until they are destroyed."

"You are correct, of course. Gare did his best and spoke to Stanton's wife, but she didn't know anything about the documents. He was about to work on Stanton himself, and the personal guard you may recall he sent to London after Margaret died, but unfortunately one of Stanton's servants got away and alerted the local sheriff. He turned up in force before Gare could question them."

"Question them? You mean torture them, Father. But I agree, sometimes his methods are what we need. We just don't want to know the details."

"Quite. Anyway, Gare was injured in the fight with the guard and Howard. The captain stayed behind and showed the sheriff the papers I had made in the king's name, showing his authority to kill or capture anyone associated with John Howard."

"Did the sheriff accept them as genuine?"

"Of course he did, without question. Who dares question a duke? Certainly not a sheriff and his peasant men. The captain reported that Howard killed the wool trader and his wife because they were about to turn him over to the sheriff."

"Clever," William the younger said. "And I presume the sheriff has the cryers passing this information along all over the north?"

"Along with a small incentive from me, yes," his father said. "As a concerned citizen, it is my duty to help uphold the law."

"How much did you offer as reward?"

"Ten pounds."

"That should get the peasants searching."

"That's the plan. John Howard must not be allowed to feel safe anywhere in England. His only hope of survival should be somewhere out of the country."

"But why him, Father? I know you were close to the Colte woman, but what did John Howard ever do to you that makes you hate him so much?"

"Nothing," his father smirked. "But that isn't the point. I've spent my entire life watching the Howards flaunt themselves, thinking they're better than anyone else because they have the ear of the king. It should be me who is at the head of the privy council, not that snivelling half-breed, and I shall tolerate it no more. Robert Howard is an imposter, and his son is the way I remove him. I don't care what happens to the Howard boy after the king executes Robert for treason."

"Harsh, but it is indeed good news, Father. We should celebrate."

"There is more," William senior said, pouring them both a glass of his favourite French wine. "The wool trader's wife told Gare the whereabouts of the missing Howard girl, Sarah. So, after they left Burningtown, my men travelled to Stratford, where she was being hidden by Norfolk."

"You have the Howard girl?" William's jaw dropped.

"Yes, she is in my custody as we speak. Furthermore, the captain stayed behind and told the sheriff in Stratford about the events in Burningtown. So, now the sheriff believes Howard murdered the dozen men who were hiding his sister in Stratford, as well as the wool trader and his family in Burningtown. He is wanted everywhere for many gruesome murders."

"What do you plan to do with her?"

"Well, dear boy, I shall return her to her father like any good aristocratic man would. In fact, Robert should arrive any moment to hear the good news."

"You're handing her over? Surely, she will inform her father of what really happened? Why would you give him his daughter when we could use her as leverage to capture her brother and remove her father from the privy council?"

"You only see as far as your nose, and you need to see the entire picture. If you are to take over from me someday, you need to be a lot wiser than you are right now.

"The Howard children are a distraction that don't matter to me, but the confessions that Margaret wrote could ruin me. If we can't find them, and if the wool trader's guard doesn't have them—and believe me, if he did, they would have surfaced by now—then they are still out there somewhere. What better place to hide them than somewhere close to Robert Howard, the man who protected her the most?

If he ever finds them, we are finished, so I need to keep Robert as a close ally until we find them. Then we will destroy him."

"Very clever, Father. You are, indeed, a very wise man."

The two men raised their glasses in a toast.

The steward knocked on the door and entered.

"Sir William, Lord Howard is here to see you."

Aristocratic Discord

"Ah, Robert, please come in and take a seat," William Asheborne gestured to his illustrious guest as he entered the room.

"What is so important that it drags me away from the king's business?" Robert Howard got straight to it.

"I see you are vexed, Sir Robert, and I apologise for taking you away from our great king's side, but I think you will find this trip worth your while."

"It had better be, or the king himself will be involved. He was not pleased when I received your summons to attend here immediately."

"Again, please accept my humble apologies, but what I am about to tell you could not wait."

"Well?"

"I assume you heard about what happened to Lord Parker on the road back to London from the north?"

"Yes, of course, nasty business, but what does that have to do with me?" Robert's face was flushed red and Asheborne was enjoying every moment.

"A lot, as it turns out, Lord Howard. You see, Parker's

chief guard was friendly with my captain, and one of his men managed to escape the carnage. He sought out my captain and told him what happened before succumbing to his injuries. It seems, dear Robert, that Lord Parker was on the way back to London to see you."

"To see me? What would Parker want with me?"

"As you know, Parker had business with the wool traders in the north, and one of his stops was with a trader by the name of James Stanton."

"I know Stanton. He was close to George Boleyn before his execution. Come to think of it, wasn't he related to the Boleyns somehow?"

"I believe he was," the duke continued. "However, when Parker paid his friend a visit, he witnessed something very unexpected."

"What?"

"Your son."

Robert Howard sat bolt upright in his chair, his eyes wide, staring at William Asheborne. "John was with Stanton?"

"Indeed, he was. Parker wasn't supposed to see him, because as soon as he had, Stanton made him leave, telling him he was mistaken."

"How did he know it was John? As far as I know, he's never seen him."

"Come now, Robert. After your son's recent exploits, everybody in England knows what he looks like. Every cryer in the country has described him in great detail."

Robert shrugged. "Maybe, but it doesn't prove anything because Parker is dead. Wait a minute, you aren't saying that John killed Parker, are you?"

"I wish I wasn't, but that is what his chief guard told my captain. John ambushed them on a bend in the road. He was with the other Underling that escaped with him, and it seems he recruited Stanton's personal guard, because he was there as well."

"For the love of God, why is John doing this? What has he become?"

"He's become a man who needs to be stopped, Robert. A very dangerous man. My captain gathered his men and rode all night to the Stanton house, informing the local sheriff along the way. From what James Stanton told the sheriff with his dying breath, he was going to turn John in for what he'd done to Parker, so John killed the entire Stanton family except for his son who was hiding in a secret place John didn't know about."

Robert stared at William, unable to speak.

"It gets worse. From what I hear, John discovered from Stanton's wife that they had known all along where his sister was hiding."

Robert leapt to his feet. "You mean to tell me Stanton was harbouring both John and Sarah? Why on earth would he do that?"

"Please, Robert, sit and have a drink because you'll need it after you hear what I am about to tell you."

Robert sat down, staring at Asheborne.

"James Stanton confessed everything to my captain before he died. He'd been close to your brother, Thomas, for a long time. When Thomas reached out to him to help John escape, he agreed. Not only that, but Thomas also helped Sarah after he took her from John in London."

"Thomas helped John? Why? And why didn't he return Sarah to me if he had her? He knows I have worried myself to death trying to find her."

"That's something you will have to ask your brother," Asheborne said. "I can only report the facts as I know them."

"Go on."

My captain rode to Stratford and found Sarah, but not before John had slaughtered a dozen or more of Thomas's men who were looking after her. Well, I might add."

"What happened to Sarah?" Robert paced around the room, barely able to speak.

"I am pleased to inform you that she is in my custody. Your daughter is safe and sound, which is why I summoned you here today. I thought it best we had this conversation privately."

"Yes, thank you. I appreciate it. You have Sarah? Where is she? What do you want for her safe return?"

"Robert, you misunderstand me. What kind of man do you think I am? I want nothing more than to reunite a man with his daughter, but I must warn you in advance that Sarah is not herself."

"What do you mean, not herself?"

"You will see what I mean when you greet her. Sarah is confused, shall we say? She seems to think everything was Margaret's fault, and that John was acting in self-defence. She thinks he rescued her, rather than kidnapped her. So when Thomas offered to hide her, she jumped at the idea. I hate to tell you this, Robert, but Sarah believed her life was in mortal danger if she was around Margaret Colte."

"This is preposterous!" Robert exploded. "Thomas has a lot to answer for. Can you prove any of this? And where is my daughter? I demand to see her."

"All in good time, Robert. Unfortunately, these were the words of dying men who had nothing to gain from not telling the truth. I am merely relaying it as my captain heard it. Straight from the horse's mouth, as they say."

"Where is Sarah?" Asheborne thought Robert was about to pass out. He had never seen him as flustered in all the years he'd known him.

He was enjoying every second.

"All this happened just two days ago." Asheborne knew he had Robert right where he wanted him. "Sarah was in Stratford, so I ordered my captain to take her to Broxley. I believe you will find her waiting for you when you get there."

Robert Howard's eyes turned moist, and he blinked rapidly. "Thank you, William. Thank you for everything you have done for both myself and Sarah. If there is anything I can do in return, you only have to ask. I am forever in your debt for the kindness you have shown my family."

"You don't owe me anything, Robert. We have to stick together at times such as these. I do, however, suggest that we increase our joint efforts to find your son and bring him to justice. I mean no disrespect, but as long as he is still out there, none of us are safe."

Robert bowed his head. "You are correct, Sir William. As much as it pains me to say it, John's time on the run must come to an end. He has brought enough shame on my family, and he has used Margaret as an excuse for too long. Even after he killed her, he won't allow her to rest in peace. Margaret is innocent, and John is the one responsible for what he has done. We must put a stop to this."

"Consider it done," William said, holding onto Robert's arm. "We will get together shortly in London to discuss our plans, but not before you return to Broxley and reunite with your daughter. But please remember that she has been through so much and her thought processes are not what they should be. She will need a lot of patience if she is to fully recover."

"She will get all the help she needs, whatever the cost, and believe me, she will never be at risk again. Thank you, my old friend, from the bottom of my heart. We will meet soon, as you said, but for now I must take my leave."

Robert Howard bowed to William Asheborne and left the room. William watched as his carriage left his grand estate, heading no doubt for Broxley.

"It is done," he said to his son when he walked into the room.

London

The late October storm whipped the freezing waters of the Thames into a frenzy, and the two wherrymen struggled to keep their barge afloat in the heaving waters of the angry river.

The four passengers huddled together in a freezing mass, drenched to the skin as wave after wave crashed over the sides. All four of them threw up several times, and not one of them thought they would survive the day.

"This is as far as we can take yea," one of the wherrymen shouted. Although his head and body were soaked to the core and his fingers were blue from the cold, his face was bright red from the effort of keeping his boat afloat. "We'll sink if we go any further."

"Pull over there, at that dock," John yelled above the howling winds, pointing through the pouring rain at a dock on the north side of the river. "That's close enough."

It was close enough, because John knew exactly where they were. They had just passed his father's private dock at his home on the Stronde, and the dock he was pointing at was Temple Bridge dock.

"Praise the Lord," Isaac shouted. "I thought we were all going to die this day."

"It's a good job you're paying double, or we'd never have agreed to take you," the wherryman yelled.

"We appreciate what you have done for us this day," John said, tossing him an extra coin. "Please accept our gratitude for undertaking such a dangerous task. If we'd known it was going to be so rough, we would never have asked you to risk it."

"You're very generous, sir." The wherrymen looked at each other and smiled, showing their decayed, infected teeth.

John shivered, glad to be moving again and getting his circulation going.

"I've never been as cold and wet in my life," Catherine said, jumping up and down to create some warmth.

"So, what now?" Edward asked. "Where do we go from here?"

"Follow me and stay alert," John said. "My father's house is only a short distance away and I don't want to be seen."

"Do you think the wherrymen recognised you?" Isaac asked.

"I don't think so," John replied. "If they had, they could have held us hostage in the barge, and in the middle of that storm there would have been nothing we could have done about it."

"Do you remember the way?" Catherine asked. "I'm rather hoping you don't."

John smiled. "I know it's not pleasant, and we'll stay in the safe room rather than the crypts if we can, but it's the safest place for us right now."

John led them away from the Thames to Fletestrete and further north up Chaunceler Lane to Holbourne.

They turned right and headed towards Holbourne Bridge that would take them over the River Fleet.

The stench from the river hit John long before they got close enough to see it. His chest was already sore from throwing up in the swirling waters of the Thames, and now here he was heaving again because of the unrelenting nausea the River Fleet never failed to deliver.

"I hate London," he shouted, more to himself than to the others.

"The stench is making me sick," Edward said. "I don't know how anyone could live in this stinking city."

John was glad of the terrible weather conditions as they approached the bridge. These were always the most dangerous places for him. Guards were always on duty, watching everyone who crossed. The weather, whilst making it almost unbearable for them to travel this day, was also their best friend. The driving wind and rain would keep the guards off the bridge and force them into the shelter of the buildings on either side of the river.

At least, that was what he was hoping.

"Single file over the bridge. Keep your heads down and don't look at the guards." John snapped his orders as they approached.

The bridge was completely empty of life, and John sighed in relief. After crossing, they made their way up Cowelane to the West Smithfield Market, which was eerily quiet and empty.

It looks like London is deserted today, John thought to himself as they neared the end of their long journey from Middleton Cheney.

"Wait here," John yelled above the heavy winds. "I'll be back when I know it's safe."

He left the others in the churchyard near Aldersgate, which was one of the entrances through the old Roman

Wall into the city, and entered the small church on Britten Strete. He watched as he left wet footprints on the stone floor behind him as he made his way to the rear of the church and down some stone steps into a recess in the corner.

He tried the door, which was open, and stepped inside a small empty storeroom. It was obvious someone had been in here since they'd left. The pile of sticks he'd positioned in the corner had been removed. Other than that, everything looked fine.

Is Stephen still here? No, I doubt it. He hated this place just as much as everyone else did, and he definitely wouldn't stay here alone.

This was the first time John had thought about Stephen for months, and he wondered where he was, or even if he was still alive. He shook himself and tried the second door, which was down some stone steps at the rear of the storeroom. It was locked, just as he'd left it in the summer.

Was it only a few short months ago? It seems like a lifetime.

John's icy fingers closed around the key hanging around his neck on a piece of rope. Satisfied, he turned and went back for the others. They would be safe here until he could arrange a meeting with his uncle.

"I'm freezing," Catherine said, pushing herself as close to John as she could for warmth.

John looked at Isaac, who had become silent again. His lips were blue, and his face was as white as snow.

"Let's get out of these wet clothes and get warm," John said, opening one of the sacks they'd brought with them.

"Nothing could have stayed dry in that storm," Edward said. "Everything will be soaking wet."

"They won't be as wet as the ones we're wearing," John answered. "At least, let's get our wet clothes off and get under a dry cloak. That should help a little."

They didn't have many spare clothes, but they all carried a spare cloak in case something happened to the one they had on. At this time of year, living the way they did without a warm cloak would have been a death sentence.

They took turns rubbing Isaac's arms, hands, and legs, trying to generate some warmth for him. All the extra clothes and food they had went to him, to try and revive him and keep him warm. By the time darkness fell, he was coming around again and looking more like a human than a ghost inside a cloak.

"You had us worried there for a moment," John said, rubbing his back up and down.

"I'm fine," came the curt reply. "Stop worrying about me and take care of yourselves."

"Welcome back, my friend," John smiled and clapped Isaac on the back.

"I haven't been anywhere. It's a bit cold but nothing to worry about."

"You're a stubborn old mule," John said. He turned to Edward. "I have to leave and contact Pye. If I'm not back by sunrise, get out of here and leave London."

Edward nodded.

"Please be careful and come back to us," Catherine said, kissing John for the umpteenth time.

"I don't expect any surprises, except perhaps for the look on Gamaliell's face when he sees me," John said. "But you never know and it's always better to be prepared."

He grabbed the key and opened the door to the dreaded crypts. He walked down the stone steps into the pitch-dark abyss. At the bottom, he groped around on the ground on the right-hand side of the steps and pulled up a sack they had left behind the last time they were here. He took a candle from the bag and put the rest back where he'd found it.

Once the candle was lit, he locked the door behind him and turned into the dark, spooky crypts that made him feel like he was being watched by long forgotten spirits who resented him disturbing their resting place.

John shivered and ignored the tingling in his spine. "I'm passing through and I apologise for my intrusion," he spoke out loud.

He hurried as much as he could, and the passage through the crypts seemed to take longer than he remembered. Either that, or he just didn't want to be in there alone a second more than he had to.

Eventually, he reached the solid oak door at the other end. He once again reached for his key, and with a relieved sigh, opened the door, exposing the driving rain in the outside world.

He emerged from the hidden door behind the closed gates of a large family tomb and made his way through the mud and rain in the churchyard of Grey Friars. A few minutes later he was in the Shambles, which was the area of London where the meat traders slaughtered their animals and sold them to the people of the city.

London was a violent place, especially at night after curfew was called. The only people out after dark were either drunkards, and the muggers and robbers who preyed on them, or the Watch, who were men who worked for the city of London searching and punishing anyone caught out after curfew.

John didn't want to run into any of them, so he kept to the shadows as he carefully made the brief journey to the large house near the Old Baker's Hall. When he arrived at the house, he went to the rear. He banged on the large wooden door and stood back, hoping the old man was at home.

A few minutes later, the door hinges creaked, and the door cracked open. An old man with a long grey beard peered into the pouring rain. "Who comes here after curfew in this forsaken weather?"

"Gamaliell, it's me, John Howard."

Gamaliell Pye stepped back, his face a picture of shock and surprise. His lips curled into a frown. "Come inside and keep away from the windows."

After locking the door and taking John's soaking cloak, Pye turned to face the young man whose life he had saved several times earlier that summer.

"I thought I told you we were done. It isn't safe for you to be back in London. Don't you know what they are accusing you of now?"

"It's good to see you, too, Gamaliell," John said. "I'm sorry, and I know I said I wouldn't come here again, but I'm desperate. What are they saying about me now?"

"They say you murdered Lord Parker after he saw you sheltering with a family near Banbury, and was returning to London to inform your father. Then you butchered the family providing you shelter because they were going to turn you in for murdering Lord Parker."

"Lord Parker is dead?" John stepped back. "I didn't know that. It's all lies. Gamaliell, you know I didn't do any of those things."

"Oh, there's more. You tortured the family and made them give up the whereabouts of your sister in Stratford. Then, you rode there and murdered another twelve good men protecting her from you. The only reason Sarah got away is because Lord Asheborne's men were close on your tail and caught up with you before you could take her again."

"Asheborne is behind all this," John sighed. "He sent a man, the likes of which I've never known. He had the coldest grey eyes I've ever seen, and when he looked at me it was like I was looking into the eyes of the devil himself."

"I have no idea who that could be," Pye said. "But I never believed for a second that you did it."

"Do you know what happened to Sarah? We searched for her everywhere, but the men you mentioned were already dead when we got there. I assumed they took Sarah, so I would give myself in once they announced it. I didn't tell the others, but that is why I came here this evening, to give myself up in exchange for Sarah's safe return to my uncle."

"You really don't know, do you?"

"I really don't know what?"

"Asheborne never took Sarah so you would give yourself up. Sarah is safely back at Broxley with your father."

John slumped into a chair. "What? Why would Asheborne hand her back to my father when he knew I would hand myself in to save her? It doesn't make any sense."

"None of it makes any sense. Who killed Parker, and why? I know you didn't do it. I'm sure he didn't know you were hiding with that family. Even I didn't know where you were, and I arranged your escape."

"Abraham was there," John said. "He must have been there to identify me, but they knew where I was. I thought maybe they suspected Parker because he was friends with James Stanton and followed him on the off chance he would lead them to me, which he did, although he never knew it."

"It still doesn't explain why Asheborne gave up your sister instead of using her to bring you in, unless he had a different purpose in mind."

"What would that be?" John asked, throwing his hands in the air. "That's what I would have done."

"Asheborne is as cunning as they come. There are rumours flying around that Margaret Colte left behind her confessions, although nobody knows what they say, or who she says helped her. But Asheborne spent weeks at the house she owned in London when she was using Ren Walden and his gang to find you and murder all those innocent young boys. Perhaps he was involved in that. Who knows?"

"The confessions are genuine enough and I know what they say, because I know who found them, or at least one of them. Asheborne had been helping Margaret for years. She was his lover even before she met my father and remained so for the rest of her life. He is as guilty as she was."

Pye's mouth dropped open, and he licked his lips. "How do you know this? Do you have them? If so, why haven't you come forward and put an end to this madness?"

John let out a deep breath. "I have the covering letter that Margaret wrote, but not the actual confessions themselves. James Stanton's personal guard, Edward Johnson, found it, but Margaret hid the confessions somewhere else, and I need to find them. That's the other reason I'm here."

"Did she leave any clues as to where she hid them?"

"She said they lie safely with T.B., whatever that means."

Pye stroked his beard for a few moments before he replied. "Lies safely with T.B. That sounds like she buried them in a crypt or something similar, but who is T.B., I wonder? Do you know anyone in her past with those initials?"

John shook his head. "The only person I can think of is Thomas Boleyn, but he is still alive as far as I know."

"The queen's father? He still lives, but why would the woman hide her confessions with him? From what I gather, he wasn't exactly good friends with your father."

"No, he wasn't," John said. "So I don't think he is the right T.B. Whoever, or whatever it is, it's not Thomas Boleyn."

"I don't think I can be of any help to you."

"Yes, you can. James Stanton only agreed to shelter us because my uncle requested it from him. I want you to arrange a meeting with my uncle. I believe he might know who this mysterious person is."

"You want me to arrange a meeting with Thomas Howard? I will try, but I can't promise he will agree to it. Are you staying in the crypts? Because that is where you must be if I am to be of help."

"We are, and we hate it already."

"It is the only safe place for you."

"I know, and we will remain there until this is over."

"Wait here." Pye scurried out of sight, returning a short while later with a sack full of provisions. "This will suffice for a few days. Come back here two nights from now and I hope to have news for you."

John thanked Pye and retraced his steps back to the crypts and the comfort of his friends. It was going to be a long two days.

True Colours

Gamaliell Pye pressed a hidden lever buried in the library wall, and as if by magic, a door sprung open revealing a dark space big enough to hide a person should the need arise.

"You've been here before," Pye told John. "Stay in there until I get you tomorrow morning. Sir Thomas has arranged for a carriage to take you to a meeting with him after the curfew ends. There is a change of clothing so you don't stink out your uncle's home when you get there."

"Thank you, Gamaliell," John said, stepping inside the dark room and grabbing the candle Pye held out for him. The door closed behind him with a loud click and John settled down for the night.

The following morning, John was ready when a carriage pulled up outside Pye's home at the edge of the Shambles. He hid under a blanket on the floor of the carriage as it wound its way through London's narrow stretes before coming to a stop.

John was ushered through a side door and taken to a

familiar room deep inside the large house in Austin Friars, which was where many of the senior aristocrats had their London homes.

Thomas Cromwell himself had a home somewhere around here, but John had never seen it because, even before all his troubles had begun, his father had never associated with Cromwell. He hated him.

He waited in his uncle's plush study, enjoying the soft leather chairs and admiring the many books on the shelves of his personal library. Memories of his former life filled his thoughts before he was pulled back to reality with the opening of a door.

"I can't say it is a pleasure to see you again, John." An elderly man with long greying hair stood before him, his clothes a statement of both fashion and status. John reckoned his velvet hat alone cost more than an average man's yearly wage.

"Thank you for seeing me again, Uncle. I wouldn't have come if it wasn't urgent."

"We need to get this over with quickly, because you can't be seen here. My family is at war, and even the king is growing tired of me. What do you want, John?"

"I'm sorry you are having problems, Uncle, but what I came here for cannot wait. Not if I am to find justice, not only for myself, but for many others murdered in my name."

"Yes, yes, I know all about your little story, and quite frankly, I'm tired of hearing it. You brought this upon yourself, and if you'd stayed with Stanton like I'd arranged, you would have enjoyed a life. Now you are back in London, begging for my help again."

"That's harsh, Uncle," John cut Thomas Howard off from his next words. "Especially since you were supposed to be looking after my sister and failed to do even that. You kept her whereabouts from me, yet somehow Asheborne's men found out and took her from right under your nose."

"How dare you?" Thomas Howard shouted. "How dare you speak to me like this? I shall have you arrested, and then you shall be hanged, drawn, and quartered, which is no less than you deserve."

"Go ahead, Uncle, have me arrested, and then see what happens to you when I tell them how you helped both Sarah and I escape. I'll even tell them how I came to know about Margaret's movements the night she died. If the king is already tired of you, he will surely take your head after he hears about that."

Thomas Howard's face turned a strange shade of purple. "How dare you come here and insult me in this manner? Nobody speaks to me like this."

"I'm sorry, Uncle, but you asked for it. You walked in and immediately attacked me as though I'm guilty, which you know perfectly well I am not."

"Did you not kill James Stanton before he could give you up? Did you murder Lord Parker, ambushing him like a coward at a bend in a road? And did you not murder twelve of my men who were looking after your sister? Tell me, nephew, why should I trust you? Have you come here to finish me off as well?"

"If you truly thought that, Uncle, you would have sent guards in here already and had me arrested before you arrived. You know I'm not guilty of what you have just accused me. Lord Asheborne's men were behind all of it, and I know why. With your help, I believe I can prove he was behind the murders you have just described and many more as well."

"You didn't kill Parker or Stanton?" his uncle blinked.

"Of course I didn't." John pursed his lips. "I liked and admired the Stantons a lot, so why would I kill them?"

"According to Stanton's son you did."

"He's angry because his parents are dead, and he blames me because if I wasn't there, they would still be alive. On that count, he is absolutely correct. I shall carry the guilt of losing their innocent lives until my dying day. But I didn't kill them, Uncle, I swear to you."

"What makes you say Asheborne was behind it?"

"Several reasons. For one, Abraham, the Underling who betrayed us, was there, and he went to work for Asheborne for the reward. Another reason is that Asheborne's captain is known to Stanton's personal guard, and he was there too. One other man I didn't know was there as well, and he was the most evil creature I've ever set eyes on. He tortured Joan Stanton in a manner that defies both God and humanity itself."

"I heard about that and was told you had done it."

"I couldn't do that if my life depended on it, Uncle. You had to see it to behold it, and I wish I hadn't seen it. He did something similar to one of your men in Stratford, too."

"And Parker. The same thing happened to Parker."

"Do you know who this man could be?" John asked.

"I have no clue. I did not know such a man could exist, and if I did, I certainly wouldn't be associated with him. What do you know of Asheborne's guilt in any of this?"

"First, please tell me that my sister is alright. My heart is heavy enough knowing I placed her in the middle of this to begin with."

"She is back at Broxley with your father, and she is fine from what I can gather. Your father knows I helped you escape London, and he knows I kept her safe, away from him in Stratford. He says he knows this because of the last confessions of James Stanton."

"James Stanton died telling me what I needed to do to prove my innocence, so yet again, my father is either lying or has been told the wrong information."

"Robert has joined forces with Lord Asheborne, and they are doing everything in their considerable powers to find you and bring you to justice for the many murders they say you committed. The only reason I am not in the Tower right now is because I told them I have knowledge of Margaret Colte's confessions, and that I know where they are.

"I told them that if anything should happen to me, the confessions will be released and all the information they contain will be shown to the king.

"I never believed them to be true, but they must be. Whatever information they contain must involve both my brother and Asheborne, because for now at least, they do not pursue me. As they are the only protection I possess, I intend to keep it that way. I cannot help you again. Surely you must understand."

"I do understand, Uncle, but what I have to say should help you in these matters greatly. You see, not only are the rumours of Margaret's confessions true, but I have proof of their existence."

"You have proof?" Thomas Howard's mouth dropped open. "How? Do you have them?"

"Margaret left a covering letter in which she explains what her confessions are about. It seems most of the confessions will show that Asheborne had been involved with her since before she even met my father. She mentioned me a lot, and I believe their contents would prove, not only my innocence, but also that Lord Asheborne was as guilty as she is. Hence the reason he is sending men all over the country trying to find them and using me as an excuse."

"How do you know this?"

"James Stanton's personal guard found it and delivered it to him after you asked him to shelter me."

"Why didn't he give it to me? I could have stopped this immediately, and he would still be alive."

"I'm sorry, Uncle, but I must be truthful with you. James said that after Anne and George Boleyn were executed, he didn't trust you anymore. He feared that if it were found that you had helped me, you would betray him as you did your niece. So, he kept the letter for leverage against you, should the need arise."

John realised he had gone too far. Thomas Howard leapt up from his seat and shook his fists at John. His knuckles cracked, and his voice was hoarse as he spoke through bared teeth. "Your insolence will cost you your life, John Howard. How dare you accuse me of betraying my niece and nephew?" He was screaming, and John thought he was going to collapse under the strain.

"Uncle, please," John stood up and placed his arms in front of him, his palms facing out in a gesture of surrender. "I didn't say that was my opinion. I said that is what James Stanton said to me in conversation. Please forgive me if you thought I was overstepping my boundaries, because that was not my intention."

"I shall tell you this only once, and then we are done. I forbid you to ever mention their names again in my presence, do you hear? As Lord High Steward, I did not sit on the jury for the trials of Anne and George. It was my duty to represent the king and read the verdicts, which I did with a heavy heart. Barely a day goes by that I do not grieve for my niece and nephew, and I shall challenge any man who dares to say otherwise."

"Yes, Uncle. Once again, I am sorry if I offended you."

"Where are they? Give me the letter you already have, and tell me where the rest of them are."

"The letter is in a safe location and shall remain there for my protection. I'm sorry, Uncle, but it remains with me until this is over."

"How dare you?" Thomas Howard was shaking, his face so red John thought he was about to suffer a heart attack. "You walk in here seeking my help, yet you insult me and then tell me you don't trust me?"

John looked down at the ground.

"Get out! Get out of here now, before I have you arrested and hanged."

"If I leave now, neither of us will get what we need. Whether or not you want to, you have to help me find the confessions, or we will both end up on the end of a rope."

"Where are they?" Spittle flew from the duke's mouth, as he spat the words out. The hatred was obvious through his intense, fevered stare.

"I don't know where they are, and that is why I am here. I was hoping you knew something I don't that could tell us where she hid them."

"What else did she write?"

"She said that the rest of her confessions lie in her past, and that is what I need help with. You said you knew her before she met my father, so what could this possibly mean?"

"Is that all she wrote? That her confessions lie in her past? What kind of clue is that? I knew her, but not that well. I'm afraid I can't help you."

"Can't you think of something, anything, that will get me closer to finding them? If I fail, then we are all going to die, you included, Uncle."

Thomas Howard stomped to the door of his study and

threw it open. "We are done here, John Howard. I don't want to ever see you again."

John opened his mouth to speak, but his uncle cut him off.

"Speak to the Elder at the Steelyard. I believe you have met before."

Steelyard Elder

Gamaliell Pye stood with his hands on his hips, shaking his head at John. "How did you think he would react when you told him he had betrayed his niece? Everyone knows that is the one name you never mention around the duke. He's probably had people killed for the mere hint of his betrayal, so you are fortunate to walk out with your head still attached."

"I didn't accuse him of anything. He asked me why Stanton didn't give Margaret's letter to him, that's all."

"Perhaps you should have worded it differently."

"Maybe, but the time for being careful so as not to hurt people's feelings is long gone. Too many people are dead because of Margaret and Lord Asheborne, and if I don't find these letters, no doubt many more will follow."

"Tell me what he said again?"

"She said the confessions lie safely with T.B."

"No, I meant your uncle."

"He told me to speak to the elder at the Steelyard. I don't know what he can do, but we have met before, so I will seek him out."

"Why did you lie to your uncle?"

"I told him Margaret's letter said the confessions lie in her past, which is almost the truth. I fear if I told him everything, then he would know the answer, find the confessions for himself, and throw me to the gallows."

"You may have a point."

"I know where to find the Steelyard elder, so that's what I shall do."

"What do you hope to discover from him?"

"There is much that is not known about Margaret's past before she met my father, and somewhere hidden in there are the reasons why she destroyed my life and murdered so many innocent people. I need to learn more of her past, so I can have a future. That's what I want to learn from him if I can."

"What about the mysterious T.B?"

"I'm at a loss." John scratched his head. "It has to be linked to something in her past, but I have no clue who or what this T.B can be. If I can't find her letters, then I'll never be able to prove Asheborne's guilt in helping her."

John waved his finger in the air. "Unless, that is, I can dig into Margaret's past deep enough to find the connection to Asheborne. Even if I can't find her confessions, I might still prove their guilt by uncovering their past."

"An excellent idea, John, and very clever of you to think of it. I wish you luck on your quest. Come back here tomorrow night and I shall have more supplies for you."

"Thank you, Gamaliell, you are the only loyal friend we have left in this world, and we cannot do this without you."

"You will do well to remember that when choosing your words around your superiors."

John nodded and headed out into the night.

THE NEXT MORNING, John, Edward, Isaac, and Catherine entered the city through Cripplegate and made their way towards Cheppes Syed and the markets.

London's stretes were exactly as John remembered: narrow, dark, and smelly. He tried hard to hold on to the contents of his stomach, but Edward didn't manage it. Several times he had to stop and bend over, cursing the city on each occasion.

The upper floors of the houses reached out to each other across the narrow stretes, blocking what little light the heavy clouds allowed in late October.

It was another miserable day in London.

When they arrived at the busy market stalls in Cheppes Syed, Catherine gave John a hug and pulled herself close to his ear.

"Please be careful my love, and don't get caught."

"I won't," John replied. "I hope you enjoy your time away from the church and I'll see you later. Don't forget to store the food in the crypts and keep the door locked until our return."

"You worry too much. I know what to do, so take care of yourself and I'll see you later."

John kissed Catherine one last time. He left her browsing the market stalls and hopefully enjoying a normal day for the first time in ages.

John, Isaac, and Edward made their way down Bred Strete to Thames Strete, where they turned left and followed the river to the Steelyard, which was a German-run, city tax-exempt, walled community that the locals described as a city within a city. That was what the Steel-yard was: a community of Hanseatic traders who kept themselves to themselves as much as they could, although the elders had close connections with England's elite.

"Stay around here and watch for anyone who might have been following," John said to Edward and Isaac. "If I don't see one of you standing outside the Chequer Inn on my return, I shall assume the worst and get out of the city by barge. If that should happen, go back to the crypts and I'll join you there."

Edward nodded. Isaac seemed happy, even though he still looked pale and drawn.

"It's good to be useful again, and back to the places we know," Isaac said.

"Indeed, but if something happens, I don't want you getting involved. You're still recovering from the last time, and I want you to stay safe."

"Got it." Isaac saluted John. "I heard you the first ten times you told me."

"Just making sure." John smiled at his friend. "I'll see you shortly."

John approached the familiar gates at the entrance of the Steelyard, his stomach in knots, hoping they didn't recognise him.

"What business do you have here?" the gruff voice of a guard snapped out in German.

"I have friends here who have contact with my family in Cologne," John replied in fluent German, glad of the personal tutor he had benefitted from when he had lived a different life as the heir to an earl's great wealth.

"What is your name, and who do you seek here?"

"My name is John Broxley, and I seek Hans." John used the name he'd given when he was last here, before the elder helped him escape and told him never to return.

"Wait here," the guard snapped and ran into the walled city.

A few minutes later, a startled teenager ran up to the gates from inside the city. "John? What are you doing here? You know I can't let you in."

"Hans, it's great to see you again," John spoke in a low voice so the guard couldn't hear what he was saying. "I'm sorry, but I wouldn't come here if it wasn't urgent. My uncle, the Duke of Norwich, has sent me here. I have urgent business with your elder that cannot wait. Please allow me access so I may request a moment of his time."

Hans moved his shoulders from side to side as if he was trying to decide what to do. "The elder told me you were not to be allowed in here again, but if you are here on urgent business, I think I might be able to let you in."

Hans gestured to the guard, who stood aside and allowed the dirty-looking strete urchin into the city.

"It's great to see you again, John. Much has been said about you, although I refuse to believe any of it. What business do you have with the elder of the Steelyard?"

"You are wise to ignore what they say, Hans, and it is good to see you again, too. What they say is not true, and even though my stepmother is dead, she continues to haunt me from beyond the grave. The business I have with your elder is in connection with her."

"With your dead stepmother? I don't know how much help he can be, but I'll do my best. Wait here."

Hans left John outside a German shoppe and ran off up some steps to a large building overlooking the Thames. Several minutes later, he appeared, waving for John to join him.

"He is very busy, but he said he would spare you a moment."

"Thank you, Hans. It is really good to see you. I hope we can meet again in better circumstances and continue our friendship."

"I would like that." Hans shook hands with his friend and gestured to the open doorway. "The elder is waiting for you."

John entered a large office inside the building that reminded him of his father's study in Broxley. He approached the old man seated behind a desk who sat with his hands crossed, staring at John as he approached.

"I thought we agreed you were not to come here again after last time," the old man said in broken English. "Your father made it very clear to us we were not to harbour you."

"Thank you for seeing me, sir. I know you are busy, and I won't take much of your time. I am very grateful for your help earlier this year, but it is not that kind of help I seek from you."

"What can I do for you, John Howard? It seems you have built a sizeable reputation for yourself since we last met."

"None of it is true, sir. I have many powerful enemies who won't stop until I am dead, but proof exists of my innocence and that is why I am here today."

The elder scrunched his face and looked at John in surprise. "What do I know of this? I cannot possibly be of any help to you."

"It seems you can, sir. I believe you are acquainted with my uncle, Thomas Howard, and it was he who sent me here to learn what you know of Margaret Colte's past. Somewhere buried in her past is the information I seek to clear my name."

John was about to ask if the elder knew who the mysterious T.B. was, but stopped himself. He didn't want any mention of this name getting back to his uncle, because he knew everything discussed today would end being whispered in his ear in quick order.

"Margaret Colte? The lady is dead, so what can I possibly tell you about her you don't already know?"

"She left her confessions behind after her death, and I believe they will clear my name of the crimes for which I stand accused. My uncle seems to think you know of her past."

"I'm surprised your esteemed uncle would send you here when he knows more about the woman than I do. Rumours abound he is not in favour with the king or your father over matters pertaining to you, so is this why he sent you here? I have no wish to involve myself in the Howard family squabbles, especially when it involves King Henry VIII."

"Sir, it is true he wishes to not involve himself in my quest, but the confessions are real and can save many lives. I implore you to tell me what you know about her, and I shall leave, never to return."

"You said that last time, and yet here you are again. All I can tell you is that her name was Margaret Shipley. She arrived at Saddleworth as a penniless young girl before taking the eye of Thomas Colte, the master of the house. They married and had a child before Thomas died, supposedly of the sweating sickness. That's all I can tell you about her past."

"There was some suspicion regarding Thomas's death," John probed. "Is there something you know about that?"

"Now you mention it, there was something. Thomas was a horse trader, and I and many of my colleagues traded with him. It was said he had a child out of wedlock with one of his servants. She fled Saddleworth after Thomas's death, apparently terrified of his wife, which was unusual because they had been friends before his death.

That's all I can tell you, although I'm sure it's of no use to you."

John thought for a moment, his shoulders hunched. He was hoping for something more startling than this, which told him nothing.

"Do you know what happened to her?"

"No, but Hans might. His father and Thomas Colte were close friends, and I believe Hans stayed in touch with the servant girl for a while when she moved to London."

"She's here in London?" John perked up.

"She was, but I can't tell you where she is now."

"Thank you, sir." John backed out of the Elder's house. "You have been a great help. I promise never to come here again."

"See to it you don't."

"Well?" Hans asked. "Did you get what you came for?"

"Not yet, but I'm hoping you can help."

"Me? What can I do?"

"You were friends with a servant from Saddleworth that had a child with Thomas Colte out of wedlock. Is this true?"

"Yes, but what . . ?"

"Do you know where I can find her? She might be the answer to all of this."

"I haven't seen her for a long time, but the last time I saw her she was living in poverty in Longhornes Alley with her child."

"What is her name?"

"Her name is Alice. What does any of this have to do with her?"

"Nothing, but she might know something of my step-mother's past that can prove my innocence. Thank you, Hans. I have to go, but I am hopeful we can meet again in better times."

John ran off without waiting for a reply. He stopped at the gate and noticed Isaac stood outside the Chequer Inn, so he ran out of the gates and crossed Roper Strete, dodging people and horses to get to him.

"What happened?" Isaac asked. "What did he tell you?"

"We're going to Longhornes Alley."

John strode off without waiting for Isaac or Edward to say another word.

Longhornes Alley

John, Edward, and Isaac found Longhornes Alley between Cornhull and Bradstrete. It was one of those alleys that John despised—short, narrow, dark, and crowded.

John shivered. "I hate these alleyways. They're always full of deviants who want to relieve you of your coin."

"We stick together and go from door to door," Edward said. "If anyone tries anything we'll be ready."

John sighed. "Ready?" He took a deep breath and entered the alley.

Even though it was early afternoon, John could barely see where he was going. He knocked on the door of the first house, and an old woman with no teeth came to the door.

"What do yer want?"

"I'm trying to find someone called Alice?" John inquired. "She might have a son living with her."

"I don't know who yer talkin' about," the old woman said, slamming the door in his face.

He got a similar response from the next two houses

until he knocked on the fourth door down the alley. A man the size of a tree trunk answered and stared at John.

"Excuse me, sir. We're trying to find a woman called Alice, who we're told lives in this alley."

"What do yer want wiv her?" the giant asked.

"We believe she knows someone we're looking for, and we've been searching for her all over London."

"Alice," the giant shouted. "There's some boys 'ere who say they're looking fer someone you know. Get out 'ere and talk to 'em."

The giant turned to John. "Lay a finger on her and I'll break yer neck."

John nodded. He wanted nothing to do with this giant of a man.

A woman who looked to be somewhere above thirty years of age came to the door. John felt sorry for her because she looked like life had taken a toll on her and that she had seen better days.

She stood at the doorway, fidgeting, and looking like she might pee herself at any moment. "What do you want wiv me?" she asked.

"Are you the same Alice that knew Margaret Shipley at a place called Saddleworth?"

Alice's face turned ashen, and she shoved John, sending him flying out of the doorway. She ran down the alley, leaving John staring after her. He got up to chase after her when a giant hand grabbed his cloak and pulled him back.

"I told yer not to touch her," he said as a huge hand crashed down on John's head, making him see stars.

The man went to hit John a second time, but Edward held a knife to the man's throat. "Let my friend go or I'll sever your neck."

The man glared at Edward for a long moment before

letting go of John, who immediately bolted after the running woman.

Isaac was already in pursuit, and he was right behind her when she crossed Bradstrete into the next alleyway. She veered right into a churchyard, heading towards St Bartholomew-the Less Church. Isaac threw himself at her, and they both tumbled into the mud in the churchyard.

"Stop," Isaac yelled. "We're not going to hurt you."

John caught up, panting and trying to catch his breath. "Alice, please stop. We're not here to hurt you. We just wanted to ask you about Margaret."

"I don't know anyone called Margaret." Alice's lips were trembling, but at least she had some colour back in her cheeks.

"Then why did you run when I mentioned her name?" John asked. "What are you scared of? I already told you we're not here to hurt you."

"Do yer think I fear you when I'm married to that big lump?" Alice yelled. "He'd rip yer head off for even looking at me."

"Then why did you run?" John asked.

Edward joined them and nodded at John to tell him everything was good with Alice's giant husband.

"I don't want to speak about her," Alice said. "She'll kill me if I say a single word."

"Margaret is dead," John said. "So she can't hurt you anymore."

"I know she's dead. It's all anyone's talked about since it 'appened. That John Howard killed her. Say, that's not you, is it? You're not that John Howard, are you?" She pulled back and struggled to get away again. Isaac held her down.

"No, I'm not him, although I don't blame him for killing her. She was evil and deserved to die."

"She was more than evil. She was the devil's daughter."

"What did she do to you that made you so frightened of her?"

"I can't talk about it. She told me if I ever said a word about her someone would come and cut me 'ead off, and I believed her, I did."

"Nobody is coming to cut your head off, Alice," John reassured her. "Margaret is gone, and nobody is going to hurt you. In any case, nobody knows we're here so they can't possibly hurt you."

"What do you want with Margaret?" Alice asked, looking all around her like a lost puppy.

"She hid something before she died, and I'm trying to find it. Please, tell me what happened between you two. I heard you used to be friends?"

"We were until she married Master Thomas. Then she changed and became evil."

"I heard stories she killed Thomas. Is that true? Did she kill her husband, or did he die of the sweating sickness like she said he did?"

Alice turned white again. "Master Thomas was a good man, and he didn't deserve to die like that. He didn't die of no sweating sickness. She killed him, she did, with that poison she made. Even used it on her young boy and almost killed him as well."

"She used it on Mark?" John stiffened. "He said he was ill as a child and his mother gave him medicine to make him better."

"You knew her?" Alice thrashed about, trying to escape from Isaac. "You're here to kill me."

"No, Alice, I'm not. I knew Mark before he died, and that's what he told me. I'm just trying to find the truth."

"What did she hide that you want?"

"Did she feed Thomas and Mark honey by any chance?" John ignored her question. "Is that what killed them?"

Alice stopped dead in her tracks and stared at John. "How did you know that? Nobody but me ever knew that, and that's why she found me and told me that if I ever said a word about her, she'd send someone to cut me head off."

"Mark told me, but I wasn't listening," John said. "But I am now. Do you know anyone with the initials T.B?"

Alice turned white before her eyes filled with tears. She sobbed as they ran down her face. "Why are you doing this to me?" she asked.

"Doing what, Alice? I'm just trying to find out about her past, that's all."

"Thomas was my son, named after his father, Thomas Colte."

"Your son is dead? I'm so sorry, I didn't know that."

"Yeah, he died when he was young. Died of the bloody flux if you want to know what happened."

"I'm so sorry, Alice, and I don't mean to be harsh on you, but what has that got to do with someone with the initials T.B?"

"Because I'm Alice Burnham. My son was Thomas Burnham."

"My God, I'm so sorry. Where is he buried?"

"Sir Henry let me bury him next to his father at Saddleworth. Why? Yer not going to dig 'im up are yea?"

"No, Alice, we're not going to dig him up."

London Reunion

Daylight welcomed them as the narrow alley ended at Lothebury Strete. John shivered and shook himself, glad to be back in the open where he could at least see where he was going.

They turned right and headed towards Bishopgate and the way out of the city walls.

"Do you think her son is the T.B we've been looking for?" Isaac asked when they were back in clear daylight.

"I don't know," John answered. "But it's exactly the sort of thing Margaret would do. Her cruelty knew no bounds, and the thought of hiding her confessions at the grave of her husband's bastard son might have been something she couldn't resist."

"Are we going to Saddleworth then?" Isaac asked.

"We have too, there's no other choice. Unless you want to end your days at Tyburn, we have to find those confessions before anyone else does. Sooner or later Asheborne will find Alice, and if we don't get there first, we're done for."

"We go to this place called Saddleworth and find the

woman's confessions if they are there," Edward Johnson spoke up. "My wife and unborn child shall be avenged, either by the law, or by my own hand, but one way or the other, I shall not rest until the men who murdered Sybil and our child lay dead on the ground."

"We leave for Sadd . . ."

"John!" Edward cut in. "We are being followed. Look over there." He pointed to his right across the field at Bradstrete that ran parallel with Lothebury.

John stopped to see where Edward was pointing. At least seven men were walking swiftly up Bradstrete towards the intersection with their own strete. Most of them looked straight ahead, but at least two of them stared at John, Isaac, and Edward, watching their every move.

The men were too far away for John to make out who they were, but he sensed the hostility and knew they were preparing to ambush them at the intersection.

"Run," John shouted, turning and running in the opposite direction towards the stinking city.

Edward and Isaac ran after him, but after a short distance, John glanced back and saw Isaac lagging behind, holding his arm. The men were now in full pursuit and had almost caught up to Isaac.

"Get Isaac back to the crypts," John ordered Edward. "It's me they're after and I'll keep them away from you."

"I'm not leaving you," Edward shouted back.

"We don't have time for this. Isaac's injured, so you either get him away from here or they'll get him. If they do, he's a dead man. Don't worry about me, I'll be fine. Just get him out of here."

Edward scowled and ran back for Isaac, grabbing him by the hood of his cloak and dragging him down a side strete towards the Guildhall.

"Hey! Over here." John shouted at the men running

after them. He ran as fast as he could into the dark alley-ways he hated so much and skidded down the side of the Windmill Inn.

He saw three of the men break off and follow Edward and Isaac, and he gave a silent prayer that his friend was strong enough to help Edward deal with them.

The other four kept after John, who ran behind the Grocer's Hall and came to a halt at the culvert on the muddy banks of the River Walbrook. He stopped and confronted the four menacing figures who approached him.

"Hello, John." The man at the front threw back his cloak, revealing a face John recognised instantly.

"Abraham!" John spat the words on the ground.

"I knew you'd come back, and I've been waiting for a chance to get to you ever since. My boys saw you and Isaac earlier today, and I have to admit I'm surprised to see Isaac still walking after the beating he took the last time we met."

"For a coward and a betrayer, you talk too much," John said, giving Abraham an intense, fevered stare.

"If you give yourself up, I can save you from the same heavy beating," Abraham said. "Although after all the grief you've given me since Andrew took you in, I'd rather you didn't."

John resisted the urge to throw himself at Abraham and chose instead to live and fight another day. He ran along the muddy conduit to the north and turned up the opposite side of the Grocer's Hall.

As he ran to the rear of the Windmill Inn, his head exploded, turning day into night. He felt himself falling, and there was nothing he could do about it as his scram-bled senses fought to regain control of his mind and body.

Another rock crashed into his back, sending him sprawling into the mud-soaked earth below. Warm, sticky fluid ran down the back of his neck, and John knew he was in trouble. He reached inside his cloak for his knife, but a large foot smashed into his midriff, knocking all the wind out of his lungs.

This is it. This is the moment I die.

John lay on his back, beaten and defeated. Abraham had won.

"Pick him up, boys," Abraham's voice sounded far away. "We're going to be rich."

John heard laughs as hands reached down for him. From out of nowhere, he heard a thud and a soft moan, and he felt himself falling back to the ground. He shook his head, struggling to clear the fog that engulfed his mind, blinking as his vision slowly returned.

Two men lay next to John, one of them moaning in agony as their blood mixed with mud in a dark crimson pool that slowly drained out of sight. John's senses jumped back into focus, and what were dull sounds moments ago became loud noises in his ears.

One of the two men lay dead, his eyes wide open in a death mask all too familiar to John. The other thrashed about in agony, the wounds to his body draining his life away from him. John knew it wouldn't be long before he joined his fellow knave in death.

He scrambled to his feet, grasping the sides of the Grocer's Hall for support. He felt the back of his head, and his hand was immediately soaked with blood. His senses returned, John reached again for the knife inside his cloak. He'd worry about his wounds later; right now, he had to find a way to escape Abraham and recover.

Abraham! No, he has to die.

John shook himself once more and ran back to the culvert and the rear of the Grocer's Hall.

Where is he, and why hasn't he finished me off already while he had the chance?

Two men faced off against each other with knives drawn. John didn't know who one of them was because he had his back to him, but the other was Edward.

What is he doing here? The other must be Abraham.

John ran to his friend's aid, yanking the man's head back and thrusting his knife against his neck.

"I've got you, Abraham, and before you die, you're going to tell me everything you know about Margaret and Asheborne."

"John, stop. I'm not Abraham, It's me, Ste . . ."

John let go and stepped back, his muscles suddenly weak and numb. The man's hood had fallen from his face when he had pulled his head back, revealing a long scar that ran all the way down the right side of his face. John would recognise that scar anywhere.

"Stephen! What are you doing here?"

"You know this man?" Edward asked, still holding his knife as though poised to attack.

"Yes, this is Stephen Cullane, and he's a friend." John shook his head one more time to make sure he wasn't seeing things. "What are you doing here?"

"Who is this fool?" Stephen pointed at Edward. "He was trying to kill you."

John laughed through the pain. "No, he wasn't. Edward is a good friend, although he was supposed to be taking care of Isaac?" It was more of a question than a statement.

"I suggest we get out of here before they catch us, and then we can discuss what happened," John said, nodding his head towards a growing crowd.

"What about these two?" Stephen gestured towards the two dead bodies lying on the ground.

"They've already been seen, so we need to get out of here before the constable arrives," John said.

They ran into the heavy crowds of Cheppes Syed, losing themselves in the heaving masses of Londoners going about their daily business of buying and bartering at the market stalls.

"Where's Isaac?" John asked. "Is he safe?"

"Of course," Edward shot John a dark look. "I got him outside the city gates to where he was safe and told him to get back to the crypts. I returned to search for you, and when I found you, I saw this knave creeping around and looking like he was about to join in the attack on you."

"Let's get outside the city walls. They'll lock them down after news of the murders gets out," John said. "No doubt my name will be shouted all over London by night-fall. We can talk about this once we're safe."

They made their way through Aldersgate without incident. There they vanished into the small church on Britten Strete and into the safety of their storeroom and the crypts.

"John, you're back." Catherine threw herself at him before pulling back when she saw who was with him.

"Stephen? Is that you?"

"Stephen!" Isaac leapt to his feet. "I never expected to see you again."

Everyone spoke at once, so John held his hands up to quieten them down. "Please, let's speak one at a time. To begin, I need to know what happened to Abraham. Then we can find out how these two came to blows."

"He ran off when he saw me," Stephen said. "I tried running after him, but this fool got in my way and held me back."

"I thought you were with them," Edward said. "And I thought you were going to kill John when you raised your knife. I didn't know you were friends. How could I? I was trying to protect John, that's all."

Stephen scowled. "I could have caught the coward if you hadn't stopped me."

"I am sorry," Edward said. "I didn't know who you were."

"Well, at least we know how you two met and how Abraham got away," John said. "But it doesn't explain how you knew I was back in London or how you found me?" He looked at Stephen.

"Pye told me you were back and asked me to look out for you if I saw you. We all know how reckless you are when you're on a mission, so I searched everywhere, and to be frank, you're not hard to find. I followed you this morning and saw you in Longhornes Alley talking to a giant of a man and a woman. I followed you after you chased the girl, until they attacked you at the Grocer's Hall. I was coming to help you when I was stopped by him." Stephen pointed at Edward.

"What have you been up to since we last saw you?" Isaac asked.

"Not much," Stephen replied. "Certainly nothing like what you've been doing, from what I've heard from the cryers."

"None of it is true," John said. "Asheborne is responsible for all of it and blamed it on me. So, what have you been doing since we left?"

"I stayed out of the way for a while until it died down a bit. I used your treehouse, and I liked it there." He shot John a sly smile. John ignored him.

"When things got quiet, I moved back into the city and went after the rest of the gang leaders. Although there weren't many left after you'd finished with them. They're all dead now."

"Is the gang still going?' Catherine asked.

"Yea, there will always be gangs about, no matter how much we wish there weren't. But at least I kept them quiet for a while."

"What did Pye tell you about us?" Isaac asked. "If you knew we were back, why didn't you come here and join us again?"

"I thought about it, but I was busy with other things. And before you ask, don't. It's none of your business."

"Probably best we don't know," John said.

"So, what have you really been doing?" Stephen asked.

"It's a long story." John sat down and began telling Stephen everything that had happened since they had last met.

Once he had finished, Stephen let out a low whistle. "So, the bitch left her confessions and now you know where they are?"

"Maybe," John said. "If they're not there, then we are lost and right back at the beginning again. Are you staying with us?"

"I have no choice. I'm a wanted man after killing one of the men who attacked you today." Stephen looked at Edward, who just stared back at him.

"If it's okay with your guard over there," Stephen added. "After all, we're both in the same boat because he killed the other one this day."

Johnson nodded. "I'm sorry for stopping you, but I didn't know who you were."

"And I'm sorry for what happened to your family." Stephen offered his hand to Edward. "It will honour me to help you avenge them. Asheborne killed my brother, so I want him dead just as much as you do."

Edward took Stephen's hand and nodded his approval.

"What are your plans?" Edward turned to John. "Are we going to Saddleworth?"

"I regret not killing Abraham, but we will get more chances, and we need to be better prepared next time because he has to die. But for now, we ride to Horsham to find Thomas Burnham's grave. I'll get the provisions from Pye, and we leave the day after tomorrow."

Digging up Bones

The setting sun shimmered on the calm waters of the River Arum, reflecting the peaceful feeling that John had enjoyed during the two-day ride from London down to Horsham.

It was good to get away from the depressing loneliness of the crypts that had protected and isolated them so well. He took a deep breath and tasted the fresh air as if it was his first time.

"When this is over, this is how we are going to live," he spoke to his beloved Catherine, who was riding alongside him. "We are going to be free, where we can ride our horses and go for long walks along a river somewhere without a care in the world."

"That sounds like heaven on earth," Catherine replied. "I pray that life is meant for us after we find Margaret's confessions."

"If we find them," Edward spoke up. "Let us pray that our ride here was not in vain. Come, let's find somewhere to rest for the night before our day of destiny tomorrow." Edward kicked his horse forward along the muddy road that meandered into the small town, following the path of the River Arum.

The narrow stretes of Horsham felt welcoming and happy, or at least that was the message John's soul was receiving as they made their way to an inn where they planned to spend the night. Edward and Catherine left to trade out the horses, and Isaac took the coin from John to pay for their lodgings.

John kept himself out of sight, hidden behind his hood, to avoid any contact with the locals. Even though it was unlikely, he didn't want anyone to recognise him from the cryers' descriptions and turn him in.

Once they were safely in their lodging, John pulled off his cloak and relaxed. "I like this place," he said. "It reminds me of the peacefulness I enjoyed in a different life."

"I wouldn't know," Stephen said. "Strife and danger are all I've ever known. I find places like this difficult because I'm not used to it."

"Neither am I these days," John replied. "But it is something I look forward to in days to come."

"Just not today," Stephen added, almost to himself.

"No, not today," John agreed.

The next morning, they walked up to the market traders setting up for the day and talked one of them into selling them some fresh fruit. After giving directions to Saddleworth, the ragtag group of five dishevelled misfits made their way towards the impressive house that lay beyond their vision, further along the banks of the Arum.

A while later, the traders thinned, and they left them behind. Open fields took their place, and John once again revelled in the fresh air that filled every space in his body. A building in the distance took their eye.

"Is that it?" Isaac pointed towards a smoking chimney in the distance.

"It looks a little small to be a grand manor house," John said. "We'll be able to tell better when we're closer."

As they got nearer, they realised it was a farmhouse that must belong to the bigger house they could now see further down the road beside a small lake a short way from the river.

John threw off his cloak to reveal the clothing Pye had given him for his meeting with his uncle a few days prior. A silk shirt under a woollen doublet and hose made him look every inch the wandering aristocrat he intended to be this day.

"You look like you're back in Broxley as the heir to the estate," Isaac taunted his friend. "You won't want to know us now."

"Although it shouldn't, I feel strangely out of place, like I don't belong." John said in his old, aristocratic accent. "Who would have ever thought I'd feel like this one day?"

"You look like you're better than us, which is what you're supposed to be," Edward said.

"How may I be of service?" Stephen prodded John.

"Alright, stop it," John said. "It's time to get to business. Wait here."

John carefully adjusted his hat to hide his features and made his way along the narrow approach lane that was barely wide enough for a single horse and carriage. Three large chimneys towered above the four angled gables jutting out from the front, giving the house a character all of its own.

John had seen this design before, and the house seemed to fit in with the peace and tranquillity of the nearby town. Whoever lived here now, John hoped they took good care of it.

The gardens looked like they needed a little attention, which took John by surprise. In his experience, the noble houses were always maintained immaculately.

Then he noticed how quiet the chimneys were. As he got closer, the house looked dark and empty. Nobody came to greet him at the front door, not even after he had knocked several times.

He went around to the rear of the house, past a beautiful private chapel that was built on the side of the house.

That, too, was empty.

The once impressive gardens at the rear of the house were in a state of disrepair, and it was obvious to John that the house lay abandoned and empty.

What a shame.

The stables were the last clue that the grand house was derelict. So much straw lay piled up inside the stables that it was impossible to enter them. Off to the right, he saw a cross in a small, walled-off part of the estate. He ran over and entered through the open gate.

He was in the graveyard.

One gravesite was newer than the rest, so he looked to see what was written on the headstone.

Sir Henry Colte, Earl of Farnborough.

John's eyes filled with tears as the memories of that dreadful day shattered the tranquillity in his mind.

"Rest in peace, Sir Henry. I'm so sorry." He spoke out loud.

Another fresh gravesite close by caught his attention. This time, John collapsed to the ground and threw his hands together in prayer. Tears fell freely down his face as John read the inscription.

Mark Colte. Son of Thomas and Margaret Colte, and nephew of Sir Henry Colte. 1522-1536.

John knelt beside Mark's grave. "I'm so sorry for dragging you into this," he said aloud. "And I'm so sorry for letting you die. Please forgive me."

John pulled himself away from Mark's gravesite and looked around. He found the grave of Thomas Colte next to his brother's, and then further back away from the family, he found what he was looking for.

Thomas Burnham. 1532-1534.

John ran back to get the others.

"The house is empty and abandoned, but I found the boy's gravesite." John threw his dirty old cloak back over his clothes to gather some warmth on this cold late autumn morning. "Let's get this over with."

"What's wrong, John?" Catherine asked. "You look upset."

"Mark lies in there, close to his father, and I wasn't prepared for the shock when I saw his grave. Sir Henry lies there too, and the sight of their graves brought it all back."

Catherine squeezed John's hand and bowed her head.

"I'm glad you warned us," Isaac said. "I didn't know him well, but it was our fault he died. I'm glad we're here, if only to pay our respects to Mark and his uncle for what they did for us."

The procession to the graveyard was sombre. They stopped at the stables and grabbed some shovels that had been left and made their way through the gate to the graves of several generations of the Colte family.

"Why do you think the house is empty?" Isaac asked. "If it were mine, I'd never leave here."

"I don't know," John said. "Sir Henry has a son, so this will all be his now. Perhaps he is still young and has a guardian until he is older. Whatever the reason, it is sad to see a once grand estate fall to ruin in this manner."

"It's only been a few months since Sir Henry died,"

Stephen said. "So why does it look like no one has lived here for years?"

"It doesn't take long for the gardens to fall into a state of disrepair," John said. "I remember how hard the servants worked at Broxley to keep the gardens in working order, although I barely noticed at the time."

Stephen gave John a withering look and turned his back to look at the gravestones. "I see the new ones," he said, pointing at Sir Henry's and Mark's graves. "Which one is Mark's?"

John pointed at Mark's grave, and the rest of them, bar Edward, knelt beside it in silent prayer.

"I'm sorry for your loss," Edward said. John noticed a pained expression on his face and realised how difficult it must be for him, having only recently buried his wife and unborn child, as well as the family that he had grown to love in the Stantons.

"I'm sorry for your loss too, my friend," John said softly. "I know this is difficult, but we must find the confessions and avenge our families' murders."

Edward bowed his head and joined the others in prayer.

"Where is the grave of the little one?" Isaac asked, standing to his feet.

John pointed to a grave behind the family and off to the right. "Thomas Burnham lies there."

They gathered around the small headstone and held hands while John led them in a quick prayer.

Requiem æternam dona ei, Domine
Et lux perpetua luceat
Requiescat in pace.
Amen.
Eternal rest, grant unto him, O LORD,
And let perpetual light shine upon him.

May he rest in peace.

Amen.

"Amen."

"Let's get this done and get out of here." Stephen picked up his shovel and began digging, with the rest of them following.

"Stop." John held up his hand. "I just hit something solid."

He threw his shovel to the side and fell to his knees, digging in the soil with his bare hands. The others joined him.

They pulled on the object until it slowly began to emerge from beneath the earth. It was a small coffin, and Catherine clapped her hands together and looked up to the heavens.

"Please forgive this desecration, Lord. Please forgive us for our sins."

John's spine tingled as he and everyone else stopped what they were doing and joined together to pray for forgiveness. He felt around inside the gravesite for anything else—a pouch, a box, anything that might conceal Margaret's confessions, but there was nothing.

"Nothing," he said, allowing his breath to escape through his teeth in a loud hiss.

"Now what?" Stephen asked.

"Not even Margaret would desecrate the child's coffin," John said. "Even she wouldn't have gone that far."

"Are you sure?" Stephen pressed.

"I'm sure, and even if I wasn't, we're not doing it. We would be damned for eternity if we opened the lid on that coffin, so let's put it back and pray for our souls."

"I'll do it," Stephen offered, but the look on his face told John a different story.

"I'm convinced Margaret wouldn't have opened his

coffin, and we're not going to either. Wherever they are, her confessions are not here."

John lowered the coffin back to its resting place and began pushing the earth back over it. The others joined in, and soon Thomas Burnham's grave was back to how it was before their desecration.

They joined hands once more and prayed for forgiveness, which John doubted they'd receive. If God was listening, he would probably ensure that after what they had just done, they would all suffer in eternal damnation.

So be it. It seems Margaret has won, both in this life and now the next. Please, Lord, forgive the others for they only do as I asked of them. Punish me for our sins as it was I who commanded this unholy act.

They walked with heads bowed to the stables and threw their shovels into the straw before making their way back to the road leading to Horsham.

"Wait," John commanded. "There might be something else."

The Chapel

"I'm not going back to that grave," Isaac said. "I feel like I've done the devil's work today, and I'm never doing that again. I'm sorry, John, but I feel terrible for what we have done here."

"I do, too," John said. "We all do. I feel unclean, and I shall pray hard for forgiveness, but remember, this is all Margaret's doing, and if it is indeed the work of the devil, then it is Margaret herself who is the devil."

"Even she didn't dig up the grave of a young boy." Isaac's face was contorted as though he was in great pain.

"She wouldn't have hesitated if it suited her to do so, and you know it," John replied.

"So, what else might there be?" Edward asked. "I'm sorry, John, but I'm with Isaac. I'm not digging up any more graves."

"I'm not asking you to. There's a chapel built onto the side of the house, and I was thinking there might be a memorial to the child in there. If there is, it would have made a perfect hiding place."

"You go," Isaac said. "I'm not feeling too good to be truthful. I'll wait here and keep watch."

John placed his hand on his friend's shoulder. "You do look a little pale," he said. "Take a rest and I'll be right back."

Catherine stayed with Isaac, while John, Edward, and Stephen ran back to the house.

"There it is." John pointed at the small chapel that had been added to the side of the house.

Without another word, Edward tried the heavy oak doors, but they were locked. John tried the windows, but all the ones at the front were shut tight as well.

"Here," Stephen shouted.

A small window on the side of the chapel, barely big enough for a person to crawl through, was cracked open. Stephen pulled hard, and it opened all the way out.

"We can get in here," he said triumphantly.

"Wait here," John said. "There's no need for us all to go in. If anything is there, I will find it. Help me up."

Stephen and Edward held their hands so John could stand on them and squeeze his way inside the window.

Once inside, John waited a moment for his eyes to adjust to the darkness. He peered around, scratching at his chin at the unexpected sight before him.

The room was long and narrow. It had a large fireplace on the inside wall that had to be connected to a fireplace inside the house itself. A long table with several chairs was the only furniture in the room, and a large candle lantern hovered above the table.

The far side from where John stood had a small balcony, and beneath that was a doorway that must lead into the house.

This isn't a chapel: it's the great hall! It looks like a chapel from the outside, but from the inside there is no doubt.

John backed away to the window and returned from whence he had come.

"It's not a chapel," he declared to the surprised faces waiting outside. "It looks like one from out here, but it's the great hall. All that's in there is the table and that's it. There's nothing in there that mentions Thomas Burnham."

The trio rejoined Isaac and Catherine, waiting for them at the side of the road leading to Horsham.

"It's not a chapel," John explained to them. "It's the great hall to the house, so wherever Margaret hid her confessions, they are not here."

"Maybe they're not real after all," Isaac said. "She probably spread those rumours so fools like us would run all over the country digging up graves and committing as many crimes against God and king as we can. I'll wager Margaret is laughing at us from beyond the grave."

"The thought had crossed my mind," John said. "But as long as there is even a slight chance the story is true, we must pursue it. It's our only hope of salvation."

"There is no salvation for what we just did." Isaac's shoulders drooped, and he held his head low.

"What do we do now?" Stephen asked.

"We go back to London and start again, although from where I don't know," John said.

THE RIDE back to London stood in stark contrast to the ride down to Horsham. Barely a word was spoken, especially by Isaac, who remained deep in prayer almost the entire time. Even Catherine was distant from John, who felt the weight of the guilt for what they had done.

Stephen tried making conversation, but nobody took the bait. After a while, even he fell silent.

Isaac didn't even complain when they entered the dreaded crypts. Instead, he went down the stone steps and spent the night alone deep inside the dark cavernous hole they all despised. John could hear him praying throughout the night, and he felt a lump form in his throat at the thought of what he'd forced his best friend to do for him.

I'll make it up to him. I have to.

"What now?" Stephen whispered to John in the middle of the night. "We can't just stay here forever, feeling sorry for ourselves."

"I agree, and we won't. Tomorrow evening I'll visit with Gamaliell and see what he has to say. Right now, that's all I can think of."

"It's a good start," Stephen said. "I'll come with you. I'd rather be anywhere than here."

.

.

Souls of the Dead

The next evening after curfew, three bodies silently exited the crypts through a solid oak door hidden deep within a family tomb in the churchyard of Grey Friars. They kept to the shadows as they entered the Shambles, scurrying behind the large house next to the Old Baker's Hall and banging on the door.

Gamaliell Pye greeted them and ushered them in with haste. "I've been waiting for you to get back. Did you find the confessions?"

The look on their faces must have already told Pye the answer, but John spoke up. "No, we didn't. I fear the only thing we did was desecrate a grave and condemn all our souls to damnation."

"I can't help with your souls," Pye said. "But don't think for a moment that Margaret wouldn't have done such a thing if it suited her purpose. If she hadn't put you in this situation, then you wouldn't have desecrated the boy's grave."

"Tell that to Isaac," John said, casting a look towards

his friend sitting next to him. "He's taken this badly and barely speaks to us anymore."

"He must understand that whatever else you are, you are not sinners against God. What you did, you did for a reason. A good, honest reason, and for that your souls can rest assured of their cleanliness in the eyes of the Lord."

Isaac stared at Pye, and then at John. His eyes filled with tears that flowed softly down his cheeks. "Thank you, Gamaliell. I needed to hear that. I know what we did was wrong, but I also know why we did it. For that reason, I have forgiven myself and I have made my peace with God."

He stood up and hugged his greatest friend. "I'm sorry if I have been distant these past few days."

"I understand, and there is nothing to be sorry for." John was glad his friend was back.

"What are you going to do next?" Pye asked.

"I thought I'd go back and visit the girl again. She's the only one who can tell us about Margaret's past, and she knows more than anyone where she went and what she did."

Pye's eyes hardened, and he looked beseechingly at John.

"You haven't heard, have you? You couldn't have."

"I haven't heard what?"

"During your absence, the girl and her giant husband were brutally murdered in their home in Longhornes Alley. They say someone horribly tortured the girl before she died."

"They were murdered?" John jumped out of his chair. He clenched his fists and pushed them against his forehead. "This was all my fault, for I was the one who pressed her for information about Margaret. She was terrified that someone would come and cut her head off if she spoke about her."

Pye dropped his gaze to the floor. "I hate to tell you that her fears were well founded."

"She was beheaded?" Stephen's eyes were wide open.

Pye nodded.

"That's something you know a lot about." Isaac stared at Stephen. "Was this your work?"

Stephen rose to confront Isaac, but John got in the middle. "Stop this, now," he ordered. "That was uncalled for, Isaac, and you should apologise. You know Stephen didn't do it, because he was with us."

"He beheaded Margaret," Isaac said.

"That was different," Stephen said. "She deserved it."

Isaac went to say something else, but John cut him off. "We all know who did this to the poor girl. It was the man with cold grey eyes we met in Burningtown. He's the cruellest man I've ever known. It must have been him."

"But why would he kill her like that?" Isaac asked. "What did she do to him to deserve that?"

"Abraham said he saw you and I the day we spoke to her. He must have found out who she was and sent the evil one to torture her. This is all my fault, and her death is on my hands." John slumped to the chair, his face ashen. "I shall give myself up tonight, because too many good people have died in my name while I continue to live like a rat in the dark corners of the city. I must put a stop to this."

"I understand your sentiment, John," Pye said. "But realise that if you hand yourself in, you will be tortured, perhaps even by this man you talk about. When you are, you will have no choice other than to give up people like myself and your uncle. Then we shall die as traitors for doing nothing more than helping you."

"Then what do I do?" John asked. "People die if I do nothing, and good people I love will die if I do. What am I supposed to do?"

"You find those confessions and put an end to this once and for all," Pye said. "That is what you must do."

"How? If the girl is dead, then how can I find out about Margaret's past? Even from behind her mask of death, she has found a way to win."

"There's more," Pye said softly. "During your absence, the cryers have been all over London blaming you for the murders. They say you were seen in the alley the day they died and that you killed them because the girl was friends with Margaret Colte."

John's head sunk to his chest. "I am defeated and don't know what to do. The weight of the souls of the dead weigh too heavily on me and I can no longer carry this burden."

"There is one more piece of news," Pye said.

"What more can there be?" John closed his eyes tightly, creasing his face into a tight ball.

"You may like this piece of news. I heard from a close friend of a guarded secret."

"What? Don't play games with me, Gamaliell, please."

"Your sister is in residence at your home on the Stronde. I received word she is looking for you in the treehouse."

"How do you know this?" John sat upright and stared at Pye.

"It seems you have a friendly guard that remains loyal to you in the earl's household."

"Willis," John said. "It must be Willis."

"Go see your sister," Pye said. "Clear your head of the guilt, and then you might think clearer of what to do next."

John stood up.

Treehouse

The Stronde was an area reserved for aristocracy. East of Temple Bar and the River Fleet, the Stronde followed the path of the Thames in an idyllic setting, perfect for the large houses of the entitled elite of Henry VIII's England.

Robert Howard, Earl of Coventry, and head of the King's Privy Council, owned the largest of them all.

Extensive gardens backed up to the Thames, allowing the elite access to the river and to their private barges. The gardens produced the seasonal fruit and vegetables for the household, and tall trees separated each section.

One tree stood taller than the rest, and high in the branches was the treehouse that had provided shelter for John during the early days of his life as a fugitive.

Built by a now-deceased groundsman several years earlier, the treehouse was a place where John and Sarah could meet in safety when she was in London. Sarah had stocked it with food and clothes so John could survive, and it wasn't until John had met Andrew and the Underlings that he had finally moved out of it.

The treehouse was John's favourite place on earth, and

he couldn't wait to see it again. More importantly, he couldn't wait to see Sarah again after all that had happened since they last met.

"It's better I go alone, because Father is sure to have posted guards all around the house, especially if Sarah is in residence. I took her from under his nose once, and he'll be sure I don't do it again."

"If you think we're staying in these nasty crypts while you're up there enjoying yourself at the top of the world, you can think again," Isaac said. "We're coming with you and you're not stopping us."

"But what if we're captured?" John asked. "What if we're seen? We'll all be executed."

"What do you think will happen if you're caught and we're here?" Isaac fired back. "You'll tell them where we're hiding, and we won't even know they're coming for us. We're coming, and that's final."

"He's right," Catherine said. "If I'm to be arrested, I want to be with you when it happens."

John looked at Stephen.

"I'm not staying here if you're all in the treehouse. I stayed there for a while after you left in the summer, and I liked it. It's safe as long as we're quiet, so I'm with Isaac and Catherine."

John shrugged his shoulders. "That's settled, then. It's too dangerous for us to use any of the city gates. Now that everyone thinks we're back in London after the murder of the girl and her husband, the entire city will be searching for us. The rewards on offer are too great for anyone to ignore, so we will have to be very careful from now on. We can't even cross the Fleet over the bridges where guards are posted anymore."

"How much is the reward now?" Isaac asked.

"The last I heard, my father and Lord Asheborne

have combined to offer anyone who finds me fifteen pounds a year for life if I'm alive and ten pounds a year if I'm dead. Gamaliell is about the only person outside of Sarah and my uncle who will turn that down, and we must assume anyone else we meet who knows who we are will betray us. Nobody can afford to turn down that much coin."

"If we can't use the city gates or the river crossings, then how are we supposed to get around?" Stephen asked.

"London has many secrets if you know where to look," John said. "And we know quite a few of them. How do you think we avoided you when you worked for Ren Walden?"

"I often wondered," Stephen said. "But there were many times I saw you and looked the other way. I caused a scene sometimes to create a diversion so the other chiefs wouldn't see you, so I did more for your survival than you'll ever know."

"Don't be so defensive," John said. "We know now that you risked a lot to help us, but back then we didn't. You were our archenemy, so we did everything we could to get away from you."

Stephen shrugged his shoulders. "It worked, didn't it?"

"Not without the loss of many lives," John answered. "How many boys died just because they looked like me? Forty or more?"

"I had nothing to do with that," Stephen retorted. "It would have been a lot more if I hadn't been there. I did all I could to help you."

"It's not over yet." John changed the subject. "Not until we find her confessions and prove Asheborne was helping her all those years, even during the worst periods of her crimes."

"So how do we get around if we can't use the gates or bridges?" Stephen asked again.

"We'll show you, but there is one thing I have to say before we do this, although you might not like it."

Four expectant faces stared back at John.

"I'm the one they're after, not you. Everyone in England knows what I look like, but few know who you are. This might be your last chance to enjoy a normal life. If you leave here now, you can deny ever knowing me, and enjoy a full life. At least then I shall die knowing you are safe."

"Not that again," Isaac said. "You bring this up all the time, and I'm tired of hearing it. The cryers talk about me as well and call me the fat one. We're in this together, and we either win or we lose, but whichever it is, we do it together."

"I can't even think of life without you," Catherine said. "Anyway, we're married, remember? You got on your knees in front of everybody and proposed to me. I accepted, so in the eyes of the king and the Lord, we're married. We belong together, John Howard."

"What about you, Edward? Are you still with us?"

Edward nodded his head. "I shall remain with you until I avenge my honour. After that I cannot say."

"Fair enough." A lump formed in John's throat. "I have never known a more trustworthy and loyal group of people. It is an honour to call you friends, even though you are all as stubborn as mules."

"What's the plan?" Edward asked, his words carving through the heavy emotion hanging in the air.

"We separate and make our way from the crypts to our secret passage through the wall. Then we wait until dark to climb the tree, where we wait for Sarah."

"You know a secret way through the wall?" Stephen's eyes bulged. "Why haven't you told me this before?"

"When could I have told you secrets such as this? We

barely knew you before we killed Margaret, and we left London shortly after, so we never got the chance."

"Fair enough."

"Stephen, you come with me and Catherine. Edward, you go with Isaac. We meet at the secret passage and wait for nightfall."

They gathered enough supplies to last for several days, locked the doors to the storeroom from the church and from the entrance to the crypts, and waited until late afternoon before making their move.

Around two hours before curfew, which wasn't late now that the nights were drawing in quickly in the late autumn, five bodies emerged from Grey Friars. They joined the last of the people buying their meat and wares in the Shambles before splitting up and taking separate directions around St Paul's Cathedral.

John, Catherine, and Stephen headed towards Watelying Strete and the West Fish Market.

John stopped and cupped his ear.

"Listen, do you hear that?"

Stephen and Catherine indicated that they did. The town cryer was in full-throated voice, yelling out John's name.

"We need to hear what he's saying," John said.

They walked to St Paul's Cross and stayed at the back of the large crowds that had gathered to hear the cryer's words.

John Howard and the Underlings back in London. Oh yea, good people of London, the murdering runaway aristocrat and his gang of cutthroats returned to London to murder Lady Margaret Colte's dear old friend and her husband in cold blood. Howard tortured Alice Burnham and her husband in ways only the devil himself would command. John Howard is said to have long dark hair and an injured shoulder. His female companion and fellow Underling has long blonde hair, and the short fat one called Isaac has a wound to his neck from the courageous battle in the north where Lord Asheborne's men died trying to prevent another massacre. Lord Asheborne and Howard's father, Sir Robert Howard, have joined forces and generously offered fifteen pounds a year for life for the capture of Howard alive, and ten pounds a year for life if he's killed while being captured.

Oh yeah, oh yeah, oh yeah, hear me, good people of the city. A woman and her husband brutally murdered by John Howard and the Underlings, who are back in London.

John pulled the others away. "There's nothing new here. Abraham must have told them what happened in Burningtown, or at least what he says happened."

"All lies." Catherine's face was flushed red.

"We've got to get out of here," Stephen said. "Come on."

John hurried his steps and made sure to go a long way around before heading to the secret passageway. Nobody seemed to be following them, so he led them down Garlyk Hill to Thames Strete, where they turned right towards Baynard's Castle and Sir Henry Colte's home in London.

John stiffened when they reached the large house close to the Somerset Inn. "This is, or was, Sir Henry's home. It's where he first saw us and agreed to help Mark clear our name."

Catherine squeezed his hand hard. "This city carries only terrible memories for us. When this is over, we need to leave here and never come back."

They turned right, back towards St Paul's, and John stopped again. "Right there," he pointed, his eyes heavy with burden and guilt. "That's where we were ambushed."

"Remember this when the time comes for revenge," Stephen said. "That is when you will need these memories, not now. It's getting dark and it will be curfew soon."

"We're almost there." John pulled them past the Black

Friars smithy and its workshops, towards the stinking River Fleet that made John want to bend over and empty his stomach every time he went near it.

"I know this place," Stephen said. "It's a bridge alright, but it's covered and heavily guarded. It isn't much of a secret, and we'll never get across without being seen."

"Things are not as they seem," John said.

He led them to a huge bush growing against the side of the old Roman wall and pushed his way inside until they were up against the ancient stones themselves.

"Now what?" Stephen hissed.

"See that hole in the wall behind you?" John asked.

"Yes," Stephen turned.

"That's a secret passage that takes us underneath the bridge and leads into Bridewell Palace. We'll go over one at a time after the others join us and darkness falls."

But Isaac and Edward didn't appear.

Darkness fell and there was no sign of either of them.

"What do we do?" Catherine asked.

John thought for a moment. "We carry on as planned. We'll find out what happened to them later. Someone probably spotted them after the cryers were out yelling our names, so they turned around and went back to the crypts."

"Why don't you take Catherine to the treehouse and see your sister," Stephen said. "I might not have known about this secret passage, but I know London very well. I'll go back to the crypts and find Isaac and Edward, then we'll all join you tomorrow night at the treehouse."

"I thought you didn't want to stay in the crypts." John said.

"I don't, but this is different. Isaac and Edward are friends, and I'm going to find out what happened to them."

"That's a good idea," John said. "Be careful going back. Curfew has been called. We'll see you tomorrow after dark. Hopefully, by then, we will have some better news ourselves."

"Be safe," Stephen said, backing out of the bush into the darkness of the night.

"Let's go." John grasped Catherine's hand. "They can take care of themselves, especially Edward and Stephen."

"I know, but I worry about them all the same," Catherine said.

John looked up through the branches and closed his eyes, praying for his friend's good grace.

"Let's go," he whispered.

They stepped into the black hole inside the ancient Roman wall.

Calm Before the Storm

The sound of oars splashing in the waters of the Thames roused John from a deep sleep, and for a moment he didn't know where he was. The familiarity of the treehouse wrapped around him like a warm blanket, and for a few seconds at least, he felt at peace with the world.

He rose from his pallet and stopped to look at the sleeping figure of Catherine beside him. Butterflies danced in his stomach, and his heart skipped a beat as he gazed down at her.

"Oh, how I love thee," he whispered softly so as not to wake her. "I promise that one day, should we survive this ordeal, I shall make you proud of me."

"I already am proud of you, silly." Catherine opened her eyes and smiled up at John. "You didn't think I would sleep through such kind words, did you?"

John fell forwards and playfully tickled her, enjoying the intimacy of her touch. The rhythmic sound of the oars on the river seemed to beat in unison with his heart, and for the first time in many months, John had no desire to be anywhere else on earth. He was exactly where he wanted to be.

The early morning wherries taking passengers to who knows where were a tiny speck on the vast river when John finally got to his feet and looked around at the place he'd called home for so long. He turned in a circle, taking in all the familiar, and yet strangely foreign, sights that unfolded in front of him.

The large vegetable gardens hadn't changed at all, but the extension on the east side of the house looked, from the outside at least, like it was finished. The large house to the left of theirs that had been partially built the last time he'd been here was almost completed, but almost everything else remained exactly as John remembered it.

And none of it felt like his anymore.

A faint scratching and scraping sound below him jerked his mind alert, and he grabbed his sword. "Someone's climbing the tree," he hissed.

John hovered at the entrance in the middle of the big treehouse with his sword at the ready, hoping for the best and preparing for the worst. A head emerged out of the branches, and John dropped his sword in delight. The shoulder-length dark hair and those dark eyes that always saw right through him were sights John recognised immediately.

"Sarah! Sarah, it's so good to see you at last. I've scoured England trying to find you, but Uncle Thomas would never tell me where you were."

"John! You're here. I can't believe it." Sarah pulled herself into the treehouse with John's help and hugged her brother tightly. Tears flowed freely from both of them. "Although I could smell you before I could see you."

"You never change, dear sister, and nor should you ever

do so. You've met Catherine before." John gestured towards his beloved lady.

"Of course, it's good to see you again, Catherine. Oh, John, I thought I would never see you again, especially after that ghastly man kidnapped me and took me to Lord Asheborne."

"Did he have grey eyes that looked like they were dead?"

"He had the most frightening eyes I have ever seen, and he had a nasty wound on the side of his face that looked like it had just happened. I thought he was going to kill me."

"He probably would have if he hadn't been ordered to take you to Asheborne unharmed."

"What happened?" Sarah asked. "All I've heard is how you murdered Lord Parker and the family who sheltered you in the north somewhere."

"Don't forget, I was supposed to have killed a dozen of Uncle Thomas's men in Stratford too, but how I missed you after killing all of those men I'll never know."

"I hid in a safe place while they were fighting, just as Uncle Thomas's men had ordered me to. I never saw the fighting, but I heard it, and John, it was the most frightening thing I have ever heard. I thought I was surely going to be killed."

"How did they find you?"

"Somebody they called 'the captain' came right to me, so he knew where I was. He told me he had caught you killing all those men, and that he was there to rescue me."

"Did you believe him?"

"Of course not." Sarah hit her brother in his wounded shoulder, causing him to wince. "I knew they were the ones who had done the killing."

"Why did Father not believe you after you told him it wasn't me?"

"I tried, John, I honestly did, but Father won't listen. He's convinced that I'm protecting you and that I'm lying to stop you from being executed once you're caught. Please be careful, because Father has joined forces with Lord Asheborne and they're offering a large reward for anyone who hands you in."

"I know. The cryers are yelling it out all over England."

"I'm so glad my message got through to you and you are here. I can hardly believe it." Sarah hugged her brother once again.

"How is Willis?" John asked. "The last time I saw him, he was dying at the side of the road after we ambushed Margaret. I thought he would be surely dead by now from his injuries."

"He lives but suffers from his wounds. Father made him his chief guard in reward for his loyalty to Lady Margaret. Which is ironic given that it is he who remains loyal to you. He was the one who got word out to you that I am here in London."

"I'm glad he lives because I feel terrible guilt for his injuries. I didn't mean for him to get hurt, but my friend didn't know who he was and thought he was attacking me."

"Willis knows and understands, dear brother. He wants to meet you as he says he has vital information that might be important."

"What could Willis possibly have that I need? Does he have Margaret's confessions?"

"I have heard of those, although I doubt their existence. Margaret didn't seem the type to have remorse for her actions. Whatever the truth, they haven't been found, because Father mentions them all the time in his meetings with Asheborne. He thinks I'm not listening, but I am."

"Where can I meet Willis?"

"He said to suggest a time and place, and he will do his best to be there."

"Tomorrow after dark, by the side of the stables at the wall. Tell him I'll be on the river side of the stables behind the wall on Milford Lane. He can meet me there."

"I shall tell him. There's one more thing, and then I must go before I am missed and Father sends someone to look for me. I have had little freedom since I returned to him."

"I can imagine. The last thing he wants is for me to kidnap you again."

"He refuses to believe I went of my own accord. He's convinced you dragged both Mark and myself from our beds at the end of a sword."

"He will never believe me, no matter what I do. Before you go, how is our brother, Arthur? He must be growing tall by now."

"Arthur is well, although he isn't with us. Father sent him away to be raised somewhere in secret. He won't tell me where he is in case I tell you. He's afraid you will find him and kill him."

"Why would I kill my half-brother?"

"Because he has taken your place as the heir to father's estates."

"He can keep them. He's welcome to them."

Sarah took John's hand and looked down. "There is one more thing. I overheard father talking to Lord Asheborne about you. They agreed that once you are captured and executed, I am to be married to Asheborne's son, William, so our families are joined. John, I shall run away again before I marry that man. I despise him."

John sighed. "Don't worry, Sarah. If I can find Margaret's confessions, I believe they will prove that Asheborne is as guilty as she was. He has known her from long before she knew us, and she was his mistress for many years.

"She wrote her confessions, not to cleanse her soul, but to protect herself from Asheborne. That is why he is helping father, and trying so hard to find them.

"He knows I am trying as hard as he is, and if I get them first, he is finished. That's why he wants me dead. I shall find them, Sarah, and when I do, the Ashebornes will be done for. You won't have to worry about marrying his son."

"Stay here until after you meet with Willis. I shall try to visit again, but if I don't, it is because father is watching me too closely. I love you, John, and I hope we meet again soon."

They hugged one more time, and then she was gone. John stood in silence, staring at the Thames in deep thought.

Willis

As soon as darkness fell the next evening, John slid down the tree. He headed for the stables at the west end of the gardens. They backed up to the wall separating the property from Milford Lane. John climbed over the wall and waited, glad of the warmth of his thick cloak.

At least it isn't raining.

All day, his mind had been fixated on Isaac and Edward. *What happened to them? I hope they are safe and well. Edward wouldn't let anything happen to our friend, so they must have gone back to the crypts for some reason. They'll be there when Catherine and I finish our business here at the Stronde.*

He cleared his mind and focused on his meeting with Willis.

What did he know that could help them?

John secretly hoped Willis would just show up holding the confessions so they could get this over and done with, but he knew that was wishful thinking.

He'd been behind the wall for over an hour and was beginning to think Willis wasn't going to make it when he heard faint footsteps at the side of the stables. John crouched behind the wall, ready to run at a moment's notice.

"Master John," the welcome sound of Willis speaking softly broke the tension, but something was different.

"Master John, it is I, Willis." Willis's voice rattled as though his throat were soaked in ale. His breath rattled in his lungs, and John could clearly hear him struggling to breathe.

"Are you alone?"

"Yes, Master John, I am alone. What I have to tell you is for your ears only."

John stood and peered over the wall into the darkness. He couldn't make out much, but the shadow of Willis was a sight to behold., He jumped over the wall and embraced his former guard.

"Willis, I am so sorry for what happened that night. I tried to stop Stephen, but he didn't know who you were. He thought you were attacking me. I thought you were surely dead, and I mourned for you every night after all you had done for me."

"I lived, Master John, as you can see. Although I suffer from my injuries, I lived. I do not blame you because I know what happened. The lady was evil, and after what she had done to you, I was happy to be injured if it meant her death. It is good to see you, Master John."

"I owe you a lot, Willis. One day I hope to repay you, but for now you can see my plight; I have nothing to offer in return for your kindness."

"You owe me nothing. I consider it my duty to help clear your name because I know you are innocent of everything Lady Margaret accused you of. There isn't much time, so I must get right down to it. I have information I believe you might find useful if you are to clear your name and be rid of that woman at long last."

"What word do you bring?"

"Your father assigned me to guard Lady Margaret after you left, and my only duty was to go everywhere with her to protect her from you."

John scoffed out loud.

"I know, sir. It is ludicrous, but they were my orders from your father. I went with her everywhere she went. I was there when she buried Sir Henry and Master Mark at Saddleworth, but the one thing that I thought strange was the ride she took right before her death."

John's ears pricked up at the mention of her final trip somewhere. "Where did she go?"

"She ordered me never to tell anyone where we were going, not even your father. This was to be our secret, and if I ever told anyone, she would see to it I died a very painful death."

"Where did she go?" John repeated.

"We rode, her and I, to Malton, Yorkshire, to a place called Malton Manor. She gave no explanation as to why we were going there, and it wasn't my place to ask. I was merely there to protect her along the way.

After dark, we rode to a farmhouse several furlongs away from the manor house, where she ordered me to wait with the horses while she vanished inside. She was gone for some time, perhaps four hours or more, before she returned. Then we left and rode back to Broxley."

"What did she do for that amount of time? Did you see her?"

"No, Master John. It was dark, and I didn't see where she went."

"Did she say anything when she came back to you?"

"Only that I was never to speak of the journey to anyone or she would take my life. They were the only words she said to me for the entire ride back to Warwickshire."

"And were these types of rides unusual, or did she take them all the time?"

"She frequently rode to visit with Lord Asheborne, and often stayed at the white house in London, but this was different and very unusual. She seemed hurried and concerned until we got back to Broxley. Then she seemed a lot happier with herself."

"Where was this place you went to again?"

"Malton Manor in Malton, Yorkshire. It is a big estate, and you can't miss it."

"Thank you, Willis. This greatly interests me. I owe you an even greater debt of gratitude now."

"You owe me nothing, Master John. I don't know why she went or what she did, but I've heard the stories like everyone else. I hope I'm not sending you on a wasted journey."

"Who else knows about this?"

"Only you, Master John. I have told nobody else, not even your father."

"Please keep it that way, Willis. I fear my very future may depend on it."

"You have my word."

John thanked Willis again and kept to the darkness of the trees on the way back to the treehouse. He was brimming with eagerness and excitement when he climbed the tree and couldn't wait to tell Catherine what Willis had told him.

"John, you have to get back to the crypts."

Pye's Refusal

.

"Stephen." John was taken aback at the sight of his friend. "You took me by surprise. What's going on?"

"It's Isaac and Edward. We need to leave at first light."

"What happened?"

Catherine sat next to John and placed her arm around his shoulders.

"The traitor, Abraham, spotted Edward and Isaac. They ambushed and attacked them on the grounds of Black Friars, away from prying eyes. Isaac says he has never seen a braver, more skilled man than Edward, who killed five of Asheborne's men."

John bowed his head and clenched his fists. "What happened to them?"

"Isaac tried to help Edward, but he is still weak from his last fight, and he fell to their blades. Edward fought them off and hid Isaac in the grounds of Black Friars until after curfew, when he returned and took him to the crypts."

"Is Isaac alive?"

"He lives but is badly hurt."

"What about Abraham? Is he dead?"

Stephen shook his head. "He ran after Edward felled his men. The man is a coward to his core."

John clenched his teeth into a snarl. "Whatever else becomes of me, I swear before I die, I shall kill Abraham for what he has done to us."

"I shall be with you," Stephen said.

"We leave immediately and cross the bridge," John said. "Then we wait in the bush until curfew is lifted. I pray Isaac will pull through."

John grabbed his weapons and their meagre supplies and climbed down the tree.

"OH YEAH, OH YEAH, OH YEAH," the town cryer's distinctive shrill voice echoed in the early morning mist as a crowd gathered at St Paul's Cross to hear the morning news.

Oh yeah, oh yeah, oh yeah, good people of London. Five brave men belonging to Lord Asheborne brutally slain while trying to capture the fleeing Underlings. Although heavily outnumbered, Lord Asheborne's valiant men gave chase and cornered John Howard and his murdering gang before giving their lives for the safety of the people of London. The fat Underling who goes by the name of Isaac has a visible wound to the neck, so if he is seen, be sure to apprehend him carefully, as he is desperate and dangerous. John Howard ran away and hid like the coward he is, with the help of a new Underling who has a scar running down the right side of his face that cannot be missed. The Sheriff says the capture of John Howard is his number one priority, and Lord Asheborne and Howard's father, Lord Howard, have promised to do all they can to help rid the stretes of this dangerous villain.

Oh yeah, oh yeah, oh yeah . . .

John pulled back from the gathered crowd and melted into the early morning shadows, glad of the heavy mist that hung over them like a heavy blanket. "I've heard enough of Asheborne's lies. Let's get out of here before they see us."

"What lies." Catherine pulled her face so hard she almost turned purple with the effort. "How could you have run away and hid when you weren't even there?"

"None of it was true," John sighed. "It never is. Asheborne has everyone in London believing that all we do is run around murdering everyone we come into contact with."

"Everyone in England, you mean," Stephen corrected him. "Every cryer in England is shouting your name. We don't have much time left if we're going to find these confessions before they catch us."

"You're right." John pursed his lips. "Let's get back to the crypts."

They ran to the cemetery at Grey Friars and quickly found the hidden door to their secret crypt.

"It's locked!" John kicked the door in frustration. "Edward must have locked it behind him."

"He did the right thing," Stephen said. "We can't get in this way, so we have to use Aldersgate and get in there."

"The guards at the gates will search everyone coming in and out of the city," John said. "We can't use the gates."

"I'll go." Catherine offered. "Nobody is looking for me, especially if I'm alone. I'll find Edward and get him to open this door."

"I hate for you to go alone, but it's the only way we're getting in there," John agreed. "Please be careful my love."

They embraced. Then Catherine stepped back and was swallowed by the heavy mist that hung over London. John and Stephen hid behind the large tomb and waited.

An age later, the heavy oak door creaked open, and Edward peered outside. "John," he hissed. "Where are you?"

John and Stephen appeared from the clearing mists and stepped into the black hole that promised safety and security from the outside world.

"Isaac!" John ran to his friend, who was on the ground, propped up against an ancient tomb. "I got here as fast as I could. How are you, my friend?"

Isaac moaned softly and spoke a few words John didn't understand.

"What happened?" John turned to Edward, who stood holding a candle over them so John could better view his friend on the ground.

Edward's face glowed eerily in the candlelight and cast a ghostly shadow on the walls.. John shivered and refused to look.

"Asheborne's men saw us as we went by St Paul's," Edward explained. "We ran, but Isaac's injuries held him back and they quickly caught us. I fought them off, but Isaac was injured again and fell. I hid him until the curfew fell, and then I went back for him and brought him here. He needs a barber or a chirurgeon, and I've been waiting for you to get back ever since."

"Thank you, Edward, for you surely saved his life. You are a skilled and brave warrior, and I am glad you are here with us."

"You would do the same for me, John Howard. That much I have seen, and that is why I stay with you."

"What are his injuries?"

"A deep wound to his side from what I could see by candlelight," Edward said. "I covered him with honey, but that is all I know to do."

"You did the only thing we can do," John said, falling

to his knees beside his greatest friend. He took the candle from Edward and uncovered Isaac's wounds.

Isaac moaned as John pulled back his cloak to reveal a large wound to the left of his stomach

"He's lost a lot of blood." John turned to the others stood around him. "Which isn't good, especially on top of the wound he got at Burningtown. I need to see Pye and get him to a medic."

After dark, John quietly slipped out of the crypts and went to the home of their only friend in London, Gamaliell Pye.

"You can't come here." Pye got straight to the point. "It's too dangerous."

"Isaac is injured and needs to see a medic."

"I'm sorry, John." Pye shook his head. "I know this isn't what you want to hear, but I can't get a medic to him. The cryers are shouting his name all over the city The moment I get someone to see him, they will betray me and claim the reward. That would spell the end for all of us, and I cannot allow that to happen. I'm sorry, John."

John rubbed the back of his neck. "I understand, but Isaac needs your help. He's lost a lot of blood and he's badly injured."

'I'm sorry." Pye stared at his feet. "I will provide anything you need—linen thread to stitch the wound and as much honey as you need to cover it, but any medic would give him up in an instant. It would be more dangerous if he saw a medic than if you treat him yourself."

John bowed his head and pursed his lips. "You are correct of course, but I fear for Isaac's life if I don't get him help."

"A medic is a death sentence, but you might save him if

you treat him yourself," Pye said. "That's the best I can do for you."

"What's happening out there?"

"The people are tired of hearing your name and are demanding your capture and execution immediately. They are frightened and want you off the stretes, and who can blame them after all the lies that have been fed to them?"

"I have a plan," John said. "I might have a chance to prove our innocence and clear our names, but before I go, I have to make sure Isaac is recovering."

"What plan?"

"I have good information that Margaret may have hidden her confessions in Yorkshire, so I plan on riding there to find them."

"Where did you find this information?"

"From her personal guard who worked for my father."

"You trust this guard?"

"With my life."

"Then you might have a chance, but you must act quickly. Lord Asheborne and your father are desperate to find you, and they have men going door to door searching every place in London. I heard they are even searching the churches in case you are hiding inside one of them."

The blood drained from John's face.

"I will give you the supplies you need, but you must stay out of sight and away from here. I'm expecting them anytime."

Pye handed John a large bag of coin before he left, along with the supplies he'd promised. "This is from your uncle. He says he cannot help you directly because he is being watched closely, but he sends this to help you live."

"Thank you, Gamaliell. I hope this will be enough to save Isaac's life."

"May God's good grace be with you, John. Stay safe, and I shall see you when this is all over."

John walked out of the door into the darkness of the night. Pye had been their only salvation in this brutal city, and now it was gone.

Whatever happened from now on, they were alone.

Close Call

The door to the crypts remained open, but the small group of outlaws lived their lives in the small room. It at least had the comfort of daylight, unlike the crypts that offered only eternal darkness.

The daylight gave John the chance to see Isaac's wounds close up. The old wounds were healing, but the new one on his side was deep.

"Hold him still," John ordered the others. "This is going to hurt, my friend, but it's going to make you better."

Taking a long, deep breath, John looked up to the heavens and prayed for a steady hand. "Are you ready?"

Isaac moaned and grabbed John's hand. "Just get on with it. I'm fine, so don't worry about me."

John smiled at his stricken friend. "Ever the hero. Hold on tight."

Isaac squeezed John's arm so tightly that his knuckles turned white, as John plunged the needle into the side of his wound and began stitching it up with the linen thread Pye had provided. Time and again, Isaac stiffened and gripped John, but never one time did he utter a word or cry out in pain.

When it was over, John laid Isaac's head gently on the cloak they were using as a pillow and smeared honey over the newly stitched wound. "It's done, my friend. Now you need time to heal." Isaac, soaked with sweat, groaned and gave John the thumbs up sign.

"Is he going to be alright?" Catherine whispered.

"Yes, I believe he will." John smiled at the concerned faces staring at him. "He needs time to recover, but I do believe he will live to remember this day."

Catherine touched John's blood-soaked hands. "You are amazi . . ." Her words trailed off as footsteps echoed in the church beyond the locked door.

"Quick," John whispered. "Let's get Isaac in the crypts and clear this room."

Edward and Stephen carried Isaac down the steps into the crypts, while John and Catherine carried their supplies after them. Once they were done, the four of them ran back to the storeroom.

Heavy footsteps stomped on the stone floor of the old church on Britten Strete. John could hear muffled voices as they got nearer the rear corner and the location of their hiding place.

John watched in horror as someone tried turning the door handle to their room. Edward and Stephen held their weapons at the ready, but John held up his hands. "This is a holy place, and there shall be no bloodshed in here," he whispered, indicating that they prepare themselves to run to the crypts and make their escape to the treehouse should the men find a way through.

"What's in here?" The man's voice bounced from the walls of the church, amplifying it so it was heard clearly inside the small storeroom.

"That is an empty storeroom and nothing more." John's stomach tied itself in knots, and he tried to control the involuntary shaking in his arms and legs.

This is it! The only thing between us and gruesome death is that door. Whoever just spoke told untruths, but they were the most welcome words I've ever heard.

John held his breath as a foot crashed into the door. "Open this door now, or we knock it down." Another foot crashed into the thick door.

"You dare desecrate the house of God?"

The man who lied must be the priest!

"Do not test my patience, Warden. Open the door."

"That room has not heard footsteps in a hundred years. The key is long lost to history and cannot be opened. I assure you, gentlemen, no man can hide in there because it hasn't been opened since the days of Henry the Sixth."

"You are testing my tolerance, Warden. I give you one more chance to open the door, or it gets knocked down."

"You dare desecrate God in his own house?" the Warden raised his voice to fever pitch. "Eternal damnation awaits any man who commits acts of violence on holy grounds."

"Open this door. Lord Asheborne commands it."

"Lord Asheborne does not command God to do anything!" the Warden roared.

A loud crash came from the door.

"Commander, it isn't unusual for old churches to have rooms that haven't been opened in centuries," another voice echoed around the walls and ceilings. "We've found several ourselves already that don't have keys."

"What are you saying?" the Commander barked.

"I'm saying that we don't need to desecrate this church. The Warden has no reason to lie, and whatever lies beyond that door is of no interest to us. If no man has entered in a hundred years, then John Howard is not behind that door."

"Lord Asheborne ordered us to search every room in London, no matter where it was."

"Lord Asheborne did not tell us to destroy God's holy houses."

A loud sigh followed by silence. John closed his eyes and prayed hard.

"Very well, Warden, we have no reason to doubt your word, but if we find that Howard is here, you will hang with the rest of them."

The footsteps clattered out of the church and silence returned to their little corner of London.

John let out a gasp of air and allowed his shoulders to slump. "That was a close call," he whispered.

"Why did the churchwarden lie for us?" Catherine asked. "How did he even know we're in here?"

"He must have seen us," John replied. "And he protected us. Why, I don't know, but we owe him our lives."

"Do we go out and thank him?" Catherine asked.

"No." John shook his head. "If he wanted contact with us, he would have already spoken to us. By avoiding us, he can truthfully deny ever knowing us."

"So, what now?" Stephen asked.

"Until Isaac recovers, we can't do anything. We're not leaving him here alone. Not even Pye, will take him in and care for him. So, we're staying here until he gets better."

"That may be awhile," Edward said.

"Then so be it. I'm not leaving my friend when he needs me the most."

They made sure Isaac was never alone by taking turns sitting with him and mopping his sweat soaked brow with the remaining linen given to them by Gamaliell Pye.

Finally, after four days, Isaac seemed to be improving. He sat up and drank ale, and for the first time since his injury, he took notice of what was going on around him.

"I'm sorry if I've been a burden," he said. "I feel much better now, so what's going on? Did you find the confessions?"

"It's good to have you back, my friend," John said. "We were worried about you, and feared we were going to lose you."

"It'll take more than a blade from Abraham's men to get rid of me," Isaac scoffed, and then burst into a fit of coughing and spluttering, forcing him into the foetal position as agony raged throughout his body.

"You need to rest," John said. "We're almost out of food, so I'm going to go for more. It'll also be a good chance to hear what the cryers are saying about us while I'm out there."

"I'm going too. Four days down here is enough for anyone," Stephen said.

"If Catherine is alright with it, I'd like to go, too," Edward said. "It's too dangerous for any of us to be out there alone."

"Someone has to stay with Catherine in case we're caught," John said.

"Then you stay," Stephen scowled.

"Then I'll stay." John rolled his eyes at Stephen. "You two go and I'll stay here."

"I will remain," Edward said. "I don't know London, and if we get split up, I wouldn't be able to find this place again. You two go get us more supplies, and I will remain with Catherine and Isaac."

"Are you sure?" John asked.

"Isaac is recovering well," Edward said. "We will leave

soon to find the confessions, so we won't be down here much longer."

"We leave after curfew is lifted." John said.

Secrets

John and Stephen joined the busy throngs of people in the Shambles going about their daily routines of buying meat and bread. John held his head high, enjoying the feel of the wind on his face for the first time in an age.

The weak autumn sunshine soothed John's soul, and he took deep breaths with his eyes closed in an attempt to absorb as much fresh air as he could.

After filling a sack with meat and bread in the Shambles, they made their way past St Paul's towards the West Fish Market to stock up with the salty fish they hated so much, but which lasted them for several days without spoiling.

Once they'd finished, they turned up Bred Strete towards Cheppes Syed and their last stop of the morning.

"John, we're being followed." Stephen indicated with his head towards a group of five or six men wearing hoods, pushing their way through the crowds in the heaving markets.

"Are you sure they're following us?" John asked.

"I know London, and I know when I'm being followed. They've been watching us since we got down here."

"Let's go then," John quickened his pace and continued along Bred Strete.

The cramped houses along the left-hand side blocked the sunlight, throwing shadows across the narrow strete. Someone threw liquid waste from a pot from an upstairs window that splashed down onto the muddy strete. The splashback soaked John as it hit the ground. He shivered and moved further over to the more open side on his right.

The men following them turned onto Bred Strete and tried closing the gap between them. "That's them! Don't let them get away." One of them yelled, pointing right at them.

"Follow me," John shouted and ran off the strete into a building on his right. Once Stephen joined him, he slammed the door shut behind them.

"Where are we going?" Stephen asked. "They'll trap us in here."

"No, they won't," John said, running towards the back of the building, closing the doors behind them to confuse their pursuers.

At the rear of the house, John opened a window and jumped down into the grounds of Holy Trinity the Less churchyard.

"Throw me your sack and get down here," John yelled at Stephen.

Without hesitating, Stephen did as he was told and quickly jumped out of the window.

"This way," John said, running towards the tombs at the rear of the graveyard.

The men following them burst through the doors and hung their heads out of the window just as John and Stephen hid behind the tombs. "They jumped down here," the man at the front yelled, jumping out of the window, quickly followed by the rest of them.

"Now what?" Stephen asked, reaching for the knife tucked away inside his cloak. "Do we fight?"

"No need." John searched the names on the tombs close to where they hid. "That one."

Whittington

Crouching so he couldn't be seen, John pushed on the large stone slab covering the tomb until it began to drift to the side.

"In here, quick," John whispered.

"What's down there?"

"Our way out."

John gestured for Stephen to climb into the gap he'd opened up. John jumped in behind him and slipped on the rough steps carved into the abyss. He stumbled and grabbed onto the side of the tomb to stop himself from falling all the way to the bottom. Once he'd regained his footing, he reached up and pushed with all his might on the stone above their heads.

"Where did they go?" one of the men chasing them shouted. "They've got to be here because we'd have seen them if they'd run off."

"Where are they, then?" another shouted.

John slid the stone slab back into place and hoped the men hadn't heard the noises he'd made. He stood there, stooping in the pitch darkness and held his breath, waiting to hear the sound of the tombstone sliding open again.

Muffled shouts grew softer and quieter until they eventually disappeared altogether. When he was sure the men had given up and left, John sighed loudly.

"That was too close. I never even saw them, so I'm glad you were with me."

"What is this place? You knew it was here, so what is it and where does it lead to?"

"Me and Isaac found it when we were hiding from your strete gang. It's saved us a few times from capture."

"Where does it lead to? It's completely black in here, and I can't see a thing. Do we just wait and get out the same way?"

"No. Be careful, and go down the steps. At the bottom, grab the sides and walk carefully until you find some more steps at the other end. You won't be able to see anything, but trust me, there's a way out of here."

John heard Stephen muttering and breathing hard in front of him, and he held on to his cloak, so he didn't lose him in the darkness.

After what seemed an age, Stephen stumbled and fell. "I think I found the steps."

At the top, John helped Stephen push the heavy stone slab above their heads until slowly, inch by inch, daylight appeared. It took a moment for them to adjust their eyes, and John had to blink hard a few times so he could see. Once they'd adjusted, he pushed Stephen out of the secret passage and fell beside him on the outside of another tomb.

They both took a moment's silence as fresh air entered their lungs.

"Where are we?" Stephen finally asked.

"We're in St Aldermary's Churchyard. See, that's Watelying Strete, and over there is the Star inn."

"Wow, you really do know London's secrets. No wonder we had a hard time finding you. I know where we are. Look, that's the white house your stepmother used when she had us bring her the boys that looked like you." Stephen pointed at the little white house on the corner of Watelying Strete and Soperlane.

"You mean where she ordered them to be murdered?" John ground his teeth together. "John Two and the rest of them were innocent boys who didn't deserve to die."

"No, they didn't." Stephen looked at the ground and closed his eyes for a few moments.

John looked around for signs of the men chasing them and saw them on Garlyk Hill a few furlongs away. "They're still there. Let's get the sacks and get out of here."

They grabbed their sacks and ran back to the Shambles without another word. Once back inside the crypts, John slumped to the floor.

"That was close. London is too dangerous for us, and we need to get away from here. The answer might be in Yorkshire, but even if it isn't, we have to find a new town to call home. As soon as Isaac can move, we're leaving London for good."

End of the Line

During the night, Isaac shouted and screamed, and thrashed about as if he was fighting an imaginary battle. John carried him into the crypts so he wouldn't be heard inside the church.

"It's alright, Isaac, I'm here," he said soothingly. "Nobody is going to hurt you while we are beside you."

Isaac's head and body were soaked with sweat, and he drifted in and out of consciousness while John mopped his brow to cool him down, but nothing seemed to work.

"I fear we are losing him," John whispered to Catherine when they were alone. "I don't know what to do, but I cannot lose my best friend.

"I'm trying to be strong for him," John continued. "But it breaks my heart to see him lying there broken and bleeding, gasping for air one moment and then shouting at the top of his lungs the next."

"We need to cover his wound with more honey as soon as daylight comes," Catherine said. "That's the only thing we can do."

"His actions remind me of my mother when she died

of the bloody flux," John said. "She was mad one moment and then quiet the next, just like Isaac. I thought losing her would be the hardest thing I would ever endure, but losing Isaac would be just as hard."

"Don't think that way," Catherine stroked John's head. "His fever will break, and then he will be his old self again, just you wait and see."

Isaac's fever didn't break. Instead, it got worse. John could feel the heat from his body two paces away, so he poured water over him gently, trying to bring him relief.

Angry shadows whipped around the walls, reminding John of a Bard's play, where soldiers floundered in the blood of their fallen comrades during the battle of Agincourt. He forced himself to look away from the morbid scenes playing out by candlelight in front of him. Instead, he fixed his eyes on Isaac's very real battle for his own life.

The moment daylight appeared, John carried his friend back into the storeroom so he could see what he was doing.

"What about the noise?" Stephen asked. "Someone will hear him if he keeps screaming out like he has all night."

"I don't care," John said. "I need to see his wound, and I want to cover it with more honey."

The others stood and watched John gently pull Isaac's tunic away from his drenched body. The stench hit him instantly, and John turned away so Isaac couldn't see the expression on his face.

The wound was surrounded by a deep, inflamed redness that spread out in streaks like tentacles reaching around his body. Green puss oozed from the linen stitches that had been so crudely inserted, and John pulled back, grimacing. He tried looking away, but he couldn't. He just sat there, open-mouthed, staring at the ghastly aberration on Isaac's body.

225

Finally, he tore himself away and looked at the others, who stared back at him. Edward nodded at John and closed his eyes. Tears rolled down Catherine's face, and Stephen's face was as white as snow. They knew, just as he did: his best friend was in serious trouble.

Isaac was dying.

In a rare moment of comprehension, Isaac gripped John's arm and pulled him forward. John lowered his head so he could hear the hoarse whispers as Isaac struggled to speak.

"I'm so sorry," John's voice broke as he spoke. "It's all my fault."

"I'm dying, John," he gasped. "Don't mourn me, but rather avenge me by clearing your name and living as a free man. You're the best friend I ever had, and I had the best time of my life with you."

John's fingertips trembled as he held onto his friend. "Isaac, I . . ." He broke off, unable to speak.

"Not your fault," Isaac struggled for breath. "Abraham's fault. Make him pay, John. That's all I ask."

"It shall be done." John clenched his fist as hard as he could. "What can I do to make it better for you?"

"Just be here with me when it happens, that's all."

Tears welled in John's eyes, and he held Isaac's hand tightly. "Always, my friend, always."

Isaac's eyes rolled back into the top of his head, and he lurched forward in one final, breathless spasm. When he fell back down, his eyes locked one more time with John's before closing for the final time.

Isaac was dead.

Ashes to Ashes

Nobody spoke for the rest of the morning. They sat, lost in their own thoughts. John looked at Edward, who looked distant, as though he were reliving the murder of Sybil and his unborn child.

"The men who did this will pay," John finally broke the silence. "Not only for Isaac, but for Sybil and her child, James and Joan Stanton, and all the men who guarded Sarah."

Edward closed his eyes as if in prayer, and even Stephen placed his hand on his shoulder to comfort him.

"Every last one of them will pay for what they have done," John continued. "But especially Abraham, because without his betrayal, none of this would have happened. Andrew, David, Helena, and now Isaac. I thought killing Margaret would put an end to it, but it didn't. It just made it worse, and every one of them died because of me."

"It isn't your fault, John, so stop blaming yourself." Catherine said.

"How is it not my fault when so many people have died

in my name? What about John Two and all the other boys who died just because they looked like me?"

"And who killed them?" Stephen shouted at John. "Was it you? No, it wasn't. It was that evil bitch of a stepmother you had, as well as Ren Walden, Rolf the German, and all the other men and women who killed in your name. Remember, you're not the only one who lost someone close to you. It was because of Abraham that my brother was killed, so if we're going to blame anyone, let's start with him."

"Lord Asheborne is the main culprit," Edward finally spoke. "Him and that evil man he unleashed on us. Asheborne was behind just about all of it, and it is he who has the most blood on his hands, if only we could prove it."

"We will prove it if we can find the confessions," John said. "That's how we avenge Isaac and the others."

A hard knock on the door to the storeroom made John freeze on the spot. Edward was the first to react as he grabbed his sword and held it at the ready.

"What do we do now?" Catherine asked. "We can't run and leave Isaac here."

"We fight." John's grief gave way to revenge as he joined Edward and Stephen, prepared to battle anyone who entered through that door.

"It is I, the churchwarden." A voice spoke to them. "I mean no harm, but I couldn't help but overhear your friend in trouble. I can help."

John, Edward, Stephen, and Catherine stared at the door, each waiting for someone else to say something and break the deadlock.

Finally, after a long pause, John was the first to speak.

"How do we know it's you and that you mean us no harm?"

"You heard me defend you when Lord Asheborne's

men came here some days ago. I knew you were behind the door, but I protected you and sent them away."

John looked at the others and held up his hands. "What do you want?"

"I can help with your friend."

"Why do you want to help us?"

"You are in God's holy house. I help anyone who is in need."

"Even us?"

"Especially you."

John stepped forward and unlocked the door. Edward and Stephen stood ready to strike at a moment's notice. A tall, thin man of middle age stood before them with kindly eyes and heavy creases that told of a hard life.

"I'm sorry about your friend," the churchwarden said as he stepped into the storeroom. "He needs a proper burial in consecrated ground, and that is how I can help."

"Thank you." John dropped his sword and fell to his knees in prayer.

"Please, stand," the man said. "It is dangerous for that door to remain unlocked for any length of time, so place your friend in the crypts for a day or two and I shall arrange his burial."

"Why are you helping us?" Stephen asked.

"Every man deserves a proper burial."

"How long have you known we were here?" John changed the subject.

"Ever since you returned to London. I hear and see everything that goes on in this church, and I knew you were here from the very moment you left wet footprints on the stone floor."

"Why didn't you give us up if you knew we were here?" John asked. "Do you know who we are?"

"Of course I do, John Howard. I am not here to judge

229

anyone, not that I believed any of it in the first place. I've heard your conversations in here, so I know you tell the truth when you say you are innocent."

"How did you hear our conversations?" John's mouth dropped open.

"You are not the only one with a key to the crypts, Master Howard."

"You were in here with us and we didn't know it?"

"Please keep your friend in the crypts for a day or two." The Warden ignored the question. "That is the only thing I ask of you. What you do afterwards is your own choice, but rest assured you will always be welcome in this house."

"Thank you, Churchwarden," John said. "We will be waiting for you."

At dawn three days later, John, Edward, and Stephen stood back after digging a gravesite in the corner of the small churchyard outside the city walls on Britten Strete. They stood with Catherine, Gamaliell Pye, and the church-warden, who spoke a few words before they lowered the earth onto Isaac's shrouded body.

After a small prayer given by the churchwarden, John stepped forward. "Most of you here remember how comforted Isaac was when we spoke the Lord's Prayer in the crypts during the summer. Those words brought comfort to him them, and I hope they will bring comfort to his soul now."

John bowed his head and began reciting the Lord's Prayer in Latin. His voice cracked with pain and emotion, but he held himself together just long enough to recite his final words to his greatest friend.

Pater noster, qui es in caelis,
sanctificetur nomen tuum.
Adveniat regnum tuum.

Fiat voluntas tua,
sicut in caelo et in terra.
Panem nostrum quotidianum da nobis hodie,
et dimitte nobis debita nostra,
sicut et nos dimittimus debitoribus nostris.
Et ne nos inducas in tentationem,
sed libera nos a malo.
Amen.

John sank to his knees and gathered a handful of wet, muddy earth. "Sleep well, my friend, for you shall never be forgotten as long as we draw breath. We shall try to live up to your strong sense of loyalty and friendship, and we shall always love you. Rest in peace, Isaac."

John threw the muddy earth onto his friend.

No More Hiding

Something was missing when the beleaguered group returned to the crypts. They were dark, lonely, and empty, as if something tangible was absent. Everyone knew exactly what it was: Isaac.

"I need to clear my head," John said after pacing around the crypts all morning. "I'm going to the markets on Cheppes Syed."

He walked back into the crypts but was called back by Catherine. "I'll go with you," she said. "I need the fresh air and I can't stand it in here."

"Please, my love, allow me to go alone," John said. "My heart hurts and I need to clear it before I do something I might regret later."

"I'll go with Catherine to the markets," Edward said. "You go, John, but be careful and be sure to be back here before curfew."

"Thank you." John turned and vanished into the black hole that was the crypts. When he got outside, he walked. Where, he neither noticed nor cared. He pulled the hood of his cape over his head so as not to be recognised, but otherwise, he just wandered aimlessly.

By the time he reached the Thames, his chest was heaving, and he was struggling to catch his breath. Even though it was cold, John was sweating profusely, and he felt damp, cold, and clammy.

But he didn't care. At least he was feeling something, which was more than his best friend was doing right now.

What happened? What did I not do that could have saved him? Why couldn't it have been me who died and not Isaac?

These thoughts and many others filled his mind. He wandered for hours along the stretes of London, not caring who saw him or where he was going. He felt helpless and chastised himself for being a failure, although deep down he knew it wasn't his fault.

He stepped into horse manure strewn across the filthy stretes like he didn't even care, and he didn't even try to dodge out of the way when a woman emptied her piss pot from an upstairs window onto the grimy, stench-filled strete he wandered down.

At least I'm feeling something. Anything. Is this how it's going to be for the rest of my life? Living like a rat in the darkest corners of the city, covered in shit and piss as though somehow all of this will atone for the lives that have been lost in my name?

No, this world is better off without me in it.

His thoughts turned to Catherine. She had been through so much, and she made him so happy. If he gave his life today, what would that do to her?

He thought of the day he had saved her from Ren Walden, the Strete Master who had been dragging her to work in a brothel on the south side of the river after murdering her father.

She'd watched in horror as John killed Walden, and

then went with him because she had nobody else in the entire world she could turn to.

Is she better off with me? Or have I allowed her to fall in love with a dead man walking? Would my death also mean hers?

Eventually, he found a small building and took refuge inside. Grief fell out of him like a toxic river emptying itself into the wide expanse of the oceans. Months of pent-up grief, anger, and misfortune came pouring out.

He saw the faces of all those who had lost their lives because of him. John Two, Andrew, Helena, David, Mark, Sir Henry Colte, as well as the forty or more boys who had died for nothing more than resembling John Howard.

And now Isaac.

I promised Isaac I would avenge him.

He slapped his head to clear his mind of any thoughts of giving up. The people he cared about depended not only on him surviving, but surviving long enough to clear his name and find the proof of Asheborne's involvement with Margaret's crimes.

That is worth living for.

John shook himself to stop the dark thoughts from returning and hurried back to the crypts. The sun was setting, and it wouldn't be long before curfew would be called. He knew the others would be worried about him, so he ran as fast as he could.

He ran far to the north and crossed the River Fleet over an old cow road that was in the middle of nowhere. Then he ran back through West Smithfield Market, and finally back to the little church they called home on Britten Strete.

The churchwarden nodded at him as he entered the church and made his way to the storeroom in the rear corner.

"Thank you for all you have done for us this day," John

said. "We owe you a debt of gratitude for helping us bury Isaac in the church grounds."

"You are welcome, my son. Go in peace and be careful, because there are wicked men out there who want to see you dead."

John nodded. "I know. Thank you, Warden."

He rapped on the door to the storeroom. 'It's me, John."

"I don't know if I should be relieved or angry at you," Catherine said, throwing herself onto him as if she hadn't seen him in weeks. "Where have you been? We've been worried about you."

"You should be both," John said, pushing his way into the storeroom and locking the door behind him.

"Where have you been?" Stephen snarled. "Catherine here was worried you'd been caught, or even worse, that you'd done something stupid."

"I did do something stupid." John held Catherine to him, glad of the warmth her touch brought to his heart. "And I'm sorry I left, but I had to clear my mind. Isaac was, is, my best friend, and I struggle to know how to come to terms with his loss."

"We all do," Stephen said. "I grieve for Andrew all the time, and I'll wager you didn't see Edward run away when those men murdered his wife, did you?"

John looked at the floor. "I'm sorry, and I'll do better from now on. I wrestle with the weight of all those souls bearing down on me. They all died because of me, and I don't know how to contain my feelings sometimes."

"Welcome back," Edward said. "I hope you found what you were seeking."

"I did." John's eyes lit up for the first time in days. "And my mind is clear. There is to be no more hiding in the shadows. From this moment on, we fight back.I If that means giving our lives, then we shall die as brave and true warriors, and not as rats living in the dark."

"When do we leave?" Edward asked.

"Soon, but there is one more thing I must do this night."

"What?" all three asked at the same time.

"I need to see Gamaliell and tell him of our plans, and to seek his help."

"What plans?" Stephen asked.

"We gather the horses and supplies we need, and then we leave at dawn the following morn."

"We go to Yorkshire?" Edward asked.

"We go to Yorkshire," John pursed his lips. "And we hide no longer. We end this by finding Margaret's confessions and bringing justice to bear on Asheborne and his men."

"Welcome back, John," Stephen said. "This is the John Howard I remember: bold and not afraid to do what needs to be done."

"Then we avenge Isaac, Sybil, and the Stantons by finding Abraham and the man with the cold grey eyes." John ignored the interruption.

"Then we kill them." Edward gave an icy stare.

"Then we kill them."

Espied

As dawn broke, four hooded figures paid their respects to their fallen friend one last time. Then they made their way north through West Smithfield Market, carrying bulging sacks over their shoulders. There was nothing unusual about this, and the early morning risers didn't give them a second glance.

As the procession headed north on Clerkenwell Strete, they passed the Charterhouse Priory on their right-hand side. One of the monks looked up and observed them as they trotted past.

The monk fixed his cold, lifeless grey eyes on the rider at the back of the small group. His hood had fallen off his head, and the rider looked familiar.

Edward must have sensed the monk's eyes burning into him, because he looked over at the monk and waved as he rode past.

The monk looked away and continued his tasks, ignoring the friendly rider on the road north. He knew who this man was.

Oswyn Gare never forgot a face.

Malton

The journey north took twelve days to reach the outskirts of Malton, Yorkshire. Edward and Catherine swapped out the horses four times. The small group reached their destination tired, cold, and yet glad to have left London and the constant dangers they faced behind them.

John and Catherine huddled together under their combined cloaks and blankets for warmth, but still they shivered. It was snowing hard and everywhere was white all over, wet, and freezing cold.

"As pretty as this place is, it's way too cold for me," Stephen said, rubbing his hands together and blowing on them. "I swear, if it gets any colder, I'm going to cuddle up with Edward for warmth."

John laughed, and even Edward gave a faint smile.

"Not unless you want your entrails melting the snow," Edward said. "I don't care how cold it is, you're not bringing that scar anywhere near me."

Stephen laughed and pulled a blanket over his head. "I'll see you knaves in the morn, when I hope this dreary weather will change and give some warmth."

It didn't. Instead, it got worse.

"If this is what November is like, I'd hate to be here in deep winter," John said the next morning, as he peered out of the stables they had availed themselves of the night before.

Shivering, they struggled to maintain their footing while they slipped and fell in the foot-deep snow, getting their horses ready for the final push into Malton.

Wind whipped the driving snow into their faces, and they buried their heads deep into their hoods, which provided scant protection from the early winter storm.

John couldn't feel his fingers, so he clenched and unclenched his fists, but nothing worked. His feet felt like blocks of ice, and he knew his beloved Catherine on the horse behind him must be suffering as well.

The town square was empty, and the driving snow made it almost impossible to see anything. John thought he could make out what looked like a church tower ahead of him.

He stopped to raise a frozen finger in the direction of the tower. "See over there? It looks like a church tower. We might be able to find shelter until the storm passes. If we stay out here, we'll all freeze to death."

"What's a church doing in the middle of a town square?" Stephen shouted through the howling winds.

"I don't know, but I'm grateful it's there," John shouted back.

The visibility was so poor that, even when they got right up to it, John could barely make out what it looked like. All he saw was the welcoming sight of a large oak door set into a stone doorway that came to a point at the top. It looked old, more than likely built many centuries ago, although he didn't stop to admire the view.

They tethered the horses on the side of the church

where they were protected from the whipping winds and slid their way through the deep snow to the front door. John silently prayed that it was open, and he forced his frozen fingers to turn the handle and push on the door.

To everyone's great relief, the door swung open, and the magnificent, welcome views inside were a joyful sight for the four frozen transients.

"Who comes here on this terrible morn?" a voice shouted out from an unseen place at the rear of the church.

"We are four weary travellers who seek refuge from the storm," John shouted back. "We have been freezing to death out there and seek shelter in your wonderful church."

"Everyone is welcome in the house of God." A small, squat man, who looked to John like he was somewhere in his mid-thirties, approached them down the centre aisle. His straw-coloured hair was long, and he wore a heavy cloak over his clothing.

"Where do you travel from in this unholy weather?"

"We travel from London, but we were not expecting to ride into such a fierce storm so early in November. May we stay here until it passes?"

"What is your business here?" the priest eyed the four freezing figures in front of him jumping up and down, trying to generate some warmth and get the feeling back in their hands and toes.

"We seek Malton Manor, if you can tell us where it is. Although we'd be eternally grateful if we could shelter here until the storm passes."

"What business do you have with Malton Manor?"

"I seek to find a family member who I didn't know existed until recently." John crossed his fingers as he lied inside a church.

"Then you are most welcome here," the priest said. "Come, I have a fire going where you can find warmth and dry out."

The priest led the four bedraggled travellers to a side room at the rear of the church where he had a roaring fire going. All four of them got as near as they could, and John could see the colour returning to Catherine's cheeks as she warmed herself in front of it. John's face stung as the fire melted the ice that had frozen to his face.

"The storm should pass in a day or so. I have food and ale, and if you will join me in prayer, you are most welcome to stay."

"Thank you for your kindness," John said. They joined with the priest in prayer and said their thanks to the Almighty for providing them shelter from the storm.

"I am Father Browne," the priest said. "What may I call you?"

"I'm John, and this is my good wife, Catherine."

Catherine curtseyed at the priest, who nodded at her. His eyes strayed to the scar on Stephen's face.

Stephen ignored his stares and introduced himself. "I'm Stephen, and this is Edward."

Edward bowed his head. "Thank you for allowing us shelter, Father. We are indebted to you."

"So, tell me." John changed the subject and tried to avert the priest's eyes from Stephen's telltale scar. "What is this church doing in the middle of the town square?"

"That's a question I often get asked," the priest chuckled. "And the answer is simple. This church is called St Michael's Church, and it has been here a long time—almost from the very beginnings of Malton itself after it was settled many centuries ago. It is a fine example of a Norman building, and people will still come here five hundred years from now, long after we are all gone."

John walked away from the fire and looked at the magnificent stained-glass windows, lighting the altar to his left in the main part of the church. Heavy oak pews lined both sides of the walls that held descriptions of important dignitaries long since gone, but never forgotten. It reminded John so much of another church that bore the same name. A place that he had once called home in a different life.

His thoughts turned to Sarah and the many times he and his family had visited St Michael's at Broxley Hall in happier times. He looked at the floor and blinked, hiding the sadness in his eyes from the others.

He shook his head and forced himself back to the here and now. "So, where will we find Malton Manor?" he asked the priest.

"You can't miss it," Father Browne said. "Once the storm clears, look up the hill. The Manor dominates everything around here. Sir William Pitts and his family take great pride in Malton Manor."

"Is there a farmhouse a few furlongs away from it?"

The priest's eyes opened wide, and he stared at John. "There is. Why do you seek Tristan?"

"I have reason to believe he knows the person who I seek. This Tristan lives at the farmhouse?"

"Yes," the priest answered. "He is the beekeeper for his lordship. A kindly man who has known great hardship in his life."

"I'll be sure to be thoughtful in our dealings with him," John reassured the priest. "How do I find him?"

"Follow the road past the manor house until you come to a crossroads. Turn right, and Maltune Farm is the first place you'll see on the left side of the road before you come back to Malton Manor."

The storm finally cleared, leaving the rolling hills of

North Yorkshire covered in a fresh coating of pure white snow. John thought it looked beautiful, at least while stood in front of a warm fireplace looking out of the window.

After thanking the priest for his warm hospitality, John led them out into the bitter, frosty morning. "At least it isn't snowing," he said, feeling a sharp pain as the freezing air burned his lungs.

"It's pretty here, but it's far too cold for me." Catherine stayed close to John.

"You'll get no arguments from any of us," Stephen said. "Let's find what we came for and get out of here."

Edward and Catherine swapped out the horses one last time, and they carefully made their way up the steep hill. The snow was knee-deep in places, and it was hard going. Steam rose from the horses' nostrils as they battled against the freezing conditions, and John wrapped himself as deep as he could inside his cloak.

The massive stone house dominated the landscape where they stood. Double Roman-style pillars reached up to the heavens on both sides of the large front door, and the house stretched out on both sides for what seemed forever. John lost count of the number of rooms it must have had.

The roof had been decorated like a castle, with small turrets sticking upwards every five or six feet. Woodlands surrounded the house on all sides, one of them leading down to what John assumed would be the River Derwent that the priest had told them about.

As they got closer, John saw that the long winding entrance was wide enough for two carriages to pass with plenty of room to spare, and he noted the magnificent view the important visitors would have seen with the huge pillars.

"This place is amazing," Stephen said. "It's the finest house I've ever seen."

"It's almost as nice as Broxley." Catherine playfully jabbed John in the ribs.

"We need to find the farmhouse and speak to the beekeeper, Tristan." John ignored the playful barbs. "I'm hoping he can tell us why Margaret would come back here, and where she might hide something as important as her confessions."

"After all we've been through to get here, he'd better tell us," Stephen said.

"We're not here to hurt anyone," John reminded him. "If he doesn't want to help us, or if he genuinely doesn't know, then we'll find another way."

"Whatever you say, boss," Stephen said sarcastically, referring to John by the term the gang had used to address their leader, Ren Walden.

John jolted to a halt. "Don't ever compare me to Ren Walden. He was evil, and I'm nothing like him."

"I was kidding," Stephen said. "Don't get your hooves in a twist."

John took a deep breath. "We've all been through a lot to get here, and this weather isn't helping. Let's find the beekeeper and see what he has to say."

John kicked his horse on up the icy road and looked for the crossroads ahead of him.

Tristan

The whitewashed farmhouse stood by itself on top of a small hill overlooking the town of Malton below. A few furlongs further along the road, two of the turrets from Malton Manor rose above the tree line, announcing its grandiose location to the world.

John dismounted from his horse and gathered them all around. "It's probably better if just Catherine and I go first, at least until we see if he's going to talk to us or not. It might overwhelm him if we're all there."

"You want us to stand out here and freeze to death while you sit in front of a roaring fire talking to the beekeeper?" Stephen snarled. "Just exactly who do you think you are?"

"Fair point," John said. "And no, I don't expect you to stay out here while I'm talking to him. I'm going to ask him if he will allow us all inside."

"Just make sure you do."

John grasped Catherine's frozen hand and headed for the front door of the beekeeper's house, trying not to slip along the way.

245

After several loud raps, the door inched open to reveal an old man who John guessed was in the twilight years of his life. His hair was as grey as the English clouds, and his face was lined from many years of working outside in all weathers. He was around John's height, and although portly, he looked to still be in good physical shape.

"Sir, we're sorry to bother you on this cold morn, but would you be Tristan, the beekeeper of Malton Manor?"

"That is me," the old man answered in a rasping, high-pitched voice. "What do you want of me?"

"Sir, we are four weary travellers who have ridden a long way in this appalling weather to seek you out. I hate to ask, but might we be invited inside so we don't freeze to death out here in the cold?"

"There are four of you?" the man said, looking around for the other two.

"They are tethering our horses," John explained.

"What do you want of me?" Tristan asked, cocking his head to the side and glaring at John.

"A family member of mine came here right before she died, and I believe you may shed some light on why she was here."

"Who was this family member you speak of?"

John hesitated. "Margaret Colte."

Tristan bit his bottom lip and stood there for a moment before answering. "I'm sorry, I can't help you."

He tried closing the door, but John threw his frozen foot in the way. "Please, sir, I beg of you, we mean you no harm. You must have known Margaret, or she wouldn't have come here before she died, and the information we seek is vital to us. We have travelled a long way to see you, and if you could spare us a few moments of your time, we would be grateful. I can assure you, sir, if it wasn't so important, we wouldn't be here."

The beekeeper stared at John. "I don't know how I can help you, but please come inside and get yourselves out of this dreadful weather."

John shouted for Stephen and Edward to join them and entered the small but comfortable farmhouse Tristan called home. They stood in front of a crackling fire that instantly warmed them, and John took a moment to prepare himself for what he was about to say.

He looked around the room, taking a moment to gather his thoughts before speaking. The only items in the room were a table with four chairs in the middle of the floor. A window looked out over the pretty North Yorkshire Moors.

John turned his attention back to the beekeeper. He still hadn't made his mind up on the best way to approach the subject, and he stood there, staring at Tristan, rocking his head from side to side.

"Well, it's always nice to have company," Tristan said. "Especially on days like this, but I don't know how I can help you."

"Sir, we have come a long way to find you. I'm here to find out why Margaret Colte came here shortly before her death. How did you know her?" John sighed. He decided to just spill it all out and see what happened.

The beekeeper ground his teeth and stared at his strange visitors. "I don't know anyone of that name, so I don't know how I can help you. You've found the wrong farmhouse, I'm afraid."

"Sir," John said. "I—we—know for a fact that Margaret was here in the summer. She entered this very house and spent some considerable time here, as I under-stand from a man I trust with my life. You may know her by a different name. Margaret Shipley?"

Tristan's face turned as white as the blankets of snow

outside the window. "Margaret Shipley? How do you know her, and how did you know she was here?"

"Sir, it's a matter of life and death that we find what we came for. Margaret Colte, or Shipley as you knew her, caused much heartache to my family, and I need your help. Her personal guard escorted her here in the summer, and he is loyal to me and would never lie, so why was she here and how did you know her?"

"Wait a moment," Tristan backed off, but Stephen blocked his path. "You're not? Oh, my God! You are. You're that John Howard everybody in the country is shouting about, aren't you?"

John bowed his head. "I am he, but don't believe everything you hear. Even in death, Margaret still continues to destroy my life. I am innocent of everything of which I am accused. It is Margaret who is guilty, not me, or anyone else standing before you today. We buried our best friend just a few days ago, and even though she is dead, it was Margaret who was responsible. She has the blood of many people on her hands."

Tristan sighed and slumped into a chair. "If you're here to kill me, then get on with it. I am not a wealthy man, and I have nothing to offer to save my life."

"We are not here to harm you," John said, sitting beside the beekeeper. "It is information we seek, vital information that will bring the real evildoers to justice and clear our names. That is why we're here. Will you help us?"

"Margaret was always trouble, right from the moment I first saw her as a young girl. What do you want to know?"

"How did you know her, and why did she come here in the summer?"

"She came here as a young girl with her family. Her parents were good people, and Margaret became close to my daughter. They went everywhere together and were as close as two girls could be." Tears filled his eyes as he recalled the memories of Margaret and his daughter.

Catherine sat close to him and placed her hand on his knee. "I'm sorry," she whispered gently. "I know this must be difficult for you, but we wouldn't be here if it wasn't important. Margaret caused so much death and heartache for all of us, not just John. So please tell us what you know, so we can put her memory behind us and move on."

Tristan's shoulders drooped as his head lowered to his chest. "There were always rumours when she first came here that she'd done something terrible somewhere else. I ignored it and put it down to jealous gossip because both Margaret and her mother were such pretty ladies.

"After my wife died, I thought it would be good for my daughter to have a good friend, so I encouraged Margaret to spend time with us and stay close to Dawn. It was the biggest mistake I ever made."

"Your daughter is called Dawn?" Catherine asked.

John touched Catherine's shoulders and looked at her with renewed admiration. She was taking charge of this discussion, and she was handling it with a grace and compassion that he never could. He sighed and allowed himself to become lost in her presence.

"Dawn was the name we always called her, because she was born as the sun rose in the sky. I always called her my little ray of sunshine." Tristan covered his eyes and broke down in floods of tears.

"What happened?" Catherine gently prodded Tristan.

"She killed her. Margaret Shipley killed my beautiful girl."

"Margaret killed your daughter?" John leant forward.

Tristan nodded through his tears. "She fed her poisoned honey and killed her."

John stumbled back, hitting the table with his legs.

"You're telling us that Margaret used poisoned honey to kill your daughter?"

Tristan nodded, unable to speak.

"That's exactly what she did to her son, Mark, and I got the blame for it. Before we knew her, I have sound reason to believe she killed her first husband with poisoned honey and blamed it on the sweating sickness." John forced out a deep sigh. "She was truly the most evil woman I've ever met."

"That's what they said my Dawn died of," Tristan struggled to get his words out. "The medics said it was the sweating sickness, but I didn't believe them. I knew it was Margaret and her poisoned honey."

"Why didn't you have her arrested?" John asked. "It would have saved a lot of people much heartache later on when she got older."

"I tried, but I couldn't prove it. It was my word against hers, and she fooled them all."

"What happened to Margaret after Dawn died?" Catherine asked.

John went to say something, but Catherine shot him a dirty look and waved him off. "We're really sorry about Dawn, and we share your grief, but can you tell us what happened after she died? We know it's difficult, but it's important, and we wouldn't ask if it wasn't."

"Margaret took her poison with her and ran away. She left her mother behind, and she never got over it. She died soon after of a broken heart."

"Where did Margaret go?" John asked, ignoring Catherine's stares.

"I never knew," Tristan said. "I spent my life searching for her, and I never stopped looking. At least not until I found her years later, but by then she was too powerful, and I couldn't get near her."

"You found her?" Catherine asked. "Where? Was she in Saddleworth?"

"I don't know nothing about any Saddleworth," Tristan shook his head. "The cryers in Malton shouted out the news about John Howard and what he'd done to his brother. They said his mother offered a big reward for his capture."

Tristan looked John in the eyes. "They said her name was Margaret Colte, but I knew who she was. It was Margaret, alright. Margaret Shipley, who'd done the same thing to my Dawn."

Now it was John's turn to slump into a chair and hold his head in his hands. "Finally, someone other than my closest friends believes I'm not guilty. Sir, I'm really sorry for your daughter's loss, but what you have told us has been most useful, and if we find what we came here for, we should be able to prove Margaret killed her. It won't bring her back, but it might allow you to be at peace with her memory."

"What did you come here to find?" Tristan asked. "You said you came here to find out about Margaret."

"We did," John said. "But we believe she came here to hide the confessions she wrote before her death. Do you know why she was here?"

Tristan rubbed his hands together and sighed. "She made her confessions and hid them here? She did pay me an unexpected visit a few months ago, and I wanted to kill her as soon as I saw her. But I'm old now, and not as able as I once was. She told me there was a guard outside who would kill everyone in Lord Pitt's Manor if I touched her, and I believed her. If you've known Margaret, you know she doesn't make idle threats."

John scoffed. "The man outside was Willis, and he is loyal to me. My father assigned him to Margaret after I ran away. I can assure you, Tristan, he would never hurt anyone in Malton Manor. He is one of the good people in this world."

"I couldn't have known that," Tristan answered. "In any case, I thought she was here because she felt guilt for what she'd done to my Dawn. She wanted to know where she could pay her last respects, so I told her, and she vanished into the night. I was glad when I heard you'd killed her a few weeks later."

"That one I am guilty of," John said, squeezing Catherine's hand. He knew she still had nightmares over the slaying of Margaret Colte.

"You did the world an excellent service by killing her," Tristan said.

"It will be for nothing if we don't find what we came for. What did she say to you exactly?"

"She came in the middle of the night and woke me from my sleep. It stunned me to see it was her. She told me she'd regretted Dawn's death all her life and came here to pay her respects to her best friend. I didn't believe her, but what was I to do? I told her where Dawn was buried, and I slammed the door in her face. She said that if I ever told anyone of her visit that she would ensure I died a terrible death, but I didn't care. I told Lord Pitts, but he said it didn't matter after you'd killed her. He told me to forget it and allow Dawn to rest in peace."

"She came to visit Dawn's grave in the middle of the night?" John sat forward.

"Yes, she went to her grave and then went to pay her respects at the memorial Lord Pitts donated to Dawn in St Michael's church."

"How do you know where she went if you slammed the door on her?"

"I didn't trust her, so I followed her."

"What is your last name?" John asked.

"Browne," Tristan said, pulling his eyebrows together in a frown. "Why?"

"Dawn Browne," John said, looking around the table at the others. "That's D.B, not the T.B. we're looking for."

"T.B?" Tristan asked. "We called our daughter Dawn because she was born as the sun rose, but her real name is Trayce. Her grave gives her real name, which is Trayce Browne, if that is any help to you. Do you think Margaret hid her confessions in Dawn's grave?"

"That's it." John slammed his hand on the table, making everyone jump. "That's why she came here. T.B. must be Dawn's gravesite."

"What are you going to do?" Tristan looked worried. "What did she do to Dawn's grave?"

"Have you been to her grave since Margaret was here?" Stephen spoke up.

"Of course," Tristan answered. "I go to her every day."

"Did you see anything different about it?"

Tristan shook his head. "No, nothing."

"So, she didn't disturb it at all?"

"No." Tristan shook his head again.

"Where does she rest?" John asked.

"I'll take you," Tristan said.

A few minutes later, they all stepped outside into the freezing cold, and Tristan led them towards a graveyard at the rear of the farmhouse.

Revelations

Tristan Browne fell to his knees beside two small crosses in the rear row of the graveyard behind the farmhouse. John wiped the snow from the wooden crosses and read the simple inscriptions.

Joan Browne

Tracye "Dawn" Browne.

"I'm sorry, Tristan, but we have to look at Dawn's grave to see if it has been disturbed."

"You're not desecrating my daughter's grave." Tristan threw himself onto his daughter's gravesite. "That is a crime against God, and I will not allow it."

"We won't desecrate her grave," John assured the beekeeper. "If what you say is true, and it lays undisturbed after Margaret's visit, then we won't touch it at all."

Stephen and Edward helped Tristan to his feet and then helped John remove the snow from Dawn's resting place. When it was down to the freezing soil, John looked at Tristan.

"Are you sure Margaret didn't disturb anything here?"

"I'm sure. She's my daughter and I come here every day, so yes, I would know."

"Well, we have no reason to doubt you," John said. "And I can't see any signs of anything either, so if she didn't put them here, then where are they?"

"Wait," Edward said. "Did you say there was a memorial to your daughter in the church?"

"Yes, Lord Pitts kindly paid for one for me so I could remember her. My nephew is the priest there, and he persuaded his lordship to pay for it."

John thumped his forehead with his fist. "Of course, that makes more sense. Her confessions would be protected from the weather if she hid them inside the church."

He turned to Tristan. "Where is her memorial in the church?"

"It's right at the back, next to the door to my nephew's private quarters. What are these confessions Margaret is supposed to have written?"

"They are the documents we need to prove she is guilty of her crimes, which should include your daughter's murder," John said. "It's time to go back to the church."

"I would love to go with you," Tristan said. "But I have to prepare some honey for his lordship, and I cannot keep him waiting. May I ask that you return here to tell me what you find?"

"Of course," John said. "Rest assured, Tristan, we shall let you know what we discover."

John led the way back to the church, making sure to close the door behind them when they got there to keep out both the cold and any prying eyes that might be watching four strangers prowling around the town centre.

To John's relief, there wasn't any sign of Father Browne, which meant that he didn't have to explain why he was digging about inside the wall of his ancient church.

The door to his private apartment was closed, so John put his finger to his lips and pointed at the closed door. Stephen, Edward, and Catherine nodded back at him, signalling they understood.

The others couldn't read, so they stood back and allowed John to look at the inscriptions on the wall remembering the generations of men and women who had lived in Malton over the centuries.

Several of the stones along the back wall were inscribed with names, and John ran his finger up and down, trying to find the one that remembered Tracye, or Dawn, Browne.

John searched all over the wall until Stephen pulled his cloak to get his attention. "The beekeeper said it was next to the priest's private door, which is over there." Stephen pointed to the doorway to John's left. "You're looking in the wrong place."

John threw his hand in the air in frustration. "Of course, thank you, Stephen."

He shuffled to where the wall met the doorway and started looking again. He let out a stifled yell when he touched the stone at the bottom of the wall. "Here it is," he exclaimed, leaning forward to get a closer look.

The stone was roughly ten inches long and about eight wide, which was plenty big enough to hide something behind. It was located in the bottom left corner of the wall, right next to the doorway to the priest's private room.

In loving memory of Tracye Browne, 1506-1521.

"It's short and sweet," John whispered, reading the inscription aloud for the others.

He looked closer and ran his fingers around the stone. "Look!" he said, far too loudly for Edward, who looked around the church as though John's voice was waking the souls of the dead.

"Look," John said again, ignoring Edward's stare. "Someone has moved this stone recently. There's a gap around it that isn't there on any of the others."

They all crowded around and helped John pry the stone back and forward until they felt it wobble and move. Slowly, the stone came towards them, until it finally fell onto the floor with a loud thud.

The four looked at each other, and John felt the familiar tingling in his arms and legs as he reached inside the gap in the wall. His fingers clamped around a soft pouch, and he slowly pulled his hand back, revealing what he'd found.

"It's a pouch," he whispered.

John turned the pouch over in his hands. The letters *M.C.* were embroidered in big gold letters on the front.

"See this? These are Margaret's initials! The pouch definitely belonged to her."

"It doesn't look like it's full of any confessions," Edward said. "It looks empty."

It was empty. John opened the pouch and turned it inside out to make sure they weren't missing anything He felt around inside the hole in the wall, but there was nothing.

"It's empty," he said, closing his eyes. "Somebody beat us to it. Whatever was here, and make no mistake, I do believe this is where Margaret hid her confessions, somebody else found them before we did. We have lost."

He sat on the floor, broken and defeated. "Without the confessions, we are done. It's over for us, and there's no point carrying on. Once we get back to London, I'm handing myself in to my father so we can end this. At least that way all three of you can have a life."

"No, John. I won't allow it." Catherine threw her arms around the love of her life. "You promised me you would be with me for the rest of our lives, and I demand you keep that promise. I don't want to live without you."

Edward and Stephen didn't say anything, but John could tell from their faces that, like him, they knew it was over. "You will be free to pursue Abraham and the grey-eyed evil one without the weight of the world chasing you down. That is how we must gain our vengeance. It is too dangerous for me to remain with you, so I ask that you take care of Catherine when I'm gone."

"It will be done," Edward agreed.

"You have my word," Stephen said.

"No, this cannot happen!" Catherine sobbed, but John cut her off.

"You know it's the only option we have left now that the confessions are gone. It's the only way I can guarantee your safety. I'm sorry, my love, for I have failed you."

"Who do you think has them?" Stephen changed the subject.

"It has to be Asheborne," John answered. "He's the one with most to gain by finding them. I'd wager that Margaret's confessions have been destroyed, leaving Asheborne in the clear. They were our only chance of beating him, and we have to accept that we have lost."

"What are you doing here?" The voice of Father Browne disturbed the crestfallen quartet, and John sat back in surprise, banging his head against the wall.

"Well? Why are you damaging my church? Did I not show you kindness and give you shelter when you needed it?"

"Father, we are indebted to you for your kindness," John said. "And we mean no disrespect to your church. We came here to find some documents that would prove not only our innocence, but also that Dawn Browne was murdered by Margaret Shipley all those years ago. This pouch held Margaret's confessions, but alas, someone beat us to it, and now they are gone."

"What are you talking about?" The priest pulled a face and stared at the small group. "What is going on here? We are a small, peaceful community, not used to strangers in our midst, and yet recently it seems everyone in England is taking an interest in us. What did you mean when you said you can prove Margaret Shipley murdered Dawn? Tristan has been saying that for years, but nobody ever believed him."

"It's most likely true, Father," John said. "I knew Margaret, and she was evil. Who else has been here?"

"Well, first there was a man I never knew the name of, that was digging around in the exact spot you are at now, and then you came a few days ago. Now, a new group of men I didn't recognise stopped to ask where they could find the beekeeper. I'm confused, and I demand to know what's going on."

John clenched his fists together as the four of them looked at each other.

"Who came here first?" Stephen asked.

"What is going on? I demand you tell me what is going on here."

"Father, you have been very kind to us," John said. "But we are here on an urgent matter of life and death. Please, tell us who was here first, and then we'll tell you everything we know."

"A man came here towards the end of summer. A tall man who never gave his name. I caught him in the exact spot you are at now, and when I cornered him, he mumbled an apology and left. I never saw him again."

"Did he tell you what he was doing here?" John asked.

"No. He mumbled something I took as an apology and

left. I never saw him again, but I knew he'd been digging around that wall."

"Didn't you look to see what he was digging for?" Stephen asked.

"I do not desecrate the house of God. No, I did not pull the wall down."

"Who on earth could that be?" Catherine asked.

"Who are the men who just asked directions to the beekeeper?" Edward asked.

"I don't know," the priest answered. "One of them they called the captain, but another looked ungodly. I swear he had the most evil grey eyes I have ever seen."

Edward leapt up and shot a look at John before running past the priest.

"What is going on?" Father Browne demanded. "Who are these men?"

"Evil men who will harm Tristan," John said, running past him. "Stay here, Catherine, and don't leave. If we're not back by dark, get away from here. I love you, my brave lady."

John tossed the bag of coins to Catherine, who stood open-mouthed as John and Stephen raced out of the church after Edward.

The Devil's Work

John counted eight horses in the small yard at the front of the farmhouse. Four men were posted outside. The remaining four men were nowhere to be seen, although the front door to the farmhouse was open.

John, Edward, and Stephen hid behind the stone wall across the narrow lane leading up from the crossroads towards the farmhouse and Malton Manor further down the hill.

"Spread out and take out the guards," Edward whispered. "Then meet me at the farmhouse."

They nodded to each other and spread out along the wall to get good vantage points. John took the middle position, with Edward to his left and Stephen on his right. He peered over the wall and readied his longbow, waiting for Edward's signal.

Edward raised his hand, and a hail of arrows silently whooshed through the air, burying themselves in three of the guards. The men fell, and before the fourth could raise the alarm, Edward unleashed another arrow, silencing the man forever.

They threw their longbows over their backs, jumped over the wall, and ran to the beekeeper's house. Edward led the way as they burst through the open doorway and charged into the cosy room they had shared with Tristan just a few hours earlier.

Except this time, it looked completely different. The chairs were knocked over and lay on the ground on their sides. Someone had swiped the contents of the table onto the floor. Blood was all over the top of the table, and it dripped onto the floor in an ever-widening pool of dark red liquid.

A deep growl emanated from Edward's throat as he looked out of the window towards the snow-covered hills and the graveyard that lay at the rear of the farmhouse.

"There they are." He pointed at the graveyard. "They have the beekeeper out there."

They raced out of the rear door and slid to a halt as the attackers turned to face them. The men's hoods had fallen off in the melee, and John shivered when he looked into the cold grey eyes of the most evil man he'd ever seen.

It's as though I'm staring into the eyes of the devil himself.

Edward and Stephen didn't hesitate and ran right at the men. John followed and looked to find Tristan.

Edward and Stephen can divert their attention while I rescue the beekeeper.

Two of Asheborne's men ran towards them, and John looked to see if Abraham was amongst them, but he was disappointed when he didn't see him.

Edward feigned a move, and Stephen rammed his sword straight through one of the men, almost severing his torso when he sliced his sword towards the ground before snatching it out again.

The pure white snow turned a deep crimson as the battle heated. The second attacker made a beeline for

John, but he never made it. In one swoop, Edward severed his head with his sword. John had to jump back so the head with a mouth that was still moving didn't land on him.

John ran to Tristan, who was standing over Dawn's grave, holding something that John couldn't make out.

Perhaps the men made him carry a shovel out there?

Then he saw it, and it was all John could do not to throw up. Tristan turned to stare at John, his face as white as the virgin snow on the hills. The look he gave John was one of total shock at what was happening to him, but it was the sight of what he was holding that took John's attention.

Tristan, the kindly, innocent beekeeper, stood, leaning onto the cross at his daughter's grave, holding his severed right arm in his other hand! Blood poured from the open wound, drenching the graves of both his wife and daughter with his own lifeblood. His mouth opened and closed, but no words came out.

A red mist came over John, and he screamed out loud, throwing himself at the small, powerful man who seemed to delight in committing the vilest acts John had ever seen.

The man snatched Tristan by the neck and held a knife against his neck. "Stop right there, or I'll sever his head, right over the graves of his wife and daughter."

John, Edward, and Stephen all stopped, because they knew there was no doubt he would do what he threatened.

"You murdered my wife and unborn child." Edward's eyes almost glowed with anger and hatred. "You are not leaving here alive."

"Oh, I think I will," the evil monk replied.

"This is the third time we have met," the man standing next to the evil one said to Edward. "And this is the last time."

John knew this must be the captain by the way Edward glared at him.

A noise behind John made him spin around just in time to see a huge rock inches from his head. His world went dark when it crashed into his skull, and he felt himself falling to the ground. The soft snow cushioned his fall, and he felt warm liquid running down his face.

He shook his head and tried to get his eyes to focus, while he struggled to his knees and grasped his sword. Edward and Stephen stood around him, protecting him from the four other men who had joined the fight from behind them.

Stephen threw a knife that embedded itself in the eye of one of the attackers, and John heard his screams through the mists in his own head. John felt himself being pulled to the side somewhere.

Finally, the swirling clouds cleared, and he saw what was happening, as blood poured down the side of his face. Stephen had pulled John to the side of the house while Edward fought three men on his own. Stephen dropped John in a heap and ran to Edward's aid.

John stood up and joined in. One man lay dead in the crimson snow, and John made sure a second followed when he thrust his sword deep into his throat. The third man ran back to the captain and the evil monk.

"There are a lot more of us," the captain said. "They were getting us fresh horses from the stables and will be here any moment."

A crash at the front of the house told John that he was telling the truth, and he grabbed Edward and pulled him backwards. "He's telling the truth, I can hear them," he gasped. "We've got to get out of here or they'll kill us. There's too many of them."

Edward ignored John and started towards the captain,

but Stephen wrenched him back. "We live to fight another day," he hissed. "These men will not get away with this."

Edward reluctantly gave in and backed around the side of the house just in time before another group of Asheborne's men burst through the rear door of the beekeeper's farmhouse.

"What about the beekeeper?" Edward said.

"We can't help him now," John panted, holding his head. "There's too many of them. In any case, he's badly injured. Did you see what they'd done to him?"

Grimaced faces told him they did.

Shouts and the sound of men thrashing through deep snow told them it was time to go, so they went as fast as they could through the deep snow. They clambered over walls and through hidden streams until they somehow found themselves at the banks of the freezing river.

Steam rose from the water, but there was nowhere for them to go. At least six or seven more men approached them, trapping them against the freezing river.

"We stand and fight," Edward said. "The captain and the evil one must die here today."

"I agree they must die," John said, "but not here and not today. We're half frozen, and I'm not seeing straight after that rock hit me in the head. We need to regroup and live to fight again. I know we will get another opportunity with these men before we get back to London, and the next time we'll fight them on our terms."

"He's right," Stephen said. "As much as I want to fight them, we will die if we make our stand here. Let's live and meet them again."

"Where do we go?" Edward asked. "We're trapped."

The shouts grew louder as the men got closer. The captain's orders could be heard loud and clear.

"Spread out and search the banks of the river. The

cowards are here somewhere. Make sure you don't kill them, though. Gare wants that honour for himself. And don't kill John Howard, because he's worth much more alive than he is dead."

John looked at the others and nodded towards the freezing waters of the River Derwent. Without another moment's hesitation, the three of them jumped into the arctic waters.

Freezing Waters

A loud gasp cracked out of John's open mouth as the air was pushed out of his body when he hit the freezing waters of the River Derwent. He immediately found it hard to breathe, and his chest heaved and thrashed from the cold water.

The current was stronger in the middle of the river, so John used what was left of his senses to kick himself towards it. He felt himself heaving and gasping uncontrollably for air, and he swallowed a mouthful of water every time his head dipped beneath the surface, which was way too often, as he bobbed and weaved in the mild currents of the freezing water.

John used the last of his strength to look for Edward and Stephen, and he saw them a few feet away, struggling just as much as he was. Together, they drifted down the river, vulnerable and unable to defend themselves from either man or nature.

Thick bushes and trees lined the banks of the river, making it difficult, if not impossible, for anyone to stand on the banking and use a longbow against them. John could hear faint shouts, but he'd gone past the point of caring by the time he heard them.

Now and then, a head would appear from out of the thick bushes, and a hail of arrows would follow shortly after. Like the others, John forced his head under the freezing water and hoped for the best.

He let out a yell underwater as one arrow grazed his neck, and water entered his lungs. A sensation of dread overwhelmed him momentarily before dizziness and darkness consumed him.

I'm dying.

There was a strange calmness with the sudden realisation that this was it. It was as though his body was shutting down and his mind was accepting it as his inevitable fate. He stopped struggling and allowed his body to still itself and fall limp.

A peacefulness, the likes of which he'd never known, embraced him, and his freezing body stopped all resistance. The heavy pain in his chest went away, and he felt himself floating upwards.

Hands reached down to him from above and pulled him towards the light. Images of Sarah and his mother flashed before his eyes.

This must be heaven.

A large hand slapped him hard across the face. Without warning, all the pain and hurt returned in an instant, forcing him to panic as he gasped and spewed the water out of his lungs.

At least it isn't the River Fleet. Who knows what ailment I would die of if my body was full of that foul water?

He found himself thinking wild thoughts of drowning Margaret Colte in the stink of the River Fleet, as he grabbed hold of whatever he was being pushed towards. Finally, he opened his eyes.

He wasn't in heaven at all: Edward had seen him drowning and had saved his life. Now he found himself hanging onto a large piece of driftwood with the other two.

I'm alive!

His senses slowly returned, but he was unable to feel any part of his body other than his lungs, which burned and ached like he had swallowed hot coals. He peered over the top of the thick tree trunk they were hiding behind as it drifted down the river and saw three or four men in the bushes aiming their longbows at them.

He ducked as they fired, and the thud of the arrows as they hit the tree trunk made him shrink even deeper into the deathly water.

The last he saw of Asheborne's men was before the driftwood vanished around a bend in the river, where the bushes and trees were so thick it was impossible for any of the men to get close to the banking.

An age later, the tree trunk nudged up to the side of the riverbank, its path blocked by an even bigger tree trunk. John forced himself to clamber along the thick trunk and crawl onto the bank that was thick with branches and limbs weighted down from the heavy snowstorm.

He turned and helped Edward and Stephen, whose face had turned a strange shade of blue, onto the riverbank alongside him. They crawled into the middle of a thick bush and buried themselves under the snow, leaving a gap so they could breathe.

They all lay there for a short while, but John's senses had returned enough to know they were in serious danger of dying from the cold. He tried rubbing his hands together, but he couldn't. His extremities had long since given up and helping the others out of the water had been their ultimate act before shutting down.

"We can't stay here like this," he said in a half whisper, half rasp. "We'll die if we don't find warmth and shelter soon."

"What do we do?" Edward asked. "I'm so cold that I fear I cannot fight."

"We have to get back to the church and warm ourselves in front of the fire," John said. "If we don't, we will die here."

John listened for any signs of an approaching enemy as they lay in silence. Nothing. All he heard was the sound of the birds in the trees.

He forced himself to sit up under the overhanging branches, and a shower of snow fell onto him from above, but he was too cold to even notice.

He fell on top of Stephen because his hands wouldn't work and got next to him. "Get as close to him as you can," John's hoarse voice called out to Edward. "We have to use our body heat to give ourselves a chance of warming up enough so we can move."

Edward rolled tightly up to Stephen, and the three of them lay there for some time, as what was left of their body heat combined to slowly bring some feeling back to their tortured bodies.

The weak, wintry sun was fading by the time the three men got up and prepared to move. John hadn't been able to feel his hands or feet for hours, but he forced himself up into the thick branches and winced as he felt the pain in his legs when he tried to move.

More snow fell onto them, and John shivered, forcing himself on his hands and knees through the deep snow away from the riverbank.

They found themselves on a small path in the middle of nowhere, but in the fading light John saw smoke rising in the distance. He pointed in its direction, or at least he tried to, but his hands and arms wouldn't do as he commanded.

"Over there," he said. "There's smoke, so hopefully Malton is in that direction."

They trudged slowly and painfully through the hardening snow, as the sinking sun lowered the temperature. John didn't know how much more they could take, and he knew they had to find warmth and shelter soon, or they would perish in the frozen wastelands of North Yorkshire.

The moon reflected off the snow, giving them a clear view of the picturesque northern town of Malton. As they approached St Michael's church in the town square, John thought it the most welcome sight he had ever seen.

The church door was locked, but all three of them pounded on it as hard as they could with the last vestiges of their strength. When the door slowly opened, three frozen, half dead bodies fell through the doorway into the entrance of the church.

"Good Lord." John heard Father Browne say.

"John!" A high-pitched wail told John that Catherine was alive and well. He felt hands dragging him along the ground towards a glowing warmth that stung and hurt his body as he got closer to it.

An hour later, and with a blanket around him as his clothes dried by the roaring fire, John slowly came to his senses. His body burned with explosions of sharp pain as he regained feeling, and he grasped at the ale and food offered by the priest and Catherine.

"What happened?" Father Browne asked. "The captain came here to tell me you were all presumed dead in the river. He said nobody could withstand the freezing water on such a day as this."

"He was almost right," John said. "Much longer out there and we would have frozen to death."

"What happened out there?" Catherine's eyes were red and swollen, and John could see she had been crying.

"We tried to save the beekeeper, but there were too many of them," John said. "We managed to get away and had to jump into the river to save ourselves. The thick branches and bushes thankfully kept them away from the edge of the water, and we floated downriver for an age before sheltering under a thick bush until it got dark."

"I didn't think we would survive," Stephen said, the colour finally returning to his face. "I've never been as cold in my life before."

"What happened to the beekeeper?" Edward asked.

Father Browne looked at the fireplace for a long moment, and John felt the tension rise in the silence.

"You couldn't know what happened, so I'll tell you. The captain came here after they lost you in the river and searched the wall in the same spot I caught you peering at. He demanded to know what you had found here."

"What did you tell him?" John asked.

"I told him the truth. I said that I watched you pull the stone from the wall and didn't find anything. He got angered with me when he removed the stone and found the pouch engraved with the letters 'M.C.' He threatened me, but he soon stopped when I reminded him he was desecrating the house of God."

"Did he believe you?"

"Clearly not, because he waved the empty pouch at me and demanded to know what you'd done with the contents. I told him the pouch was empty and that it had disappointed you to discover it that way."

"What happened next?" John asked.

He warned me you were dangerous and desperate. He said they had seen you leaving London, so they followed you. Once they realised you were travelling north, the captain sent for reinforcements from Lord Asheborne, and it took a while for them to arrive."

"They followed us from London?" John asked. "Why didn't they ambush us and get it over with before we got all the way up here?"

"I'm merely relaying what the captain told me. He said you came here on a fool's errand trying to find documents that don't exist, and he told me you were extremely dangerous to anyone that comes into contact with you. He said I was to turn you in the moment I saw you, should you have somehow survived the freezing river."

"So why didn't you?"

"Because I don't believe him. Young Catherine here has spent the day telling me all about your adventures and what has happened to you, and I find her much more believable than the captain and that evil man he has with him."

"Gare," Edward said. "The captain referred to him as 'Gare.'"

"Whatever his name, he is an evil man."

"So, what did happen today?" John asked.

The priest looked at the fire again. "You know that Tristan was my uncle, don't you?"

John nodded. "Tristan told us earlier this morn."

"The captain said they arrived too late to save him." Father Browne looked up at John, pain etched deep into his eyes. "Do you know what he told me?" he asked.

John could see he was finding it difficult to tell him what had happened.

"Do you know what he said you did to him?" the priest's voice cracked.

John and the others remained silent.

"He told me they found Tristan laying on top of Dawn's grave, that was soaked in his blood. He said his severed arm was laid out on his chest and that he had been gutted like a fish." His voice broke, and he held his hands to his mouth. John stared at the fireplace, unable to find the right words to say.

"Then he told me that his head had been forced onto the top of the cross over Dawn's grave." Father Browne burst into tears. "Tristan was a good man, and he didn't deserve to die like that."

John closed his eyes and lowered his head to his chest. "I'm so sorry, Father. You are right. Tristan didn't deserve to die like that."

"What did the captain say next?" Stephen looked pale again.

"He said you killed several of his men before escaping to the river, where you are believed drowned. He gave me his apologies for not getting here soon enough to stop the tyrannical John Howard and his Underlings, as he called you."

John sighed and touched the priest's shoulder. "You know we didn't do any such thing, Father. This is the work of the man they call Gare, and we can prove it if we get a chance. He's done this sort of evil murder before, and if we don't stop him, he'll do it again. I'm so sorry this happened to your uncle. It seems everywhere I go, people die a terrible death."

"I didn't believe for a moment that you did this," Father Browne said. "And I told Lord Pitts as much when I saw him earlier today. He is beside himself with anger and grief, and he has vowed to scour Malton until he finds your corpses frozen at the side of the river."

"Lord Pitts is looking for us?" Stephen asked.

"Everyone in England will look for you. By the time the sun rises, all of northern England will hear from the cryers what you did. I'm sure it will reach London soon after."

John sighed and looked at the others. "It never ends, does it? They accuse me of every evil deed they commit and there is nothing I can do about it."

"The captain said the king is furious and demands your head," Father Browne said.

"Where did the captain and Gare go?" Edward changed the subject.

"They are staying as guests of Lord Pitts this evening. They will leave for London in the morn, but they will leave two of their men behind who can identify you, should you be found."

"No doubt to collect our bodies and collect the reward," John interrupted.

"They probably have people at the stables watching, just in case," Stephen said. "And they probably saw us coming here."

"If we'd been seen, they'd have been here by now, arresting us, and dragging us outside to kill us," John said. "We're safe here for now, but we can't stay long."

"Lord Pitts is a military man, and he won't stop until he finds you," Father Browne said. "Even if the captain does as he says and leaves tomorrow, you are in grave danger if you stay here. We all are. Lord Pitts would have me hanged if he finds out I am harbouring you."

"We won't put you in any more danger, Father," John said. "You have suffered more than enough already. We shall leave at first light tomorrow. I was going to give myself up, and I shall, but not until that evil monster, Gare, has been stopped."

"And the captain," Edward added.

"No, don't leave in the morning," Father Browne said. "The captain and all his men are leaving then, and even though you want to kill them, there are too many of them for you to fight. They will kill you, and Tristan would have died for nothing."

"It is a worthy cause to die for," Edward said.

"Not only that," the priest added. "But Lord Pitts will have his men scouring the river and this entire area looking for you. You wouldn't have a chance of getting away."

"What do you suggest then?" John asked.

"Stay here tonight, so you can recover from your ordeal. Allow the captain and his men to get a head start on you, and leave tomorrow night as soon as darkness falls."

"What about our horses?" Edward asked. "What happened to them?"

"They are in the stables up the strete from here," Father Browne said. "I felt sorry for them tethered up outside in this weather, so I took them to the stables where they are safe."

"Can we get to them?" Edward asked.

"No, they will be guarded, but not to worry. Tristan and I have horses at his farm. Four will be ready for you at the rear of his house tomorrow after dark."

"You have risked much for us, Father Browne," John said. "We owe you our lives and we cannot thank you enough."

"Thank me by ridding the world of that evil man and avenging my uncle."

"It shall be done," Edward's cold eyes told everyone present he meant every word.

"What about the tall man who was here digging around the wall?" John asked. "If Asheborne had found the confessions, then he wouldn't have sent his men here after us."

"So, if he doesn't have them, then who does?" Catherine asked.

"That's what we need to find out," John said. "Who else would risk so much to find them besides Lord Asheborne and ourselves?"

"Tell us again what he looked like?" Stephen asked the priest.

"A tall, thin man about my age. That's all I can tell you."

John bolted upright in his chair. "Who else have you told about this?"

"Only Tristan, why?"

"Please keep this to yourself and don't tell anyone about it."

John turned to Catherine, Edward, and Stephen. "I know where we're going."

"Where?" Stephen asked.

"We're going to Burningtown."

York

A full moon illuminated the frozen town of Malton and a perfect landscape of snow-covered hills and trees. Steam blew out of John's mouth, and his breath froze the moment it left his body.

"I'll be glad to get back down south and away from this horrible weather," Catherine said, as she shivered in the bitterly cold November evening.

Even though nobody answered her, John knew they were all thinking the same thing.

The horses' hooves crunched through the packed ice, as they followed the barely used paths Father Browne had told them about to get out of the town and away from the prying eyes of Lord Pitts and his men.

"If we ride all night, we should be in York by the morn," John said, the freezing air burning his lungs as he breathed. "We should be safe there while we resupply ourselves and shelter until the next morn."

Nobody argued, and the four of them made good progress under the moonlight, glad of the distance they put between themselves and Malton.

As dawn approached, the famous city of the north appeared in their view. "There it is," John said. "It looks like London with the wall surrounding it."

"Yes, it does," Stephen said. "I heard stories about York when I was a boy. They said the Romans built the wall, the same as they did in London."

"They were correct," John answered. "The Romans built walls around several of our cities to defend them against attack."

"It looks like home," Catherine said.

They trotted their horses through the gates and entered the bustling city. John immediately felt at home in this ancient city.

The next morning, John heard a commotion in the small square across the road from the Inn where he was staying while the others gathered the supplies they needed for their journey south.

Oh yeah, oh yeah, oh yeah, be on the lookout, good people of York. John Howard and his Underlings, who left London and rode north to escape the king's wrath, tortured and murdered a beekeeper in Malton. The beekeeper caught them stealing horses and paid for it with his life. John Howard is the murdering son-of-an-earl who butchered Lady Margaret Colte in the summer, and is the most wanted man in England. Lord Asheborne sent men after him, but alas, they were too late, and six of his brave men paid for it with their lives during Howard's escape. Our great King, Henry VIII, demands justice, and the reward is fifteen pounds a year for life for anyone who finds the murdering scum and hands him in. It's ten pounds a year for life if you have to kill him before handing him over. Howard is said to be sixteen, tall, with long wavy dark hair, and his murdering Underlings include a man with a long scar down the right side of his face, and another tall man with long brown hair. They are travelling with a girl with blonde hair, although Lord Asheborne and Howard's father, Earl Howard of Coventry, believe Howard may have killed her and dumped her body somewhere in the great county of Yorkshire.

Oh yeah, oh yeah, oh yeah . . .

John shrank back from the window in case he was seen and paced fervently around the tiny room, worried about Catherine and the others. Word had travelled fast, and Asheborne was making sure they couldn't find safety anywhere in England. He slumped to the floor and held his head in his hands.

A short while later, Catherine, Edward, and Stephen hurried back into the room with their heads buried deep into their hoods.

"Did you hear what they are saying about us?" Catherine looked at John after she closed the door behind her. "They're saying we murdered that poor beekeeper and six of Asheborne's men. They're even saying that you killed me and dumped me somewhere in Yorkshire."

"I heard," John said. "No doubt every town and village in England is hearing the same thing. The captain must be sure we're still alive because they didn't find our bodies in the river, so he's making sure we don't find sanctuary anywhere else." He took Catherine's hands in his and looked around the room. "I have something to say that you all need to hear. Please don't argue with me or tell me I'm wrong, because you know I'm not."

"You're not leaving me." Catherine gripped his hands tightly.

"Not this again," Stephen said.

John ignored Stephen's dirty look. "This has to end, and if we enter London without the confessions, I will have no choice other than to give myself up. Catherine, I know you will suffer, but at least you will have a life, and I will die happy knowing that you walk free. If I keep running, we will be caught, and then all of us will die a terrible death. I cannot do that to any of you, but especially not to my beloved Catherine."

Catherine gripped John and kissed his head. "I love you, John Howard, and you're not going anywhere without me. I refuse to allow it, do you hear?"

"I mean what I say. This cannot carry on."

"We need to get out of York," Stephen said. "It's not safe for us here."

"It's not safe for us anywhere," John said. "And that's why I have to give myself up."

"We go to Burningtown," Edward said. "If we don't find the confessions, then we will talk about giving ourselves up, but not until Gare and the captain are dead. Then we can all hand ourselves in to the king."

"Speak for yourself," Stephen said. "I'm not giving myself up to anyone."

"Do we have what we need?" John asked.

Edward nodded.

"Then we leave York right away, in case they recognised any of you. From now on, neither Stephen nor myself can be seen in any town we ride through."

***

ALTHOUGH THE LAND was covered in frost every morning, the temperature gradually warmed the further south they went. By the time they reached the familiar sights of Burningtown Manor in the late afternoon ten days later, the snow had given way to freezing rain that soaked them through and left them shivering once darkness fell.

They watched from behind the wall where all this had started weeks earlier and watched for any signs of activity.

No smoke was rising from any of the four chimneys,

and after a while they were satisfied Burningtown Manor was empty.

"Nobody would expect us to come back here, so there's no reason for anyone to be guarding it," John said. "But to be sure, Edward and myself will look, and if everything is clear, we'll signal for you to bring the horses and join us."

Edward had gone over the wall before John finished speaking, and John went after him. They ran the hundred or so feet to the low wall that separated the house from the gardens where the Stantons had grown their own produce in better times. They hid there for a few minutes, listening for any signs of a trap.

Nothing.

Edward rose and went around the wall towards the front of the house. Shattered glass lay scattered over the once immaculate garden in front of the broken downstairs window. The front door lay smashed on its side as another reminder of the violence that had occurred there.

Edward entered the fractured doorway and looked in every room. John dashed past him and opened the door to the great hall. He immediately wished he hadn't.

The long table was stained with dried blood. John closed his eyes, shivering from the dark memories it evoked. The tapestries that once adorned the walls were missing, but otherwise, it looked just as it had before the attack.

Satisfied nobody was downstairs, John quickly checked the upstairs rooms before going down to tell Edward they were safe.

But Edward was nowhere to be seen.

John ran around the house again, his sword drawn in case someone had been lying in wait for them, but he found nothing. He ran over to the small cottage they had shared with Edward and Sybil and stopped dead in his tracks.

Sybil!

John ran around the rear of the house to the small graveyard and saw Edward on his knees, saying a prayer over his beloved Sybil's grave. John turned and went back to signal Stephen and Catherine to join them, leaving Edward to have a private moment with his wife and unborn child.

Everything about Burningtown reminded John of Isaac, and it wasn't long before he, Stephen, and Catherine were on their knees offering a prayer for their fallen friend.

"So, what now?" Edward asked, when they were all together again.

John looked at Edward. "We either find Margaret's confessions or we go to London empty-handed."

Kick in the Teeth

Edward refused to sleep in the cottage he had once called home, and Catherine was adamant she wasn't sleeping in the house where Joan Stanton had been so brutally murdered by Gare, so John arranged pallets for them all in the warm straw in the barn.

"It's probably warmer than in the house," he told them. "We can't start a fire in case we're seen, so at least we have the straw to keep us warm."

"Where do we look for the confessions?" Catherine asked.

"If he had them, why didn't he give them to you on his deathbed?" Stephen asked Edward.

Edward threw his hands in the air. "Master Stanton told me they were hidden in the wall behind the house, and we went there, as you know. We found the coin he'd left there and the letter from Margaret, but other than that I don't know where else he would have hidden them."

"The best place to start would be where we found the letter we already have," John said. "We might have missed something, but otherwise we'll pull his study apart and look there. Either we find them, or we don't."

"You don't think we'll find them, do you?" Catherine asked.

"We don't even know if the man Father Browne saw was James Stanton," John said. "So how can we be sure it was him that took them? Even if it was him, we don't know where he hid them. They could still be in Malton for all we know."

"We look at first light tomorrow," Edward said. "Then if we don't find anything, we'll talk about what we're doing next." He turned to John. "You said you will hand yourself in, but you made a promise to Isaac, James Stanton, and myself that you would not stop until they are avenged, and I aim to hold you to that promise."

"We'll talk about it tomorrow," John sighed.

Daylight brought a heavy sky but no rain, and they were all thankful for God's small mercies. The four of them went to the rear wall, where it joined the ivy-covered east wall. John fell to his knees and pulled on the third stone up from the ground. The daub around the stone was missing from the last time he and Edward were here, but the stone was intact, and it didn't look like anyone else had disturbed it.

When the stone fell to the ground, John took a deep breath and thrust his hand inside, feeling around in the dirt and the dust for anything they might have missed. He went in all the way to the back of the hole.

"There's something here!" he gasped.

His fingers clamped around a thin pouch, and he dragged it out. The others crowded around to see what he'd found. John opened the pouch and a single piece of folded parchment dropped to the ground.

"It doesn't look like a lifetime of confessions," Stephen said.

John's head dropped. He knew Stephen was right.

He picked up the parchment and unfolded it.

"Well? What does it say?" Catherine was impatient.

Look for T.B. You will find what you seek there.

J.S.

"What is that supposed to mean?" John shouted, after he'd read it out loud. "That's what Margaret wrote in her letter that Stanton left here. We're no better off now than we were before. Are they still in Malton? Surely we would have found them if they were."

John took the other sack they'd found in the wall after the attacks from his cloak. He pulled his mother's jewellery box out, taking a sharp intake of breath when he saw the carved dolphins spouting water towards the lock. He opened it and took out Margaret's letter.

"Read it to us again," Catherine said. "We might have missed something the first time."

The confessions I am writing are for God alone, as only He can grant me the forgiveness I crave. I pray I may enter His kingdom after my passing.

If someone else is reading my confessions, I am already dead, or I am about to be; the punishment for my many crimes will carry the ultimate penalty.

Either way, my soul will stand before God, waiting for His judgement. I am under no illusions as to my good Christian character because I have none, and He knows I have sinned many times during my life. My confessions are my admission of my guilt to the Lord Almighty in the hope that He forgives me.

My confessions detail the many indiscretions I committed during my life. In the physical world I bear no regret, for everything I did was for the betterment of my life, and to that end, I achieved what I wanted. That I hurt people along the way is a mere consequence that God alone may judge.

My confessions begin with Isobel and follow me throughout my life—from Dawn Browne to Henry Colte, and from Thomas Colte to Robert Howard and his son, the despicable John Howard.

God may demand atonement for what I did to John Howard, but for that I offer no apology, for I would never have achieved my objectives had I not condemned him to a life of poverty and destitution. That he still lives is my worst regret, and it remains the biggest failure of my life.

That other innocent boys had to die in his name is John's own fault and the blame must lie with him, because if he hadn't resisted the way he did, then none of this would have been necessary. He would have gone to France and died over there as he was supposed to have done. Instead, he ran away and caused me endless problems.

What else was I supposed to do?

William Asheborne agreed with me, and he assisted me every step of the way. My life would have been very different if William hadn't found me and shown me the way forward, even when it meant making the difficult decisions regarding the young boys brought to me by the Walden gang.

God alone knows that William has been involved in my life for more years than anyone could ever know. He has been my lover and my partner ever since I left Saddleworth.

Many of my confessions involve William, and he was rightly worried when he discovered I was writing them down. He insisted on keeping them for safekeeping, but as much as I love him, I don't trust him. So my confessions are as much for my protection as they are for my confession to God.

As for John Howard, I cannot find it in my heart to hold any sympathy, for I have never despised a person in my life as much as I despise that boy. My heart will not sing in peace until he is captured and killed before my very eyes.

So, my Lord, the following pages contain my confessions. My

hope is that once You have read my life story, You will find forgiveness and allow my soul to rest in Your everlasting glory.

This letter I keep here, at my little white house in London. The rest of my confessions lie safely with T.B where they will never be found during my lifetime. After my death, they will lie in darkness, waiting to be found one day to reveal the truth. The one thing of which I am certain is that history will remember my name.

Margaret Colte

"They both speak of the same thing, this mysterious T.B," Stephen said. "But neither say who nor where he is."

"I think this proves that it wasn't James Stanton who took the confessions from Malton," John said. "His letter refers to the same location as Margaret's, so if he knew where they were, the secret went with him to his grave. I do believe we found where Margaret hid them, but someone other than James Stanton removed them."

John slammed the parchment to the ground. "If it wasn't either Asheborne or Stanton, then who was it? Either way, it doesn't matter, for we are defeated."

"What do we do now?" Catherine almost whispered.

"We go to London and find Abraham and Gare." Stephen stood up. "Then we kill them."

They spent the rest of the day half-heartedly searching James Stanton's private rooms for anything to do with a T.B. but found nothing. That night, John addressed them in the stables.

"We leave in the morn for London. We need to create a diversion so Abraham and Gare will show themselves, and when they do, we kill them."

"Then what?" Catherine asked.

"If I live, I shall hand myself in to my father, so you may live. We may have lost, but we're not going down without first fulfilling our promise to take out the people who betrayed us."

Edward clapped John on the shoulder. "I knew you would see sense." He rolled over on his pallet. "We leave at daylight."

———

BY MIDMORNING, they had barely spoken a word. Catherine rode behind John, who had remained deep in thought ever since they had left Burningtown.

"It would have ended so differently if James Stanton had found the confessions and hidden them somewhere safe in Burningtown. I mean, how many T.B's can there be?" Catherine said, catching up with John.

"He didn't, so there's no point talking about it."

They rode on for another hour before John suddenly jolted upright on his horse. He stopped and waited for Catherine to catch him up.

"What did you say earlier?" he asked.

"Nothing, I was just trying to get you to talk to me."

"What did you say? Something about Stanton?"

"I asked how many T.B's can there be? That's all. I was just making conversation."

John reached forward and kissed Catherine on her lips. "Catherine, my dear, you are a genius."

He turned to Edward and Stephen, who were quite a way ahead. "Edward! Stephen! Stop and come back here."

The two riders turned their horses and trotted back to John and Catherine. "What's wrong?" Edward inquired.

"Nothing." John's face was beaming. "Catherine here is a genius. It was right there all along, and I missed it."

"What are you talking about?" Stephen asked.

"The confessions," John said, turning his horse and heading back the way they had just come.

"What is he talking about?" Stephen asked again. "Where are we going? Back to Malton?"

"We have no time to lose," John shouted back. "Follow me."

He kicked his horse and galloped off, leaving three confused faces behind him.

The Mysterious T.B.

Daylight was fading as the stone tower of St James-the-Less church came into view. John had made them leave their horses at Burningtown Manor, and he had them keep to the safety of the treeline along the short path between the two places.

The cross on top of the tower guided them to the church. John headed straight for the tower door, after he remembered Edward telling him it always remained open.

"What are we doing here?" Stephen hissed once they were safely inside. "You've not said a word since you turned us around and galloped back here. Stop treating us like fools and tell us what we're doing."

"It was Catherine who made me realise the answer was with us all along, and we missed it," John said.

"What did I say?" Catherine looked puzzled.

"You asked how many T.B.s there could be?"

"Yes," Catherine looked confused. "But how did that lead you to gallop back here like a madman?"

"You also said that it would have been a lot easier if

Stanton had found the confessions and brought them back to Burningtown."

Three blank faces stared back at him.

John pointed at a large octagonal stone font that stood in front of the altar. He showed them the exquisite pattern of oak leaves that were carved all the way around the font. Then he pointed to the words carved below the oak leaves.

"Do you see these words? I noticed them as we were about to hide in that ghastly hole underneath the oak chest." John pointed to the big oak chest they had hidden below to hide from the sheriff and his men after they were attacked at Burningtown.

"What do they say?" Edward asked, as they all peered at the incredible stone carvings on the large font.

"The font is dedicated to someone from 1348 named Ellis Blount," John said.

"Ellis Blount?" Stephen furrowed his brow. "You dragged us all the way back here to look at a stone font dedicated to someone from centuries ago called Ellis Blount? Is something ailing you?"

"The inscription is dedicated to Ellis Blount and his son," John said, his eyes sparkling. "His son's name was Tobias Blount."

He grinned at them in triumph.

"Tobias Blount," Edward said. "T.B."

"John, you're a genius," Catherine said.

"It was you who gave me the idea, so it is you who is the genius."

"It doesn't matter who's the genius," Stephen said. "Let's see if they're here before we congratulate ourselves for finding them."

They inspected the font but couldn't find anything that indicated a hiding place for Margaret's confessions.

"It might be somewhere else," Edward said. "Like in the wall or something."

John searched the wall for anything that mentioned Tobias Blount but found nothing. Then, with barely any daylight remaining, he had an idea.

"Help me move the font to the side," he said, pushing the heavy font for all he was worth. "Be careful, we don't want to damage it."

They moved it aside, and John dropped to his knees. The stone below the font held the same inscription as the one on the font:

This stone is laid in dedication to Ellis Blount and his son, Tobias, who fell to the plague in 1348.

"Look," John said, pointing at the old stone. "You can see where it has been disturbed in recent times."

He was right. The dirt around the stone was new, and it was obvious someone had removed it recently. They all got to their knees and began pulling the old stone loose.

It was dark by the time they got the stone out of the ground, but they didn't care. John thrust his hand into the black hole and felt around.

The hole was about the same size as the one in the wall at Burningtown, but not as deep. John rummaged around inside and dug in the dirt. He felt something and latched onto it. Something soft, like a pouch.

"There's something here," he gasped.

The pouch was heavy, and John felt something hard inside it. "There's a box," he said, hardly able to contain himself as he removed it from its dark hiding place.

It was too dark to see anything, so they hurriedly replaced the stone and the font, and ran outside where the moon and the stars gave them a much clearer sight of what they had discovered.

John emptied the sack onto the ground outside the

church and held up a plain-looking box about the size of his mother's jewellery box.

The box was locked, and there was no way to open it without forcing the lock, so John put it back inside the pouch and stood up.

"Let's get back to Burningtown and open it by candle-light. I'm excited to see what we have found."

They ran down the narrow path and entered a room at the back of the house, so there was less chance of their candles being seen through the windows.

"Hurry, and open the box," Stephen said. "I can barely wait to see what's inside."

They lit the candles and sat around a table. John took a deep breath and held it up for all to see. "It's plain, and nothing like my mother's box, but it's about the same size."

He got to work with his knife, and a few moments later, the lid opened with a crack.

The others stared at John as he pulled a thick pouch from inside the box.

"It's full of documents!" John exclaimed as he opened the pouch.

The air was crackling with tension as John dropped a thick wad of paper on the table in front of them. He took the top paper and began reading.

My opening letter explaining why I wrote my confessions has already been written, and I shall not explain myself again here. Just let it be known that God alone is my judge, and no man has judgement over my soul.

My name is Margaret Colte, and the following pages contain my life's story, and the confessions I make in these pages are between myself and the Lord Almighty.

If a mortal hand other than my own touches these pages, then I make no apologies for my sins, for this is how I lived my life.

I begin with Isobel and end with John Howard, and I leave

nothing out. William Asheborne, Duke of Berkshire, has been my lover and confidante ever since I left Saddleworth. It was he who came up with the plan for me to marry Robert Howard in order to create my own wealth and power, as well as to destroy the Howard family and all their disgusting offspring.

So, here they are: the confessions of my life. As I sit here now and read them back, I have to report that I am proud of my accomplishments. From the moment I was wronged as a child, right up to the years of my thirties, I have allowed no man to own me or dominate me. The wealth and power I now possess are a direct consequence of my actions throughout my life, and for that I make no apologies.

I am very proud of my achievements. One day, William Asheborne will have to die, of that I am sure, but for now he is useful to me, so I allow him to think he's in charge. But his day shall come, just as sure as Thomas Colte's did.

I'm getting ahead of myself, so allow me to go back to the beginning.

John placed the page aside and looked up at the three faces intently staring at him.

"If that's the first page, the rest of them must be as damning as they come. We have here everything we need to bring down Asheborne and clear my name, which means that all of us shall be free."

Hoots and hollers followed for a few minutes before they settled down. "There's a thick pile of papers," Stephen said. "What do the rest of them say?"

John flicked through them until he came to the ones regarding himself. He began reading out loud:

John Howard stood in the way of my destiny, and from the moment I convinced Robert to marry me, it destined him for a life of misery until his untimely death at a young age. If there is any person in this life I will despise more than John Howard, I have yet to meet him. From the very instant I stepped off the carriage at Broxley, he was difficult and hated me. In return, I hated him with a passion I had rarely felt before.

The plan to rid myself of him was easy to conjure, and he fell for it like the fool I knew him to be.

John slammed his fist into the table. "What should I have done differently with that woman?" he yelled.

Catherine put her hand on his arm. "It wasn't your fault, John. You were a young boy, and she was an evil woman. You had no chance against her."

John looked back at the page in front of him.

Suffering the entire Howard family was punishment for the crimes I committed against them. It forced me to bide my time and keep up the illusion that I was happy in my marriage to that dreadful, egotistical man until I had leverage—the leverage of a male heir to the Howard family fortune.

Once Arthur was born, I could finally carry out my carefully laid plans to bring down the family, and it didn't come a moment too soon. If it wasn't for William's encouragement, I would have done it much sooner. Had I done so, the effect wouldn't have been anywhere near as great, so I am glad I listened to the wise words of the only man I have ever truly loved—my dearest William Asheborne.

John Howard was the reason I was forced to poison my son, Mark Colte, for a second time. I never had much time for Mark, and I found him weak and spineless, but he served a purpose. John Howard should be held responsible for Mark's ailments, because if it wasn't for him then I never would have had to poison Mark again.

It was easy to convince Robert because he was never around his family enough to realise what I was doing, and he was so enamoured with me that he hung onto every word I said.

What a fool he was, and still is.

Once Robert was convinced, John should have been sent to France, where I had people in place to kill him swiftly and put an end to his miserable life.

Instead, he ran away and hid like the vermin he is, forced to live in the filth and squalor that is the dark side of London.

The irony of all this is that Robert was so caught up in pleasing his tyrannical king that he didn't stop to think that Arthur could never have been his child. If he'd considered the truth, he would have realised that he wasn't anywhere to be found during the time Arthur was conceived.

Robert Howard is raising the son of William Asheborne as his own, and he doesn't even realise it. I shall control Arthur, and all the wealth and power of the Earl of Coventry shall be mine.

As for Sarah Howard, she shall be married to William Asheborne's son, also called William, and she will not be a problem for us.

But I digress. Back to John Howard . . .

John looked up. "I can't read any more, not right now. That woman was more evil than I ever imagined, and I never thought I would say that, after all she's done to me."

"I'm so sorry, my love," Catherine touched his arm again.

Even Stephen stood with his hands over his mouth, as if in shock at what he'd heard. "No family deserves such treatment," was all he said before turning away and leaving the room.

"There's much more," John said, scanning through more pages. "Everything she ever did is here, and we have everything we need to bring Asheborne down and prove our innocence."

"What are you going to do with them?" Catherine asked. "You can't just walk up to your father and give them to him. You'll be arrested before you get anywhere near him."

"What about Duke Thomas?" Edward asked. "You are close to your uncle, are you not?"

"I can't give them to my Uncle Thomas," John scoffed. "They would vanish into the night and be used as leverage against Asheborne for the rest of his life. The confessions would never see the light of day."

"So, what then?" Catherine asked. "Can you give them to Pye?"

"Pye is a remarkable man to whom we owe so much, and I trust him with my life, but I fear he isn't well connected enough to get them to the king, which is where they need to be. These confessions are toxic and will bring down many powerful men. The mere possession of them brings grave danger to whoever has them. In the wrong hands, they would bring great power through the leverage they provide, which means that unless I get these to the right person, we are in even greater danger than we were before we found them."

"So, who is this right person?" Edward asked.

"I don't know," John answered. "I need to think about it."

"What do we do now?" Catherine asked. "Are we staying here?"

"As much as I'd like to, we can't. Now that we've found Margaret's confessions, we must act fast before Asheborne discovers we have them."

John looked at his beloved Catherine. "I'm sorry to say this, but at first light we must leave for London."

"What are we going to do when we get there?" she asked.

"I don't know. I haven't thought that far ahead."

The Right Man

The churchwarden nodded as the Underlings entered the small church on Britten Strete and made their way towards the storeroom in the rear corner. They nodded back and shuffled on without speaking.

Once they were safely inside their hated safe place, John laid out his plans for the rest of them.

"After dark, I will visit Pye to let him know we are back and hear the latest news from London. Then tomorrow, I shall endeavour to pass the confessions into the hands of someone who will do the right thing."

"Who?" the others asked in unison.

"The confessions need to reach Cromwell, the king's chief minister. I know of only one man who has those connections who might do the right thing with them."

"Who?" Stephen asked. "Your uncle?"

"I said I know of only one man who will do the right thing," John said. "That man is not my uncle."

"Who, then?" Stephen asked, red faced from impatience.

"The Steelyard Elder. He knows Cromwell and doesn't

have any reason to use Margaret's confessions to enhance his own situation. He's the only man I trust will do the right thing with them."

"The Steelyard Elder?" Stephen asked, jerking his head back in surprise. "You barely know him, so how can you trust him with something so important and dangerous as this?"

"I don't know if I can trust him," John said. "But he's the only man I know who knows the right people and isn't connected to Margaret. Henry Colte would have been the perfect man, but alas, Margaret already killed him."

"You're placing a lot of trust in someone you barely know," Stephen said.

"I know, and I have prayed hard that I am doing the right thing," John answered. "To be sure, I'm not giving him everything. I'm keeping back most of her confessions and only handing over what he needs to prove Asheborne's guilt."

"Let's hope he's worthy of your trust," Stephen said.

"He won't be happy to see me again," John said. "I've promised him twice now that I would never seek him out again, and both times I have broken those promises. He might not even agree to see me this time."

"Let's hope he does," Catherine squeezed John's hand.

Once darkness fell, John led the small group to the graveyard at the back of the church. They joined hands while John said the Lord's Prayer in Latin over Isaac's grave. When he'd finished, he fell to his knees and spoke to his departed best friend.

"We found them, Isaac. We found the confessions. I know you believed in me even when I didn't believe in myself, and I won't let you down. I miss you greatly, and what I do now, I do for you. Sleep well, my friend."

John rose to his feet and brushed the tears from his eyes. "It's time to go," he said.

Edward and Catherine remained in the storeroom while John and Stephen made their way through the dark, unwelcoming crypts that had served them so well during their times of need. As much as they hated them, they knew they would all be dead by now without them. John said a whispered prayer of thanks to the spirits as he passed by the resting places of the long-forgotten people who lay there.

"I've been waiting for you to return," Pye said, moving out of the way to allow John and Stephen into the warmth of his house. "I hear you have been actively keeping up your murdering spree during your travels north."

"All lies."

"Naturally," Pye said. "But the good people of London don't know that."

"What news do you have?" John asked.

"By the sparkle in your eyes, it appears you have more important news than I, so please tell," Gamaliell Pye said, looking at John.

"Is it that obvious?" John laughed. "We found them, Gamaliell. We found Margaret's confessions."

"You found them?" Pye's jaw dropped. "Where were they? What do they say?"

"We found them in a church near Burningtown, resting under a stone dedicated to someone named T.B., just as the documents said they were," John said. "Stanton found where Margaret hid them in Malton, and moved them to another location with T.B in the name."

"Clever," Pye said. "What did they reveal?'

"Everything. They reveal everything about her life, and I have to say it makes for very painful reading. Margaret was an evil woman."

"Do they clear your name?"

"Yes, they do, and not only that. They prove clearly that my father was tricked into marrying her, so she and Asheborne could destroy our family and take father's place next to the king. Asheborne is as guilty as she was."

"No wonder he was trying to find them so fiercely," Pye said. "Where are they? Did you bring them with you?"

"No." John shook his head. "They are so dangerous that anyone caught in possession of them is liable to meet a painful ending."

"Wise move," Pye said. "So, what do you plan on doing with them?'

"I'm taking them to the Steelyard Elder to pass onto Thomas Cromwell."

"Why him? You could just give them to your uncle."

"My uncle wouldn't hand them to Cromwell, and you know it," John retorted. "He would use them as leverage against Asheborne and my father, ensuring they never saw the light of day. I would never prove my innocence, and I would go to my grave a guilty man."

Pye looked at John for a long moment. "And Thomas Howard would watch you die without saying a word. You are wise beyond your years, John Howard, but do you trust the Steelyard Elder to deliver them to Cromwell?"

John threw his hands in the air. "I don't know, but he's the only man I know who's still alive who knows Cromwell and doesn't have any reason to keep them for himself, so unless you have any better suggestions, he's the best I can come up with."

"I can think of many men who would pay a handsome reward for Margaret's confessions, but none of them would take them for the reasons you desire. Let's hope the Steelyard Elder is the right man for the task, for I fear that if he isn't, you will live a short life."

"What news do you bring?" John changed the subject.

"Word has it you murdered a beekeeper in Yorkshire and several of Asheborne's guards who followed you on your foolish quest to find what doesn't exist."

"Every word of that is lies," Stephen said. "Not only did we find the confessions, but it was Asheborne's men who killed the beekeeper."

"There's a man." John stared at Pye. "There's a man who works for Asheborne who we think is called Gare. He has the cruellest grey eyes I have ever seen, and he carries out the devil's work. He kills with a cruelty I have never seen, as he did here in London with Margaret's old friend and her husband, and he murdered Lord Parker and Joan Stanton as well as the beekeeper in a manner none of us will ever forget."

"I have heard of this man," Pye said. "Although his name is only whispered in fear of retribution. He is a myth, and nobody knows if he really exists or is merely the dark side of their imaginations and fears."

"He's real, alright," John said. "I've seen him too many times to know he isn't a myth. Do you know where I can find him?"

Pye shook his head. "His name is a whisper in the darkness and never spoken aloud in fear that he might appear and do his work on the ones who dare speak his name."

"Well, I dare speak his name, and I wish he'd appear in front of me," Stephen said. "He's evil and needs to be sent back to the bowels of hell from whence he came."

"If I hear anything, I will let you know," Pye said.

"There is one more thing," John said. "A man they call the captain was in charge of Asheborne's men every time we've met them. Do you know anything about him?"

Pye shook his head. "Asheborne has access to many

men, and I assume this captain is just one of many he commands. I'm sorry, but I can't help you."

"I'm sure our paths will cross again," John said. "And the next time, we'll be ready."

Pye handed them a sack of supplies and grasped John's arm as he took them. "May God's good grace be with you my young friend, for I fear unless you are careful with your choices, this may be the last time we shall meet, at least in this life."

"Thank you, Gamaliell," John bowed his head. "I shall be as careful as I can, but I have to see this through and either clear my name or die trying."

"Be careful out there. The king is on the warpath and wants your head on a spike on London Bridge. As you know, the king always gets his way in the end."

"Unless I can change his mind," John said. "That's my only hope."

The next morning, John was glad of the heavy fog drenching London in a dark cloud of wet, oppressive misery.

He made his way down the half-empty stretes towards the Thames with the roll of confessions firmly tucked under his cloak. He'd left most of them behind with Catherine and taken only a selection that told of Asheborne's treasonous swathe of murders up and down the country. Murders done to cover up Margaret's scheming plans to bring down the Howard family and install Asheborne himself at the head of the king's privy council. The rest John had kept back in case the elder didn't pass them on to Thomas Cromwell. Or even worse, in case Cromwell used them for his own purposes once he got them, which wasn't outside the realm of possibility, such was the fiery power of Margaret's words.

Every time he saw someone looking at him, John

shrank deeper into his hood. The last thing he wanted was to be captured right now with the confessions in his possession. If he was, his death would be instantaneous, of that he had no doubt.

Edward and Stephen followed a short distance behind, separately and keeping to the shadows, to make sure John wasn't spotted and followed. Now and again, John would turn around to make sure they were still there and that everything was as it should be.

He took a deep breath when he reached Thames Strete and turned left. The strete was crowded with horses and people who were far too busy trying to get out of the foul weather to be looking for a wanted criminal loose on the stretes of London.

The fog was so thick over the Thames that he almost missed the entrance to the Steelyard, and he had to stop and reverse direction for a furlong or so. He nodded as he walked past Edward and Stephen, who carried on down the strete to wait in the shadows for his return.

Holding his breath, John approached the entrance to the walled Hanseatic city-within-a-city and spoke to the guards in German.

"My name is John Broxley, and I have urgent business with the Elder." John used the name he'd always given when entering the Steelyard.

This was the first time he'd ever asked for the elder by name, and he hoped he hadn't overstepped the line. He waited outside the gates, hopping from foot to foot, not so much for the cold, but from fear of being spotted by his enemies, who he was sure were out there looking for him.

The weight of Margaret's words burned a hole in his side, and he kept a hand on them so he wouldn't lose them.

After the longest wait of his life, a familiar face came to the gate. "John, it is a surprise to see you again."

"Hans!" John exclaimed. "It is good to see you again, too."

"What brings you here? It vexes the Elder that you don't keep you word and stay away."

"Hans, please tell the elder that I have vital information that is for his ears only, and that I wouldn't have come here if it wasn't so important."

"The Elder wants to know what it is you desire of him, or he refuses to see you."

John sighed. This wasn't going the way he'd hoped. "Tell the elder that I found them. He will know what I mean. Tell him I have information so sensitive that it is for his ears alone."

Hans looked at his friend with his head cocked to one side. "You are a strange man, John Broxley. Wait here and I shall convey your message, but I doubt the elder shall see you."

John said nothing, but he crossed his fingers and hoped for the best.

I've done all I can. If he refuses to see me, then I don't know what to do. I can't trust my uncle, so who do I trust? Pye can't get an audience with Cromwell, so if the elder won't see me, I'm done for.

He looked around and spotted Stephen lurking in one of the side stretes, which gave him heart and encouragement. Edward wasn't anywhere to be seen, but John knew he was there somewhere, watching over him like a guardian angel.

Eventually, Hans came back. "I'm pleased to tell you the Elder has agreed to see you," he said. "Guards, let him pass."

John sighed and closed his eyes. One hurdle was down, and now all he had to do was convince the Steelyard Elder to risk his life by taking possession of Margaret's confessions. He shook his head and cleared the doubts and fears rampaging through his mind.

"It seems you have problems keeping your promises to stay away, John Howard," the Elder said after John had closed the door to his office. "Hans tells me you have found the woman's confessions. Is this true?"

"Yes, sir, it's true, and you are the only person I trust to help me with them, which is why I am here. I'm sorry I broke my promise never to return, but what I possess is sensitive beyond imagination, as I'm sure you are well aware."

"Well, I can't say I'm not intrigued, but what do you need of me? You have them, so all you need to do is hand them over and you will be cleared, if what I hear is true."

"Sir, I can't just hand them over to anyone. The king himself needs to read them. The only way I can get to him is through Cromwell, and the only way I can get to Cromwell is through you, which is why I'm here."

"You want me to hand them to Cromwell? Why not give them to your uncle? He has access to Cromwell. Or even give them to Robert Howard, because he's your father, isn't he? He has the close ear of the king, and if these confessions say what I think they say, then you should have no problem getting either of them to listen."

"Sir, it isn't that easy." John took the confessions out from under his cloak. "I can't get near my father without risking his guards killing me on sight. I cannot trust my uncle with them, for he will no doubt use them for his own gain at my expense. You are the only man I trust with access to Cromwell. Please, sir, I need your help."

The Elder glared at John for the longest time. Finally, he broke the silence. "Let me see them." He held his hand out.

John passed over the slew of papers he'd brought with

him, and he watched as the Elder read them intently, making strange faces after reading some of Margaret's words.

"She truly was an evil woman," he said, looking up from his desk. "You realise what you are asking of me, don't you? These confessions are dangerous to any man who possesses them, and you are asking me to convey them to Thomas Cromwell, of all people."

"Sir, I wouldn't ask if it wasn't so important. I know the risks I am asking of you, but I know of no other man I can trust for such a task."

"I appreciate your belief in me, but I don't know who you think I have access to. Thomas Cromwell is a hard man to make an appointment with, and he and I aren't exactly the best of friends."

"I realise that, sir, but that's what makes it even more important that it is you who delivers them to him. Nobody would suspect you of being the bearer of such dangerous material, and Cromwell will have no choice other than to show them to the king. I know my father has enemies in the court, but so does Asheborne, and from what I can gather, few liked Margaret. So there are plenty of powerful people who would love the chance to take them down with no further involvement from you than being the man who delivered them."

"And where do I tell them I got them from?"

"Tell them the truth," John said. "Because once these are delivered, I am cleared of all charges made against me, or I die. I am done running and hiding, so this either works or it doesn't."

"You are a brave man, John Howard, and I have always believed in your innocence from the moment all this broke loose. Leave these with me and I shall ensure they reach the eyes of Thomas Cromwell. What he does with them afterwards is up to him, but I shall deliver them to him on your behalf."

John bent forwards, half in relief and the other half in a gesture of gratitude. "Thank you, sir. You do not know how much this means to me."

"I think I do, and after all you've been through, I think you deserve it. Now go, and remain hidden until this becomes public knowledge, for I fear all hell will break loose once it does."

"Thank you again." John skipped out the door with a great weight lifted from his head. Even the weather had cleared when he left the Steelyard.

He looked around for Stephen and Edward, but they were nowhere to be seen.

Trap

John ran up and down Thames Strete, but there was no sign of either Stephen or Edward. He ran back to the guards at the Steelyard gates and spoke to them in German.

"I'm sure you saw the two men keeping watch for me out here on the stretes?" he asked.

One of the guards nodded.

"Did you see where they went?"

"One of them ran that way," he pointed west along Thames Strete, towards Baynard Castle and St Paul's. "He was being chased by many men, at least seven or eight as far as I could see."

"When?"

"A few minutes ago."

"What of the other man who was watching for me? Did they chase him as well?"

The guard shook his head. "I didn't see where the other one went."

John sprinted down Thames Strete, slowing to look down the cramped, uninviting narrow side stretes as he passed them, but there was no sign of either Stephen or Edward.

Panic set in as he reached Baynard's Castle on his left. He stopped to listen, but all he could hear was his own loud pants for breath, and his heart beating out of his chest after running so hard.

Wait, what was that?

A faint shout. Another one, this time louder. John ran across the strete without looking and almost got run over by a horse and carriage travelling at speed in the direction from which John had just run.

He sprinted towards the muffled shouts that came from the field in front of the College of Physicians and hid behind the wall of the ancient St Benet Paul's Wharf Church. He peered around the side of the wall, trying to see what was happening.

Stephen was backed up to a small wall separating the college from Mountjoy's Inn, the knife in his hand raised above his head. He was shouting at five men at the top of his lungs, but John couldn't make out what he was saying.

They must be Asheborne's men.

Two men lay motionless on the ground in front of Stephen, and the others were closing in with raised swords and knives.

Stephen was in serious trouble.

John picked up a large stone from the wall and closed the gap between himself and the ferocious fight about to play out in front of him. The men were all too fixed on Stephen to notice John creeping up behind them.

He threw the rock as hard as he could at one of Asheborne's men and caught him flush on the back of the head. The man fell to the ground in a heap.

The others turned to see who their attacker was, and Stephen used the diversion to launch his assault. He dived forward, burying his knife through the neck of one man, who fell screaming before going silent.

John joined the melee, thrusting his knife into the heart of another man as hard as he could and feeling warm blood running down his arm towards his shoulders.

The man who had been hit with the stone was by John's feet, and he started to stand up. John lashed out with his foot, catching the man square in the jaw. Teeth and blood spattered from the man's mouth, and he fell back to the ground, moaning in agony.

The other three men looked at each other and ran, but not before Stephen tripped one of them as he ran past him. Stephen grabbed him by his hair and jerked his head back.

"What have you done with our friend?" he growled in the man's face.

"I don't know who you're talking about."

Stephen sliced the man's ear off, leaving him jerking uncontrollably in agony.

"It'll be your eye next if you don't tell me."

John had never seen Stephen so wild and out of control. He shivered with the ferocity of the attack, and he was glad Stephen was on his side.

"Last chance." Stephen pushed his knife towards the man's eye.

"Stop. Please, stop."

"Where's my friend?'

"We chased you for a diversion because we didn't know how many of you there were. The captain's got the other one, and that's all I know. I swear, the one we really want is John Howard."

"Where did they take him?" Stephen snarled.

"I don't kno . . ." Stephen dug the tip of his knife closer to the man's eye.

"Alright. We were going to take you to the white house on Watelying Strete that's empty after the lady died."

The man John had injured sprang forward at Stephen, but John saw him through the corner of his eye. He threw his knife, and the man fell to the ground for the last time when it buried itself between his shoulder blades.

Stephen killed the last of Asheborne's men and looked at John. "Took you long enough," he said. "I didn't think you'd get here in time."

"It took me a while to find you."

A small crowd had gathered outside Mountjoy's Inn to watch the violence unfold, and John knew the constable would be on the scene shortly, as well as more of Asheborne's men.

"We've got to get to Edward," Stephen shouted. "Come on."

They ran as fast as they could towards St Paul's and Watelying Strete.

The stretes were filling up as the heavy mist cleared and the wintry sun made an appearance. Everyday people went about their daily lives, oblivious to all the excitement going on around them. Or at least they were until men and women started shouting and screaming about a bloody murder on Thames Strete.

Crowds ran towards the grizzly scene, leaving John and Stephen struggling to get by them as they ran towards the little white house on the corner of Watelying Strete and Soperlane.

Finally, they got there, and John was surprised to find the gates at the rear of the house that opened onto Soperlane were cracked open. They slipped through, and John closed the gates behind him to stop prying eyes from seeing what they were doing.

The bodies of three dead men lay on the ground in the

small courtyard. John noticed the doors to the stables were open off to his right. The stables backed up to a tall wall behind the house. With swords drawn, John and Stephen crept towards them.

Footsteps and the sound of a closing door forced them to spin around.

"Ahh, it's good of you to join us."

A tall man with a moustache strode towards them from the house, followed by three other men. As he stepped over the dead bodies in the courtyard, the dead men miraculously stood up and fell in behind the man who'd spoken.

"It's a trap," Stephen hissed.

"I know who you are," John said. "You're the one they call captain."

"And you are John Howard, the runaway son of the earl. You're difficult to catch, but I knew I'd get to you eventually. I always do."

The men surrounded John and Stephen, who stood back-to-back with their swords at the ready.

"What do you want, Captain?" John asked. "You know I won't give myself up easily, and after what you've done to my friends, it is you who should worry."

The captain roared with laughter. "You're brave, I'll give you that. There's a big reward on your head. We'd all prefer to hand you over to Lord Asheborne alive, because you're worth more to us that way, but even dead you're worth a lot of coin, so it's up to you. I don't care either way."

The captain raised his finger in the air and pointed at John, which was the signal for his men to close in. John took a deep breath and gripped his sword in his hands, ready for the battle of his life.

Whatever happens to me now, we set the wheels in motion to bring down Lord Asheborne and his evil men. Even my father will be forced to accept he was wrong about me when he discovers what Margaret did to us. Even if I die here, I have still won.

One man suddenly screamed and fell to the ground with an arrow in his back. A split second later, another man dropped. The captain ran for cover towards the stables which were closer to him than the house.

John and Stephen used the confusion to strike at the other three men surrounding them. Stephen almost severed the head of one of them, and John struck another through the chest. The remaining one fell to yet another arrow that came from the direction of a tree that hung over the wall to the side of the stables.

John and Stephen watched as Edward climbed out of the tree and jumped down the wall, his longbow slung over his shoulder. Without a word, he nodded at them and went to the entrance of the stables.

"Captain, I know you're in there. All your men are dead, and you know you will not leave this place alive. You murdered my family, and I shall have my vengeance. Come out and tell me where I can find Gare, and I shall give you an honourable death."

A loud laugh came from inside the stables. "You think I know where to find Gare? Only one man knows where he lives, and that is Lord Asheborne himself. Gare is a monster for whom death cannot come soon enough."

"On that, we agree," Edward said. "But why should I believe you?"

"Believe me, or don't," the captain said. "It matters not. I'm here if you want to kill me."

Edward strode into the stables without another word. John and Stephen ran after him, but Edward didn't need their help. As skilled as the captain obviously was, he was no match for the powerful young warrior. One move, and the captain's sword clattered to the ground, another severed his head clean from his shoulders.

It was over in a split second, and when it was done, Edward fell to his knees in prayer.

"This is for you, my beloved Sybil, and for our unborn child that would have known as much love as any man could give. My revenge is also for Master and Lady Stanton, who were always good to us. And it was for the beekeeper of Malton, and the guards in Stratford. I hope you can all rest easier now the captain is dead. Fear not, for I shall not rest until Gare joins him in hell."

"Amen." Both John and Stephen joined him to end his prayer.

"Did the Elder agree to take the confessions?" Edward turned to John, who was standing in awe at the power and skill of his friend.

"He did. He agreed to hand them over to Cromwell."

"Where were you?" Stephen asked Edward. "Suddenly I was being chased and there was no sign of you anywhere."

"I saw the captain watching when his men chased you. He turned and walked away as soon as you ran, so I went after him. I couldn't let him get away again, and I knew John would go to your aid, so I followed him. I watched them set the trap for you, and I was about to attack them when you walked into it."

"So, what do we do now?" Stephen asked.

"We wait," John replied. "Or at least that's what the Elder said we should do."

"But we're not waiting?" Stephen asked.

"No. There's something I have to do that's much more important."

John turned on his heels and left the stables. "Let's get back to the crypts before all hell breaks loose."

Stronde

The Underlings did nothing for the next week except hide during the day and visit Gamaliell Pye every night. John was eager to learn about the furore the confessions were causing before making his next move.

"I have heard nothing yet," Pye told John every night after curfew. "But worry not, for when news breaks of what the confessions reveal, I fear every man in the land will know about it."

On the morning of the seventh day, Catherine and Edward rushed through the church towards the storeroom where Stephen and John lay in hiding. Once they identified themselves, John saw Catherine's face lit up and flushed red.

"John, it's happened! You should hear the cryers, they're shouting it all over London. The king arrested Lord Asheborne this morning."

"We've got to hear this," John said, grabbing his cloak.

"Gamaliell said to wait here until it's over," Catherine said. "John, it's only just beginning."

"I know, and it's time for us to act. We've waited long enough. Come on, let's go hear the cryers."

Oh yeah, oh yeah, oh yeah, hear this good people of London. Lord Asheborne, the Duke of Berkshire, arrested by our great king, Henry VIII, and charged with treason. Oh yeah, oh yeah, oh yeah. Lord Asheborne arrested and taken to the Tower, charged with treason against the king.

Oh yeah, oh yeah, oh yeah, Lord Asheborne, arrested by our great King Henry and charged with treason . . .

"Nothing is over for us yet," John said to Gamaliell Pye later that evening, after curfew. "There wasn't a word said about us or what Asheborne is charged with, other than treason."

"Patience, boy," Pye said. "From what I hear, the king's court is in turmoil, with many powerful men worried about what Margaret's confessions revealed about them and wondering if they are going to be next."

"They need to be worried," John said. "All of them. They're nothing but a bunch of leeches, grabbing power and influence wherever they can, and they don't care who they hurt along the way. They all deserve to be hanged."

"I know you're bitter," Pye said, "But not all of them are as two faced as you make them out to be. Cromwell came forward with the confessions, and it is he who will lead the investigation. From what I hear, both your uncle and your father will sit on the jury for Asheborne's trial, which all but guarantees his death after what he did to them."

"What he did to them? What about what he did to me?'

"Speaking of your uncle, he demands an audience with you as soon as we can arrange it."

"Does he now? He will have to wait, for I have urgent business of my own to attend to first."

"And what might that be? I thought we agreed you were to stay hidden until you are cleared and this is over?"

"We did, but you know I can never sit still. I have unfinished business I need to address."

"What are you going to do? Although, I think I already know."

"I'm going to break into the Stronde and confront my father. I kept most of Margaret's confessions back from the Elder for my own protection, and it is time some more of them are introduced to the world."

"Be careful, John. This is almost over, and you are close to being pardoned by the king. Don't ruin it for yourself now by doing something rash."

"I won't Thank you, Gamaliell. I'll see you when it's over."

"What do I tell your uncle?"

"Tell him I'll happily give him an audience once this is over."

John walked to the door. "Oh, and tell him he'll never get his hands on any of Margaret's confessions."

Pye shook his head as he walked out the door.

For the next three nights, John and the Underlings stayed at the treehouse at the Stronde. John watched carefully for any signs of either his father, Sarah, or Willis, and finally, on the fourth day, John saw Willis hanging around the side of the stables.

"Willis, it's me, John," John whispered from behind the wall on Milford Lane.

"I knew you'd be here somewhere, Master John. That's why I came here as soon as I could to find you. How are you keeping?"

"I'm fine, Willis, but more importantly, how are you?"

Willis threw a coughing fit before he answered, and

John could hear his chest wheezing as he struggled to breathe.

"I'm fine, Master John. Many things are happening behind the scenes, and I am only privy to what I hear around your father. There are a lot more words being whispered behind closed doors, but I do not know what they are."

"What do you hear?"

"Lord Asheborne is to be tried by Thomas Cromwell, and your father and uncle are both going to sit on his trial. Your father is furious with Asheborne, and he wants the death penalty. I heard the king is beside himself with anger as well, so I doubt he'll get out of this alive."

"Where is Sarah? Is she well?"

"Lady Sarah is well and always asks of you. She is at Broxley with Master Arthur under heavy guard."

"Good, I'm glad they aren't here right now. What of father? Will he be here anytime soon?"

"He will, indeed, Master John. In fact, he will be here this evening. Is there a message you wish me to relay?"

"No. I want you to leave the rear door open and unguarded after dark tonight. I want to confront my father myself."

"I fear I cannot allow that, Master John. I do work for your father, after all."

"Fear not, Willis, for I mean him no harm. I aim to give him more of Margaret's confessions, so he can see for himself what kind of woman she truly was. I want to look into his eyes when he realises I was innocent all along."

"Very well then, Master John. As long as you mean his lordship no harm. The rear door will be unlocked and unguarded after dark tonight. Your father's study is in the new wing of the house to the east of the door as you come in. At the bottom of the hall on the left-hand side."

"Thank you, Willis."

John returned to the treehouse to prepare for the most fateful night of his life.

Family Reunion

A knot formed in John Howard's stomach as darkness fell over the Thames, throwing shadows around the treehouse that had provided so many blessings over the past months.

The events that were about to unfold would result in either Robert Howard's remorseful acceptance of John's innocence and the full pardon that went with it, or a painful, torture-ridden death. Either way, John was committed to taking action, and he accepted whatever fate awaited him.

"You should leave here and wait for me in the crypts," John told the others for the hundredth time that day. "If I am arrested this night, then so too shall all of you, and there is no need for it. You can wait in the crypts, and if I haven't returned to you by daylight, then you shall know my father had me arrested. You shall have time to get out of London and escape."

"And where would you have us go?" Catherine answered. "I love you, John Howard, and I'm not going anywhere. Whatever your fate, we share it together."

"We've come this far together, and we're seeing it through to the end together," Stephen said. "We may have started out as enemies, you and I, but I now consider you to be the best friend I have ever had outside of my brother Andrew."

John looked at Edward, who placed his hand on John's shoulder. "I haven't known you long, but in the short time we've had together, you have become my closest friend and the man I trust above all others. You are an honourable man, John Howard, and both you and Stephen are men I would choose to be with when danger calls. We're staying here until this is over, whatever happens this night."

John lowered his head so nobody could see the clouds in his eyes. "I don't deserve such good friends, and I appreciate every one of you. I wish Isaac could be here to witness this night. Now, let's get this over with."

He kissed Catherine one last time and secured his weapons to his body, although he hoped with all his heart that he wouldn't need them.

He slid down the tree and stopped to listen for any unusual sounds. Satisfied, he crept slowly towards the house that he'd once called home and that he hadn't stepped foot in since the eve of Anne Boleyn's execution what seemed a lifetime ago.

He held his breath as he tried the door handle.

This is it. Once I step through this doorway, there is no going back.

John took one more deep breath and stepped inside, closing the door behind him. It was dark, and although familiar, everything seemed different.

In fact, it was different. The extension to the east wing was now complete, and John followed Willis's advice to find his father's office.

Candles lit the way, casting dark shadows in the long, narrow hallway that seemed to never end. Doors were everywhere, and John was glad Willis had told him which one belonged to his father's study, or he would have never found it.

The sound of a door opening ahead of him made him freeze. John tried the door next to his left shoulder, but it was locked. There was nowhere to hide, and he stood there with his hand on his sword as the door at the bottom of the long hall on the left-hand side opened, allowing the candles burning inside to illuminate the hallway and expose the bedraggled, filthy strete urchin stood there for everyone to see.

Willis nodded at John and beckoned him forward. "Promise me you will not harm his lordship," he said, standing in front of John, blocking his path.

"I promise, Willis. I'm not here to harm my father, although God knows he deserves it. I'm here to show him what he allowed to happen to his family after our mother died, although I do reserve the right to defend myself should the need arise."

Willis nodded. "You don't have long, one hour before a new guard takes my place, so I advise you to hurry and get this done with."

"Thank you, Willis. I shall never forget your kindness."

Willis stepped aside, and John's heart beat out of his chest as he placed his hand onto the door handle. He took a deep breath and burst through the door.

"What the—Willis!" A tall, thin man with dark hair down to his collar and a thick moustache jumped up from his desk at the sight of the unruly knave stood before him.

"Willis, where are you?" Robert Howard yelled for a second time. "And who are you? How dare you break into

324

my private study? Don't you know who I am? I shall have you hanged for your insolence. Get out of here. Willis! Where are you?"

John closed the door behind him and turned towards his father. "Willis isn't coming," he said, looking for any sign of recognition on his father's face.

There wasn't any.

His father made a guttural sound from the depths of his throat and ran around his desk, pulling a knife from under his doublet.

"What do you want, you intolerable knave? How dare you break into my home? You will swing for this."

John stared at the man he'd once idolised. Now he felt nothing more than anger and pity for the man he was about to bring to his knees.

Robert Howard approached John, still screaming for Willis, who never appeared through the door.

"What have you done to my guard?" Robert's face was deep red, and John thought his eyes were going to pop out of his head.

"Sit down, Father," John said, moving towards the enraged aristocrat.

"Wha . . . What did you just call me?" Robert Howard stuttered. His eyes blinked rapidly as he surveyed the filthy, smelly boy who'd just called him father.

"You don't even recognise your own son anymore?" John's voice raised a few notches. "It hasn't been that long, Father. Surely you haven't forgotten me already?"

"John?" Robert slumped back on his desk. "Is that you?"

"Yes, it's me." John changed his voice back to his former aristocratic accent. It felt strange and out of place, like it didn't belong to him anymore.

"What? What?" His father stood there speechless, his jaw opening and closing like a fish out of water.

"Please, sit down, Father, before you fall down. I'm not here to harm you. Rather, I'm here to educate you, and show you what a fool you've been."

Robert Howard stared at his son for a long moment. John could see his mind racing as he regained his composure. "So, it is true, then. You were the one who found Margaret's confessions. I have read them, and I am embarrassed by them. The king is angry at me and is considering my position in his privy council, and I have become a point of amusement for everyone else in the king's court. So, if you're here to gloat, enjoy your moment and get out of here."

"I'm not here to gloat, Father, and I don't care what the king thinks of you, or anyone else for that matter. I'm here to show you what you have done to me and Sarah by blindly believing that evil woman."

"Margaret and Asheborne might have fooled me, and believe me, Asheborne shall pay a heavy price for his treachery, but nothing changes between us. I still believe you poisoned Mark and, even worse, killed him. How could you do that? How could you kill your own stepbrother in cold blood like that? What changed in you that made you so cruel and heartless? You killed Mark to get back at Margaret and myself, and I can tell you it worked. Margaret was distraught with grief after you killed him."

His father's face flushed red again, and John could see the anger welling up inside him.

"You look tired, Father. You need to get some rest before you harm yourself. If you have read Margaret's confessions regarding her affairs with William Asheborne and how she used you to gain power and fortune, then you must have read that she despised our entire family. She and

Asheborne conspired to destroy us and remove you from the king's side so Asheborne could take over. You read that, didn't you?"

"Yes," his father raged. "But it doesn't change the fact that you poisoned and killed Mark Colte, does it? She didn't say anything about that in her confessions."

"And yet you show no remorse for the forty or more boys they murdered for nothing more than looking like me." John's eyes bored into his father's. "You didn't even mention it. Why was that, Father? Is it because they were poor boys who didn't deserve your sympathy? Or was that my fault as well, for not going to France as I was ordered?"

"Asheborne will pay for his crimes," Robert Howard spat the words out. "And you already killed Margaret, so I would say you're even, wouldn't you? You have murdered and killed everywhere you have been. All over the country, corpses lay mutilated because of you. Yet you have the temerity to stand in front of me and accuse me of barbarism because I didn't show pity for a few knaves who were removed from the stretes of London? I have no doubt that London is a much safer place without them."

John felt his face burning as his anger rose. "That's what you think of all those innocent boys who were murdered by your wretched whore?"

His father's face turned purple. "Guards! Guards, get in here and arrest this murdering fool before I kill him myself."

"You'll be surprised to know that I didn't kill any of those I stand accused of murdering. Margaret herself killed Sir Henry and Mark, and I can prove it. Surely you didn't miss the part where she confesses to killing her former husband, Thomas Colte?"

"Just because she admitted to killing Thomas Colte doesn't mean you are innocent. Of that I stand convinced.

Her confessions mentioned nothing regarding Thomas or Mark Colte, so why should I think you innocent? You are trying to use her confessions to blame her for your murdering crimes, and I won't allow it. You will be hanged, drawn, and quartered, like the common criminal that you've become."

John laughed, angering his father even more. John knew he wasn't used to being challenged and, in some strange way, he was enjoying it. Perhaps it was some kind of justice for all the pain he had caused John over the past months.

"Do you truly believe the confessions I gave to Cromwell were the only ones she wrote?"

John glared at his father, and he could see the momentary shock in his eyes as he blinked rapidly at John's words.

"Are you suggesting there's more?"

"I'm not suggesting anything. I'm telling you. There are many, many more. I only gave Cromwell a small sample of her confessions. Margaret Colte—or Shipley, if you prefer, was pure evil, and her confessions prove it."

"Show me. I don't believe you."

John pulled the wad of papers from under his cloak and threw them onto the desk in front of his father. "Read them and weep, Father, for they prove my innocence beyond any shadow of a doubt. They show you for the fool you have been and show how evil Margaret truly was."

His father glared at his son before reaching forward to pick up the papers spread out on his desk.

"Is this all of them?"

"Not on your life, Father. Do you think I would trust you with everything she wrote? I'm keeping most of them back for my own protection. You see, my friends have instructions to release them if I don't get back to them safely. I don't trust you. How could I after what you did to me?"

Robert Howard gave John another dirty look and then turned his attention to his dead wife's confessions. John knew what they said because he'd read them a thousand times.

Innocence

Robert Howard is the most stupid, most repulsive man I have ever met, and William was correct when he told me it would be easy for me to fool him into thinking I loved him.

I wasn't sure, bearing in mind that Robert had a reputation for being smart and clever, but William assured me that he would fall for me as soon as I smiled at him and showed my interest in him. William, as always, was correct, and as soon as I laid with him, he was mine to do with in whatever way I desired.

I was impatient, and wanted to destroy the Howards straight away, but William had other ideas and bade me to be patient. He was right, as he always is. But still, I rebelled. If I was doing this, then I wanted something to show for it after it was over. After all, I was the one who had to put up with the endless stories of how great Robert was, and I was determined to do things my way.

I waited patiently until I had leverage, and when I discovered I was with child—and even better, when the child was a boy—it was time for me to act.

Arthur didn't come a moment too soon, because I couldn't stand another moment of that infernal John Howard. I swear I would have killed him myself and made it look like an accident if Arthur hadn't come when he did. His daughter, Sarah, wasn't much better, but William and I already had plans for her, so I didn't bother her too much.

John was different. He was the heir to Robert's titles and fortunes, and he had to be removed if I was to claim the power and the coin I so deserved. John hated me, and I can't blame him for the way I treated him, but he would have cut me out of Robert's estate the moment he died, and I couldn't allow that to happen.

John Howard had to die.

Robert is a fool. I already wrote that he was stupid, but I felt the need to repeat it here, because he truly is that stupid. He was hardly ever around, and he gave me free rein to do whatever I desired with the children, which worked well for what I planned to do.

Arthur isn't even Robert's son, and that makes him even more foolish than I first thought. If he'd thought about it, he would have realised that he couldn't possibly be Arthur's father, as he wasn't around at the time of his conception. William Asheborne is the father of Arthur, and Robert is raising William's son as his own.

I never had much time for Mark, and I considered him weak and spineless, although he had been useful to me once before when it was time to rid myself of his father, Thomas Colte. I perfected my poisoning techniques on Mark when he was a young boy, and he would prove useful to me again when it was time to get rid of John Howard.

The entire family fell into my trap easily. John offered to read to Mark after I poisoned him, and he never thought it odd that I accepted his offer. Before that, I had purposely kept him as far away from Mark as I could, so Mark couldn't open his big mouth and spill everything I had done before.

As soon as I put on the fake tears, I knew Robert would believe me. And he did. John was blamed, and everything was going according to my plan.

John should have been banished to France, where I had someone *waiting to kill him upon his arrival. It wasn't my fault that he ran away at the Boleyn girl's execution.*

John became a problem for me, and I had to find him and silence him before he convinced his father of his innocence. It was William, as always, who came up with a perfect plan.

We used Ren Walden and his strete gang to round up anyone from the filthy stretes of London who looked like John Howard. We knew that eventually we would find him if we kept the pressure on Walden to keep searching.

I bought the little white house and used it as my headquarters for the search. William suggested we kill the strete vermin after we found they were not John, and I agreed. Not only would they have been able to recognise me if word had ever got out, but we were doing London an excellent service by ridding the stretes of the vermin that infested it.

It was John's own fault that so many young boys died in his name. If he'd shown the courage to give himself up, many of those boys would have survived, so the blame lies on his shoulders for their deaths.

Mark's death was most unfortunate, and I admit to feeling sadness after he died. It was an accident, of course. John was supposed to be in that carriage with my former brother-in-law, Henry Colte, a man I despised almost as much as I did John Howard. Watching him die was one of the high points of my life so far.

Watching John Howard die will be even better.

Mark shouldn't have died that day, but he had become a problem. He'd run off with John and Sarah, and I knew he was preparing to tell on me and give up his secrets, so in some ways, John did me a favour that morning.

Blaming John for the murders was easy, and everyone believed me, including the king himself. Every time someone died, William made sure that John Howard's name was mentioned, and slowly he became England's most wanted man. Surely it wouldn't be long before he was captured and executed, along with the other vermin he called friends.

Robert Howard threw down the confessions and

looked at his son. His eyes appeared dark and heavy, and he looked broken and defeated.

"I'm so sorry, John. I believed every word she ever said, and I was wrong. What have I done to you?"

"More than you can ever repay, Father. You have no idea what I've gone through these past months, and I blame you, because you are my father, and you were supposed to protect me. Instead, you believed her and threw me to the cruel stretes like I meant nothing to you."

"What can I do? Please forgive me for what I have done to you."

Robert Howard, Earl of Coventry, member of the prestigious Order of the Garter, and leader of the King's Privy council, fell to his knees on the ground in front of his son. Tears flowed uncontrollably down his face, and he rocked back and forth as he prayed for forgiveness.

Willis entered the room after John beckoned him in and told him to take care of his father.

"I'll be back in a week, Father, and I expect to see Sarah when I get here. We will talk then, as right now I have nothing else to say to you."

John Howard turned around and walked away, leaving his father a broken man behind him.

Building Bridges

Strong winds whipped the River Thames into a fury around the private quaysides of the large houses belonging to the rich and powerful aristocrats who made their homes along the Stronde, making them inaccessible by boat on this stormy day.

The trees swayed in tune with the heavy gusts, and the treehouse creaked and groaned as it moved in time with the gale force winds.

"We will do well to survive this day," Stephen said, hanging onto the walls of the treehouse for dear life. "It will be just our luck to survive all the dangerous adventures we've endured together, only to die because the treehouse breaks apart in a storm."

"Fear not, my friend," John laughed. "This tree has withstood many storms worse than this one, and it will still be here when it has passed."

"Well, I wish it would hurry up," Stephen said. "I've never liked heights, especially when I'm moving around like a leaf in the wind."

John watched as the rear doors of his father's house

opened and Sarah came into view with Willis right beside her.

"This is it," he said to the others waiting in the tree-house with him. "This is our day of destiny. Either we are free men and women, or it's over, but remember what we discussed earlier. If I'm not back by daylight get the rest of the confessions to the Steelyard Elder and tell him to give them all to Cromwell. If my father betrays us this day, I shall see that he falls with us."

He slid down the tree and ran towards his sister, who was struggling to keep her hood on her head in the strong winds.

"John!" she yelled, when he came into view from behind the stables off to her left. "John!"

They ran to each other and embraced. "John, it's so good to see you again. I never thought we would see this day when we can enter our family home together, although I have to tell you that you stink."

"You never change, dear sister, and I hope you never do," John laughed. "It's so good to see you again. How is father?"

"I've never seen him as sad and defeated in my entire life. Not even when mother died did he look like he does now."

"Good, I hope he is suffering an eternal fever," John said. "I'm sorry, Sarah, but I have no pity for the man who abandoned me and threw me away for the lust he felt for a woman who hated us."

"We both suffered, John, but he is truly remorseful for his actions."

"We'll see."

John and Sarah linked arms and walked into the house together, brother and sister reunited once again. John sighed when he looked around the house in daylight.

"It looks nothing like it did when I was last here," he said.

"You were here only two weeks ago," Sarah answered. "It has changed little in two weeks!"

John pinched Sarah on her neck. "I meant the last time we were together, silly. The east wing is now complete, and it looks a different house."

"Much is still the same," Sarah said, steering John towards his father's private study at the end of the long corridor in the east wing.

Willis knocked and waited for the command to enter. He opened the door and beckoned John and Sarah into the room. He nodded at John before closing the door behind them.

"It's good to see you again, son. How are you this stormy morn?"

Sarah was correct—Robert Howard, the strong and powerful aristocrat who once strode around like a knight of the Round Table now looked old and broken. Heavy bags hung below his bloodshot eyes, and he looked like he hadn't slept in a week. John almost felt sorry for him.

Almost.

"Please, sit," Robert gestured towards two chairs arranged for them on the opposite side of the desk. John sat, watching his father closely for any signs of betrayal.

All he saw staring back at him was the shadow of the man his father once was.

"I have done nothing this past week other than read and re-read the confessions you brought to me, and I have sat and gone over the consequences of my actions and decisions since I brought Margaret into our family. I cannot begin to understand what you must have been through—either of you. To know that I blamed you for everything when you were innocent all along breaks my heart, and I hope you can find it within yourself to one day forgive me."

"That will take a long time. You must have known that Margaret planned on killing me in France, yet you did nothing to protect me. You never once looked at the evidence and instead believed her every word, allowing her to turn everyone against me in her quest for my silence. I watched as countless innocent people died in my name, and I took the blame it all. That is a hard thing to forgive, Father, as I'm sure you understand."

Sarah sat with her head bowed. "Your actions affected me as well, Father. I tried telling you Margaret was evil, and when I told you about the argument I overheard between her and Mark, you didn't even believe me then.

"I ran away with John willingly, to help him stop her before she killed him, and you forced me to go into hiding in Stratford in fear of what you might do to me if you found me.

"If it wasn't for Uncle Thomas, I fear I would be dead by now, and when I told you I went of my own accord, you didn't believe me, instead choosing to believe I was covering for John after he had forced Mark and myself at knifepoint to leave Broxley and ride with him as prisoners."

"I have done terrible wrongs to both of you, and your mother would never forgive me if she knew what I have done to you."

"What is the latest news, Father?" John had heard enough of his self pity.

"William Asheborne has been charged with high treason, and the evidence contained in Margaret's confessions has been presented to him. He doesn't deny any of it, and has come to an agreement with Cromwell, who will lead his trial next month."

"What agreement?" John sat upright in his chair.

"He agreed to confess if we left his son alone."

"Was his son involved in this?"

"He's as guilty as his scheming father, but Cromwell accepted his plea, and William Asheborne Junior shall not be tried alongside his father."

"So, he gets to inherit his father's estates and carry on as if nothing happened?" John asked, shaking his head.

"No, that won't happen. King Henry is furious with Asheborne and has confiscated his titles and estates. William Junior will live as a homeless peasant. The king wouldn't even allow him to keep a single one of his houses."

"What of the Duke himself?" John asked. "What will become of him?"

"Once his confessions have been recorded, he will be executed at Tower Hill by beheading. That, I can guarantee you."

"It is nothing less than he deserves." John ground his teeth together as the memories of the past few months ran through his mind. "However, there are some questions he needs to answer for me before his execution."

"What would they be?" Robert raised his eyebrows.

"Two things. First, I need to know the whereabouts of the man who betrayed us when I was with the Underlings. If you recall, the leader of the Underlings was called Andrew Cullane, and I can tell you he was a great man who didn't deserve to die the way he did. Ren Walden's strete gang murdered Asheborne's brother, not the Underlings, and I want a pardon for all of them, dead or alive. The man who betrayed us is called Abraham Wylde, and he works for Asheborne. I met him several times in recent days, and each time Asheborne sent him to recognise and kill me."

"It shall be done," Robert said, making notes on the paper on his desk.

"All I want is the location of his whereabouts. I don't want anyone arresting him, do you hear? After what he did to my friends, I shall be the one who brings him the justice he deserves."

His father nodded his understanding. His eyes bore through John, making him feel uncomfortable.

"What?" John asked. "It surprises you that I learned how to take a life on the stretes? I suggest you try it for yourself and see how far you get without learning to be ruthless and without mercy."

"You have changed much, my son, and it is all my fault. I will go to my grave regretting my actions."

"And so you should." John felt his anger rising and fought to contain it. "There is another matter Asheborne needs to answer before you silence him."

Robert Howard looked at his son.

"There is another man who works for Asheborne, and it was he who carried out the brutal murders you were so happy to blame on me. He has the cruellest, coldest grey eyes I have ever seen, and he kills with the evilness of the devil himself. His name is Gare, and that is all I know of him. Once you look into those evil eyes, you will know it is him."

"I have heard whispers of such a man, but nobody knows if he is real or myth."

"He's no myth, for I have seen him with my own eyes. I have also seen what he does, and he needs to be stopped before he carries out his evil on the next poor victim."

"Consider it done. Is there anything else you need from Asheborne?"

"No, that's all."

"I have some things to tell you both." Robert scanned

his eyes from John to Sarah. "The king is angry at me for allowing Margaret to bring so much shame on our family, but he has forgiven me, and has graciously allowed me to continue in my role as the chief of his privy council."

"Why does that concern me?" John asked. "People in your position always get away with their crimes, so why should I be surprised that you do too?"

Sarah shot John a hard stare, but John's heart was hardened towards his father.

"I knew the news wouldn't mean much to you, but I tell you because I can use my position to make things right with you. I spoke to the king at length, and he read the confessions you gave to me. He understands the hardship you have been through, and he agreed to pardon you by royal decree, which you should hear about from the cryers shortly."

"So, I am a free man again?"

"Yes, John, you are a free man."

"What about my friends? Are they free as well?"

"Yes," his father nodded. "The king pardoned all of you and ordered you to be unharmed."

John allowed himself a smile for the first time. He nodded. "That is indeed good news. Please tell the king I am grateful."

"I shall pass it on to him. The other thing I wanted to tell you is that, as Arthur is not my child, he cannot inherit my titles and estates upon my death. I am drawing up new documents to restore you as the heir to my titles and estates."

"Thank you, Father, but I don't want them." John felt Sarah's eyes boring into him. "I have become used to being a peasant, and I find the people here much more honest and tolerable than they are where you reside."

"I know it's a lot to ask after all you've been through,

but you are the rightful heir to my estates, and if you refuse, then I have no one to leave it to. I ask that you give it careful consideration before turning it down."

"Give it to Sarah."

"You know that's not possible, or I would. It has to be passed down to my son, and as you are my only son, it has to be you."

"What will become of Arthur?" Sarah asked.

"He will be treated well and raised as a bastard son by another family. He shall want for nothing and will not have to bear the hardships I forced his brother to endure."

Robert's eyes clouded, and he looked down at his desk.

"Is that it?" John asked. "Are we done here?"

"There is one more thing. Please stay here at this house until I speak to Asheborne and find the answers to your questions. You and Sarah need time together, and you will be safer here from the men loyal to Asheborne who remain at large."

"What about my friends? I only go where they are welcomed, and people of our status are never welcomed anywhere."

"I can't say I am delighted, but I understand, and if it will keep you here, then your friends are welcome as well, but they are to remain away from my private quarters."

"Just remember not to treat them as your servants." John looked at his father. "Then I shall stay."

Robert Howard smiled. "We meet here in my study three days from now, when I will have the answers you seek."

Out with the Old

John, Catherine, Stephen, and Edward stayed in a downstairs room together while they waited to find out what Asheborne had to say. Sarah joined them and insisted on staying with them in the modest room with nothing other than the straw on the ground for comfort.

She also insisted on paying a visit to Isaac's grave to pay her last respects to him, and she tried her best to get along with Catherine and the others.

"There's something we need to tell you." John held Catherine's hand as he looked at his sister after they had prayed over Isaac's grave. "Catherine and I are married. We made our vows to each other during our time in Burningtown, and we love each other very much."

Sarah's jaw dropped open, and her eyes filled with tears. "You have me crying again, brother. It seems all I have done since father summoned me from Broxley is cry, but they are tears of joy, not sorrow, other than the tears I shed for a dear, departed friend in Isaac, of course."

Sarah hugged her brother and Catherine. "I know it's unlikely to please father or the aristocracy, but I am happy for you, and I can tell you are very much in love. I only hope that one day I can find such love with someone like you have."

Three days later, on a frosty November morning in the year of the Lord of 1536, Willis entered the downstairs room they shared and woke them from their slumber.

"I'm sorry to disturb you, Master John, but your father seeks your presence in his study."

"Let's hope he bears good news," John said. Sarah followed him, and the rest of them remained behind and waited for them to return.

"I have some news for you, but Asheborne wasn't helpful at all. I told him his soul would rest better if he told the truth, but he said he'd rather go to hell knowing his family is safe, than go to heaven and leave his son to the mercy of the man he calls Gare."

"So, he didn't tell you where he was?"

"No," Robert Howard shook his head. "He said Gare would hunt his son to the ends of the earth if he gave up his location, and he would torture him until he was begging to die. Even when facing his own death, he was still terrified of this man."

"Gare gets away, then," John bit his bottom lip. "Asheborne may be frightened of him, but we shall never give up trying to find him. What of Abraham? Did Asheborne at least tell us where we could find him?"

His father shook his head. "I'm sorry, John. Asheborne smiled when I asked him where I could find the man who betrayed the Underlings. He told me he would rest better knowing that as long as the Underling was out there, you could never walk the stretes in safety. He said that one day the Underling will find you, and that when he does, he will kill the girl first and watch you suffer before killing you. Asheborne is, indeed, an evil man."

John slammed the desk with his fist. "Let me speak to Asheborne and I shall save the executioner the trouble."

"There's no need," his father said. "I think I might have located the Underling myself, although I cannot promise, of course."

"Where is he?"

"Before I tell you, have you considered my offer of reclaiming your heritage?"

"I have," John leaned forward. "I have thought long and hard, and I believe I can do much good with the wealth I shall inherit after you die, so I accept my heritage and my place as the rightful heir to your titles and estates."

Robert Howard's mouth dropped open. "I feared you would refuse me. I am beyond happy you have accepted."

"There is one issue, though," John said. "I didn't tell you earlier because I considered it none of your business, but Catherine and I are married, and very much in love. Any son we have will become my heir and you will have to accept him as your grandchild should you live to see him."

"Are you telling me she is with child?"

"No, she is not with child. Having a child in our predicament would be foolish, but I warn you for the future. Do you accept, Father?"

Robert Howard pursed his lips. "I must admit it isn't what I envisioned for you, but I understand you have been through much, and have been forced to live life as a totally different person from that into which you were born. One thing I will say is that you have shown yourself to be more resourceful than I ever imagined you would, and I have no doubt that whatever you decide to do with your life, you will be successful. I accept, my son, but with regrets as you well know and understand."

"That's not all," John said. "You either accept me as I am today or not at all."

He waited for his father to acknowledge him.

"What is you desire?"

"I shall not be separated from my friends. Where I go, they go. That is not negotiable."

"You want them to move into Broxley?" John thought his father's head was about to burst.

"No. I am not living with you at Broxley. That place has too many bad memories for me."

"Where then?"

"I believe there's an empty estate in Horsham, called Saddleworth, that would be more than suitable."

"I shall look into it on your behalf. Now, regarding the Underling: I can't be certain, but I had my people go over my accounts in great detail. As well as the white house on Watelying Strete, Margaret secretly purchased another house where Asheborne's men have been seen to come and go. It's my best guess that if the Underling is hiding anywhere, that's where he's likely to be."

John stood up and offered the hand of friendship to his father. "Let us begin anew, Father. Separate, but as a family. Let us vow here and now never to allow anyone else to come between us as Margaret did."

"Agreed."

They shook hands, and Sarah hugged her brother. "Welcome back, John. I never thought this day would come."

"Now, where is this place that Margaret purchased?" John Howard asked.

Vengeance

Abraham Wylde walked out of the rear of his safe house for his early morning fresh air. He was ready to get out of this place and start anew.

Lord Asheborne had promised Abraham double pay if he stayed in London and killed John Howard after his execution. Abraham had agreed, but he intended to stay only until Asheborne's death. Then he would take his coin and run. John Howard could rot in hell as far as he was concerned.

He was ready. One more month and he would begin his new life in Norwich. It couldn't come soon enough. He wouldn't be rich, but he would be free. Howard would never find him where he was going, and he planned on living a long, peaceful life away from the violence and betrayals of London and his former life.

It was a pity Andrew and the other Underlings had had to die, but it was bound to have happened, eventually. He had just brought it about sooner. At least some good had come out of the Underlings, and he would toast their honour for the rest of his life.

That was fair, he thought.

He stood there breathing in the wintry morning air. He never saw the longbow aimed in his direction from behind the bushes in front of Currier's Hall.

He never heard the soft whoosh as the arrow left the bow.

He never saw or heard a thing.

John Howard, the fallen aristocrat now restored as one of the elites, was long gone by the time the constable found Abraham lying dead in the grounds of his safe house.

It was over.

THE END.

Epilogue

The monk with the dull grey eyes stood on the grounds of the Charterhouse Priory watching the procession of travellers coming and going along Clerkenwell Strete on their way in and out of the city.

One procession of twelve men stopped, and a man got out of the plain carriage, covered from sight by the deep hood over his head.

"Sir William," Gare nodded as the young man approached.

"Gare, rest assured my father shall not reveal your secrets."

Gare nodded, his cold eyes fixed on William Asheborne, son of the disgraced duke.

"Wait for my instructions, for they shall surely come once I am established at my new home. Howard and his son will not get away with this, and I shall have my revenge."

"I await your instructions." Oswyn Gare turned and walked back to the other monks working inside the Priory.

William Asheborne settled into his coach and prepared

for the long journey ahead, his thoughts turned towards the future.

If Margaret Colte's legacy was the damage she had done to his father with her confessions, then he would make sure that destroying Robert Howard and his peasant son would be his legacy.

Get a FREE Book!

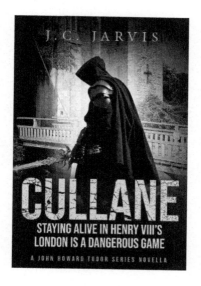

Before John Howard found sanctuary on the streets of London, Andrew Cullane formed a small band of outlawed survivors called the Underlings. Discover their fight for life for free when you join J.C. Jarvis's newsletter at jcjarvis.com/cullane

PLEASE LEAVE A REVIEW!

If you loved the book and have a moment to spare, I would really appreciate a short review.

Your help in spreading the word is gratefully appreciated and reviews make a huge difference to helping new readers find the series.

Please visit the appropriate link below to leave your review:

Amazon USA: https://geni.us/LegacyReviewUS

Amazon UK: https://geni.us/LegacyReviewUK

Other Amazon Stores: https://geni.us/JHDeception

Thank you!

MORE BOOKS BY J.C. JARVIS

John Howard Tudor Series

John Howard and the Underlings

John Howard and the Tudor Legacy

John Howard and the Tudor Deception

Fernsby's War Series

Ryskamp

Alderauge *Coming Soon…*

About the Author

J.C. Jarvis is the author of the breakout John Howard series.

He makes his home at www.jcjarvis.com

Email: jc@jcjarvis.com

Printed in Great Britain
by Amazon

24093741R00209